My Lady's Chamber

A Midtown Murder Mystery

Alan E Bailey

Each that we lose takes a part of us,

a crescent still abides,

Which like the moon, one turbid night,

Is summoned by the tides.

Emily Dickinson

PROLOGUE

December, 1953

Anger was an indulgence that Madeline Montrose rarely allowed herself, but earlier that day it had bubbled up into a white-hot rage. It was almost out of control and if she had not left when she had, walked out in fact, there was no telling what would have happened.

It was not like her and, in the aftermath, she was drained. If she was not so determined, knowing exactly what had to be done, she would have cancelled her plans for the evening, poured a strong glass of something from her husband's liquor cabinet, and put herself to bed. As it was, no one could guess what she was about to do tonight.

She leaned back from the dressing table mirror, evaluated her reflection, and was done.

She stood as she fastened the clasp on her pearls and checked her dress. The black velvet was severely tailored to the waist, then softened only by the full taffeta skirt that whispered over the stiff crinoline she wore underneath. Turning slightly she could see the low back in the mirror. She knew it was inappropriate for a woman of forty-seven, but what she was wearing was going to be the least shocking thing tonight. Satisfied, she draped the fur jacket over her shoulders. Gathering her gloves and purse she paused again at the dressing table. Even though she was running late, she stood for a long moment looking at the room.

Resolute, she snapped off the lamp and walked through the dark bedroom and down the hall. Halfway down the stairs she paused at the mirror on the landing. She checked her reflection one more time and then descended into the living room.

Tonight there would be no dowdy and out-of-date Madeline in a pleated wool skirt and gray sweater. When she arrived, she would give them all a glimpse of the woman she used to be. The Cadillac would not be hidden away in the garage while she arrived by bus. She would drive up to the front door in style and let the valet park her car. Then she would sweep up the Colonial Hotel's wide staircase to the grand ballroom and stand in the doorway for a moment, surveying the room with one eyebrow confidently raised and the diamonds at her ears sparkling in the light from the chandeliers. Only when she had their full attention would she let the maître-d remove her jacket, revealing the stunning black dress she wore underneath.

She carefully backed the car out of the garage, parking it momentarily to close the door, and then proceeded down Jefferson Avenue toward downtown.

The car radio was on, playing a sadly romantic song she remembered from the lonely war years. The dashboard clock read exactly eight o'clock. She was already running a little late for the party, but she was not going to be right on time this evening. She wanted everyone else to arrive before she made her entrance.

Turning east onto Division Street to take a more indirect route, she relaxed and began to enjoy the drive. She knew the car was old and out of style but it still made her feel pampered, gliding smoothly over the pavement. The fur on her shoulders was warm against the chill of the evening. As a light rain began, she switched on the wipers and their muted whir and thud seemed to be in perfect tempo with the old song on the radio.

When she reached National Boulevard, it was raining harder and sleet was mixed with it. Making a careful right turn, she headed south on the wide avenue that would take her about a half-mile east of the hotel. Even though it was Friday evening, there was little traffic. The street lamps glistened on the wet pavement and she hummed along with the radio as she approached the traffic light at Chestnut Street and braked to a stop.

Waiting there, she propped her elbow on the ledge of the driver's door, absently brushing the back of her gloved left forefinger against her lower lip. It was an old habit Jordan used to tease her about, and it would smudge her lipstick, but it helped soothe the dark and frightening thoughts that swirled around her. If she let them, those thoughts would force their way in and steal away the confidence she needed now.

All of her life, Madeline had been underestimated. Her widowed mother expected little of her, confident that Madeline's beauty and their distant connections to local society would assure her marriage to a wealthy man. Jordan patronized her all during their marriage, scarcely believing Madeline could make a decision of her own without his guidance. It did not stop when she was left a young widow - Jordan's bankers and lawyers and everyone else tried to tell her what was best and what to do. Even now, eleven years later, not one person really believed she could do anything important on her own. Even her youngest daughter talked down to her - except when she wanted money.

Surely everything would have been so much easier for a man, Madeline thought. It would have been easier for a man to have been left alone with young children during the war years. It would have been easier for him to work his way up in a company. Easier to be recognized for his accomplishments. Easier to have fought and clawed for everything she was going to throw away with both hands tonight.

She pushed the thoughts from her mind and, when the light changed to green, proceeded cautiously on the rapidly slickening street into the next block that was bordered on both sides by darkened warehouses. Crossing over the tracks near the limestone quarry she had a sudden panoramic view to the west. It was a view of downtown she loved and was partly why she had taken this route.

The lights of the tall Landers and Woodruff buildings hung as bright and clear as new stars in the cold night. The darkened twin minarets of the Shrine Mosque rose in silent silhouette against the low and luminous night clouds that reflected the lights of downtown. The big red letters spelling out the hotel name on the Colonial's roof dominated this cityscape, reminding her with an almost sickening dread of her destination and her purpose, but from this vantage point, the view was deceptively peaceful and inviting.

As she admired the view, Madeline did not think about the old quarry on the west side of the street, now lost in darkness. Years ago, when the quarry's excavations came within yards of the boulevard, the owners simply added a concrete wall on the west side of the street and fenced it off. If she had looked down now, the low retaining wall and rusted wire fence would have seemed out of place against the spectacular city view. The yawning abyss pulled at anyone who stared too long into its murky depths.

In the dark, she did not see the car coming up behind her too fast. Even if she had been looking at the empty street in her rear view mirror, with the rain and sleet coming down she could not have seen it coming. Its headlights were off and the hulk of the car was barely visible against the black night. Even if she had seen it, she could not have avoided the collision.

Just before impact it swerved left, catching the left side of her rear bumper. Madeline's car was thrown forward and to the right, with her front wheels jumping the curb. The tires slid over the icy sidewalk, but the car stopped with a sickening crunch when it hit the low retaining wall. It hesitated there only a second before scraping up and over the crumbling concrete edge. Bouncing up, the underside scraped over the top of the wall, slowing the car and bringing it to an abrupt and precarious stop, angled upward with the front half extended over the wall and the front wheels spinning.

When the other car hit her from behind, Madeline was slammed backward against the seat with her head snapping back painfully. Not understanding what was happening, she reflexively slammed both feet on the brake pedal. With her legs locked in place, she was thrown forward from the waist up when her car hit the wall, striking the top of her head against the steering wheel.

As the car bounced up and over the wall, the steering wheel dragged over her face, from hairline to chin. It peeled a wide strip of her forehead away from her skull and crushed the bridge of her nose. It pulverized her cheekbones, sending arrow-like slivers of bone into the back of her throat. It broke off her front teeth and shot them through her tongue, and it ultimately snapped her jawbone out of the sockets to hang open against her throat, with the lower front teeth raining down in her lap.

Dazed, she stupidly held her grip on the wheel, trying to understand what had happened. Blood streamed into her eyes, blinding her. Blood gushed from her broken nose and gaping mouth and bubbled in her throat. With her headlights reflecting off the low-hanging clouds, she struggled to collect herself. She was hurt. She had to get help. Trying to blink the loose flap of skin away from her eyes, she realized she had to shut off the engine, set the brake, and get out of the car that was now hanging out and over the quarry - if only she could let go of the steering wheel.

Behind her, the dark and unseen car ground its gears loudly into reverse and backed away wildly, as if in escape. With its engine still roaring and its gears grinding, it hesitated a moment on the deserted street. Then the gears grabbed and engaged the drive shaft and it lunged forward again, accelerating as it came.

The second impact finished what the first had not. As her rear wheels scraped heavily over the wall and the front end passed through the old wire fence like it was the delicate strands of a spider's web, Madeline realized the true horror of the situation. Her

8

frantic hands, both on the wheel, tried to steer the airborne front tires away from the fall.

From a distance, she heard the gurgling scream rising from her throat, while a calm part of her brain watched in detached fascination as her headlights reflected only a moment on the opposite rim of the quarry and then down, down, and down into its depths. Helpless, she saw her bloody, gloved hands locked on the steering wheel, the wipers swabbing senselessly at the glass, and the yellow glow of the radio that was still playing the same song. With her heart bursting in her ears, she watched the rock floor rising up in slow and silent motion to meet her.

Then, somewhere between the crushing impact that crumpled the front end of the Cadillac into the stone floor - shoving the steering wheel through her chest and driving the scalding hot engine through the firewall - with the momentum flipping the car forward to land upside down, and the brilliant explosion that followed, Madeline mercifully slipped away.

My name is Jack Jackson.

Actually, my real name is Michael Andrew Jackson. I have three older brothers and the story was that when I was born on that late-summer evening of September 18, 1954, my father, who was convinced I would be a girl, threw up his hands and told my mother to pick out the name this time. She was ready with the two names she always liked, Andrew and Michael, but my father flatly refused to name me Andrew Jackson since that had already been used. My mother thought Michael Jackson had a nice ring to it and agreed.

It did not take long for my brothers to realize that my initials, in reverse, were j-a-m, and they started calling me jelly. That stuck, and through grade school I was Jelly Jackson. I was a skinny kid, so the obvious stretch of my nickname to "Jelly Belly" never stuck. If anyone ever dared to tease me, especially with my three strapping big brothers backing me up, "Grape Jelly" was the most they would do. Then, in junior high the physical education coach got it stuck in his head that my first name was Jack and I have been Jack ever since.

I did not start out to be a detective - or as my friend in St. Louis likes to say - a sleuth. My undergraduate degree was in accounting. I began my career in public accounting, but after three jobs in three firms in three years, fired from the first two and seeing the writing on the wall at the third, I accepted that I did not fit in with certified public accountants and moved to the industry side of accounting. I got a good job keeping ledgers. Along with that, I was doing well buying "fixer-upper" houses and living in them until I had them ready to sell. The first house was a lot of trial and error, but I was getting pretty good at it.

This first case just fell into my lap - figuratively speaking, of course. After my partner, Clara, and I realized that Madeline Montrose had been murdered and then went on to identify her killer, we became something of a local sensation. We still get called in to help on cases. Actually, this isn't a stretch for Clara, who is a psychic profiler for the Kansas City police. She could probably solve these cases on her own, but we share a bond that I will explain more fully, and she really does need my help, literally speaking, from time to time. The proof is in the pudding, as they say, and right now, I can almost hear someone, somewhere, saying that they had better call Clara and Jack.

Chapter One

May, 1984

The morning sun was warm on my shoulders with the promise of a beautiful day ahead. I was already hard at work on what was looking like an endless project. Standing at the top of the extension ladder with an electric paint-stripping gun in my left hand and a paint scraper in my right, I was making slow progress in removing the thick accumulation of old paint from the strip of molding just below the roof overhang. I was glad for the breeze that murmured through the branches of the old pine tree. The sunshine was wonderful, but I needed to keep an eye on the time or risk a sunburn.

Almost fifty summer suns on the south side of the house had baked the layers of paint to a thick, crackled coating that resisted every other method to remove it. The heat from the stripping gun softened the mess to a gray, sticky putty that could be scraped away, one millimeter at a time. It was tedious work, moving the flow of hot air slowly enough to loosen the paint, but not so slowly that it scorched the wood, or worse, set it on fire. By trial and error I had developed a technique that seemed to work. At least the paint was now falling away in short strips, leaving smooth bare wood that could be sanded, primed, and painted.

Tiny paint flecks and dust covered me. On bare skin it mixed with sweat to form a sticky paste. The dust had a faint metallic taste and it filtered through the mask and collected around my lower eyelids behind the goggles. In spite of the grime, it was good to be outside after a week at the office.

Sometimes my friends teased me about my love affair with the house, or more precisely they said that it had become my mistress. Granted, it did seem to take up most of my evenings and weekends, but for three years it had been both fascinating and satisfying to see its true spirit emerge after years of neglect.

Going into the third hour with the stripping gun, a car slowed in front of the house and stopped, drawing my attention. The driver parked at the end of the walk and leaned across the front

11

seat to look up at the house as she shut off the engine. After a
moment she removed her sunglasses, opened her door, and in one
fluid motion without breaking her gaze, stepped out and stood to
look across the roof of the car at the house.

I realized she had not yet seen me. With only my head and
shoulders visible above the roof line and the pine tree behind me I
was almost invisible. I set the paint scraper on the top step of the
ladder and switched off the gun, drawing her attention when the
shrill whine stopped.

"Hello," I called, raising my right hand in a wave.

"Oh - I'm sorry," she said, like she had been caught snooping.
"I didn't see you there."

"I'll be down in a moment."

Down the ladder and pausing out of sight at the bottom, I used
the old T-shirt to brush away the dust that clung to my shoulders
and arms. Then I shook out the shirt and pulled it on over my
head. I took off the mask and was shaking the grit out my hair as I
walked around the corner of the house to meet her.

She came up the walk slowly, holding her sunglasses in her
left hand and seemed almost unable to look away from the house
to me.

From the luxury rental car and the clothes she wore, I knew
she was not from around here. The ivory color jacket was
cashmere and it matched her tailored slacks exactly. The soft,
lightweight blouse under the jacket had the sheen of silk. Her
casual leather shoes and shoulder bag looked like she bought them
to match this outfit, rather than trying to coordinate a wardrobe
around a few limited accessories. She was tall and slender and
carried herself with natural and assured grace. Her blond hair was
pulled back and secured at the nape of her neck, accentuating the
almost angular facial features and large brown eyes. Other than
the diamond anniversary band that flashed on her left hand, she
wore no jewelry.

As she came closer, with her keys jingling slightly in her right
hand, I saw that she was older than I thought at first. There were
slight lines at the corners of her eyes. I guessed she was in her
mid-to-late forties.

She seemed hesitant, as though she did not know what to say
or where to begin. "This was my parents' house," she finally said

in a quiet voice.

'So that explains it,' I thought, wondering why she had not said something like, 'I used to live here,' or even, 'This is where I grew up.' Did her wording indicate a detachment from the place?

"Well actually I once lived here, too," she continued seeming amused at her own confusion. "We moved here when I was eight."

"I didn't realize there was another daughter," I said. All I had known from the property abstract was that the woman who sold it to me had inherited it from her parents nearly thirty years ago, and that her parents built the house after buying the lot in the 1930s.

"I haven't been back here for years . . . since my mother died," she paused as if the memory of that was still painful. "It's amazing how little it has changed," she said. Then she added, "Are you the owner?"

With this woman, who looked like the most involvement she would have in a project like this would be approving her decorator's plans, I suddenly felt sweaty and dirty. I pulled off my work gloves, affirmed that I was indeed the owner, and introduced myself.

She extended her hand and introduced herself as Eva, first name only.

"I bought the house three years ago," I said, "but I am just now getting around to working on the outside. I can't seem to find anyone interested in doing this detailed type of work."

I slapped the gloves against my faded jeans. I was covered with paint chips and dust from head to toe. "I doubt if they could do it right, anyway, even if I did."

That brought a smile from her. "We had the same problem remodeling our townhouse. I'm afraid that I have scraped more old paint than I care to remember."

Subtle clues were accumulating, a townhouse, the cooler weather clothing she was wearing on this warm day, and even a slight accent - or the lack our local twang. I was beginning to suspect that she was a long way from home.

After a slight pause I asked, "Would you like to look around inside? It's fairly presentable right now."

"Oh, no! Thank you, I wouldn't want to impose," she began.

"I was just about to take a break for some iced tea, anyway," I said. "I just brewed a fresh pitcher this morning. You could join me, if you like."

"Well, alright," she agreed, "if you're sure it is not an inconvenience."

I left her standing in the living room while I went to pour the tea. After soaping my hands and arms to the elbows and rinsing them the best I could at the kitchen sink, I sliced a lemon and crushed some fresh mint in the glass before adding the ice and tea. When I returned with two glasses, she was standing at the fireplace, tracing the edge of the mantle with her fingertips, before turning to me.

"There used to be a very large mirror here," she said almost wistfully, "with two crystal sconces."

"That explains the gaps in the wallpaper when I stripped the walls," I said. "If you look closely, there are still outlines in the plaster where the lights must have been. The sconces were gone when I bought the house."

She looked appreciatively around the room as I described how the old carpet had been removed, the floors refinished, the walls stripped of layers and layers of paper and painted the soft neutral putty color they were now. I described how I had hand-finished the stair treads and bannister rail, and found an almost-exact replacement of the missing section of crown molding. She listened attentively and asked questions, showing her knowledge and experience with restoration work.

Because she was interested, I even told her that before I moved into the house, it seemed I had been collecting things for it. The dining table and chairs I bought at an estate sale, and refinished during a college summer break, had overcrowded my first apartment but now fit perfectly in the dining room. A dresser that was too big in my first house, was ideal in the master bedroom's walk-in closet.

I showed her around the rest of the house, allowing her the time she needed.

She said that her parents started building the house in 1934. She talked about the floor plan and how the windows and doors were purposely placed to maximize cross-breezes - essential when homes did not have air conditioning. She said there used to be a smaller garage and goldfish pond behind the house. Now there was a newer two-car garage. She said her sister never wanted anything she considered old-fashioned. That was why the garage did not match the house.

Over the years, or at least until she ran out of money, the sister continued to update and modernize the house. The wood shingle roof was covered with composition shingles - not as pleasing to look at, but more water repellant and less prone to fire from flying fireplace embers. In the 1960s, thick, wall-to-wall shag carpet was laid over beautiful hardwood floors. The original kitchen cabinets were torn out in the 1970s and replaced with pre-fabricated modern ones that were out of date now, and the butler's pantry was converted to a haphazard powder room. But through all those revisions, however misguided, the character of the house remained intact.

Until now, the quality of the house seemed out of sync with the half-crazed woman who sold it to me. The last ten to fifteen years she had thrown nothing away. There were pathways through the house and every room was stacked with boxes that threatened to tumble over, bundles of papers and magazines, and even paper bags stuffed full of old junk mail. By then, she was sleeping on a cot in the dining room, using the toilet and sink in the powder room, and cooking over a hot plate squeezed onto a corner of the cluttered kitchen table. The oven was stuffed with her bank statements and every square inch of the kitchen counters was piled high.

She came to the closing heavily made up and elaborately dressed in clothing that was at least thirty years old, including a fur coat that looked like she kept it under a mattress. She wore layers of cheap costume jewelry along with real gemstones. When the escrow papers were prepared, she gave her new address as a run-down travel court that was built long before the interstate replaced Route 66. It seemed she had nowhere to go when the house was sold. That alone almost voided the sale, raising the question if she really was mentally capable of signing a contract.

I always thought the house was not appreciated by its owners. Now, seeing this woman before me, I had another perspective. The couple who built the house must have been more like this daughter.

We went upstairs, and more relaxed, she told me about two little girls, sisters named Evangeline and Adelaide, who shared the front bedroom. They were close and Eva had not moved into the smaller third bedroom until her sixteenth birthday. "Mother probably would have separated us earlier, but Addie was so young when our father died during the war that mother thought we needed to be together."

I did not have to be told that Addie, as the younger sister, was competitive and jealous of Eva. The rivalry would lead to her becoming a bitter, if not insane, adult.

At only one point during the tour did Eva seem to lose her composure. As we walked through the dining room, her eyes fell on the antique silver coffee service I kept on the sideboard.

"Where did you get this?" she asked bluntly.

"I..," I struggled to remember. "I bought it at an estate auction a couple of years ago."

"It is just like the one that belonged to my mother," Eva said. "She always kept it right here, too."

I did not know what to say. I hesitated, remembering the day I had found it. I saw it across the room at a crowded estate sale. The elderly owner had died after years in a nursing home. By then the set was black with tarnish but, after examining it, I had to have it. My enthusiastic bidding ran the price up rapidly, probably more than it was worth and certainly more than I could afford at the time. But that evening when I polished the tarnish from the sterling pieces of the set, it felt like I had brought it home.

Forgetting herself, Eva picked up the coffee server, a tall and slender version of a tea pot, and ran her fingertips over it, deep in thought.

"This pattern originated in the early nineteen twenties," she said. "My parents chose and registered the pattern as their wedding silver."

She paused, holding the server up to better catch the light before continuing.

"The Wallace Silver Company used to make serving pieces like this to go with their tableware."

Although I already knew this, I let her speak.

"My mother had all the flatware, too," she said.

So did I, put away in the silver drawer of the buffet at which we were standing.

"And the crystal stemware that matched. Most of those pieces were wedding gifts. You see how the rose medallion is repeated on each piece? On the stemware, it is etched around the rim."

"Do you collect this pattern?" I asked.

"No, not really," she said, turning the server as she admired it. "I have a few pieces. The stemware is almost impossible to find these days and the company stopped making the hollowware ten or fifteen years ago. I really only wanted mother's coffee and tea service as a remembrance. My husband offered to buy it from my sister, but she would not..."

She broke off in mid-sentence, staring at the bottom of the server in astonishment. She turned the base of the pot around toward me to show the additional engraving I had never noticed before: three initials - two intertwined within a larger one - the swirling letter "M" in the middle with the smaller letters "J" and "M" intertwined on the sides.

"This was their monogram. It is definitely my mother's set," she said, setting it down carefully. Then realizing her statement must sound like an accusation that I had lied or somehow stolen it added, "Addie must have sold it after all."

We finished our tour on the patio and sat at the table, finishing our tea. Whatever emotion she had felt over the silver was under control now. She said the secluded patio was exactly like the one her mother had always wanted, down to the planters and the new French doors that opened onto the patio where the living room windows used to be. Although I was beginning to feel uneasy at yet another coincidence, I assured her that her sister had not shown me the plans her mother had drawn up, it had just seemed a natural addition to the house.

My shoulders and back were starting to itch under my shirt. It was either the early sign of sunburn, or the drying crust of paint dust. The melting ice rattled in my glass, pulling her from her reverie.

"I mustn't keep you any longer," she said, rising gracefully.

I stood to face her.

"Mother would have approved of all you've done," she said warmly. "You have excellent taste and obviously love the house. I had heard from an old friend that Addie let it go pretty badly toward the end. I am so happy, and relieved even, that you have made it into a home again."

She took my hand in hers, and for a moment there was a nagging familiarity about her. She bore no resemblance to the sister I had seen only a few times, three years earlier, but there was something about the eyes, the expression around the mouth, and the high cheekbones that struck a chord in me, even if I could not quite place it.

Then I remembered the envelope of photographs I found a year earlier wedged behind a drawer when I took it out to fix its loose dovetailing. A couple of them included the shadow of the woman taking the pictures with the sun behind her. From the looks of them, the snapshots were taken at a child's birthday party sometime during the 1930s. Was Eva one of the girls in the photographs? For a moment I thought about showing those pictures to her, but I realized it could take a while to find them.

Abruptly, she released my hand and gathered her keys and sunglasses from the table.

"I really do appreciate the tour. I am only in town for a few days. Actually, I just arrived this morning and only passed by here on a whim on my way from the airport."

I could no longer keep myself from asking, "Where is your home?"

She looked directly into my eyes, making me realize she had not done that until now. There was an intense look, making me wonder if I had offended her. After hesitating, she replied, "I have lived in San Francisco since I finished college and was married. My husband was in business there."

"Did he come with you?"

"No," she said, almost as though she had to make herself remember. "No, I am a widow - more than ten years now." Then, as if she had said too much or realized she had stared at me too long, she lowered her eyes. It was time to leave.

"Thank you again for letting me see the house," she said on the porch, offering her hand again, but unable to meet my gaze.

With the sense of too many things left unsaid, I stood on the porch, watched her walk to her car and drive away. When she was gone, I realized that I didn't even know her last name and that she had left no address.

It was later, months later in fact, that I realized the look on her face when she stared at me was one of surprised recognition.

Chapter Two

I had the dream again that night.

The dream was simple. About three in the morning, someone walked through my bedroom. I sat up in bed, turned on the light, and looked at the door to see the shadow of a woman going down the hall toward the stairs.

Then, when I really woke, I was still lying in bed and the lamp on the nightstand was off. All of it, including me sitting up in bed, turning on the light, and seeing the shadow, had been part of the dream. It was a recurring dream that began when I moved to this house. There was no particular pattern, except when I woke and looked at the clock it was always five minutes after three.

Over time, as the dream repeated, I could see that she was dressed in black. Sometimes she paused a moment with her elbows up, as if she was fastening a necklace, but the rest of it never varied. She walked in a straight line from the desk to the door, without hesitating or veering around the bed.

Even though she was walking right through me, I was never frightened. I was fascinated, especially after I was aware enough to recognize that I was having the dream. I never saw her face and I always woke when she reached the top of the stairs. If I got out of bed to investigate, all the windows and doors were locked, nothing was out of place, and the neighborhood was completely quiet.

For a while, I tried keeping a chart, but there was no identifiable pattern. The only recurring thing was that it was always 3:05 A.M. when I woke.

It got to where I would just turn on my other side and go back to sleep. If she was a ghost, then my bedroom must have been her room. It was just another part of living in my old house.

Chapter Three

From the beginning, unusual things happened in the house. Actually, they started before I set foot in it.

The picture seemed to leap off the page as I leafed through the real estate magazine in the supermarket line. I was finishing the work on my first house, building my equity, and was on the lookout for my next project. Even without an address on the listing there were enough clues that I found it without too much trouble. After stopping my car across the street and spending an hour trying to figure out the layout of the rooms from the placement of the windows and doors, and then driving by slowly several times after dark to catch a glimpse inside through the windows, I gave in and called my realtor, Paula, the next morning and asked her to set up a showing. She called me back in fifteen minutes. The earliest we could see it was almost a week later.

The appointed evening finally came and Paula was waiting beside her car when I arrived. She was on crutches, having broken an ankle while skiing a month earlier. She went in front of me, up the walk, and rang the doorbell. Standing on the wide front porch, I was overtaken by a sense of familiarity and also the feeling of having come home.

I had wondered at this unusual appointment. When I bought my first house, a small "handyman's delight," I simply looked at the house over my lunch hour. The owners were not home, evidently to keep me from negotiating with them directly and bypassing the agent. This time, Paula said the owner insisted on being home, and that the house could not be shown before six o'clock.

As we waited I could hear someone moving around behind the door. Paula waited, then whispered to me that Miss Addie must not have heard the bell, and rang it again. This time a querulous voice called out, "It's open!"

When we stepped inside, a half-blind terrier came running from the shadows, snapping at my pant cuffs until Paula scolded him away. Paula introduced me to Miss Addie, who said nothing and remained seated in a faded overstuffed chair, her face partially hidden behind a lampshade.

The front door opened directly into the living room, rather than an entry hall as I had imagined. In spite of the clutter, it was a surprisingly large room with good symmetry and proportions, focused on a carved fireplace mantle on the opposite wall and the staircase directly in front of us. Through a darkened arched doorway to our right, from where the terrier had come, I had the impression of a dining room hidden away in the shadows.

Although lamps at both ends of the lumpy sofa were on, the overhead light overpowered the room with a harsh and smoky glare. Thick, dirty carpet covered the floors and went up the stairs, almost giving an upholstered look to the staircase so that the railing appeared to float above it, rather than being solidly anchored.

I had to fight the urge to gag at the stench of the overheated room. It was a combination of old medicines, menthol cigarettes, old upholstery, and body waste. As Paula made small talk, I watched the terrier sniff around the newel post and then urinate against the carpeted step.

Paula made friendly chatter, but Miss Addie remained seated and silent, staring at me without blinking. Dirty hair was combed flat against her scalp and held back by a headband. Her makeup was almost clown-like: two circles of rouge on powdered cheeks, heavy mascara, and bright red lipstick. Her shapeless knit top and pants looked like they had been worn for several days.

A cuckoo clock wheezed and then sounded the hour, pulling me back to the conversation. Paula was telling Miss Addie that I was an accountant, a certified public accountant she said, with a verbal underline of the "certified" part.

"Great," I thought, "why don't you just tell her to jack up the asking price even more?"

"Never could stand bookkeepers," she spat out. "Ruined my husband's business."

Then she laughed, almost a cackle, and slapped the arm of her chair like she had made a joke. I had a glimpse of yellowed finger nails with black crescents under them, and inwardly cringed.

Paula, indicating her crutches, asked if I could have a look around upstairs on my own. Miss Addie waved a hand in dismissal. "Nothing he can steal up there," she said. I thought she was joking again, then saw that she wasn't. Paula nodded at me to go on up.

After the initial revulsion, I found myself captivated by the house. As I started up the stairs, my hand avoiding the gummy bannister rail, I had a full view of the living room. Perfectly symmetrical, the rectangular room was large enough to hold a piano, a long sofa, a clutter of smaller chairs and tables, and the two ancient easy chairs flanking the fireplace. The fireplace looked to be in working order, with the accumulation of recent ash on the open hearth.

The stairs creaked softly under the carpet. From this angle, I saw that the glaring overhead light was actually a flush-mounted chandelier. Its brass base was swirled in cobwebs, but miraculously not a single hanging prism seemed to be missing. It had four mismatched, high-wattage bulbs that were on now, no doubt a fire hazard, but once I cleaned it up and put in the appropriate bulbs, it could be remarkable. From this vantage point, I could also see a line, actually a ridge, on the wall about six inches from the ceiling all the way around the room, indicating the room once had a decorative crown molding.

A smaller version of the living room overhead fixture provided lighting on the stairway landing. Making the turn, I saw the hideous white and orange 1970s wallpaper of the living room abruptly stopped there, with an older and more tasteful paper continuing up the staircase and the upstairs hall.

Three bedrooms and a bath opened onto the long central hall. The largest bedroom was tucked under the dormered half story roof above the living room. I fumbled around and found the light switch, turning on the overhead fixture with only one dim bulb still working. Dark wallpaper had peeled away from the wall directly above the fireplace, showing old water stains on the plaster, likely an old leak where the roofline met the chimney. The varnish on the floors was black. My shoes stuck to it as I walked, so that I tried to stand on the scattered rugs whenever possible.

The room with its sloped roof and dormer windows was charming and cozy, but had not been used in some time. Dust lay thick everywhere, even on the bedclothes. The floor, furniture, and bed were piled high with bales of old newspapers and magazines bound with twine, old window shades and curtain rods, and stacks of cardboard boxes that were thick and soft with time and dampness. The stench was different here from downstairs, sticking to the back of my throat so that I could not swallow it away.

I opened the second bedroom door to reveal rows of shelves

made of rough lumber mounted on metal utility brackets. The shelves were filled with rocks, dried flowers, paint cans, and hand-labeled bottles whose contents had long since evaporated. On the stained desktop sat a can of watercolor brushes, colored pencils, artist paper, and a broken ruler. Watercolor trays, the kind that used to be sold in dime stores, were open with the colors crackled and dry. I wondered whose they were.

A single French door opened from this room onto a porch surrounded entirely by windows. The porch's unfinished walls, painted white decades ago, were now rain-streaked and gray. The porch was crammed with more stacks of magazines, newspapers, and boxes.

The third bedroom was nondescript other than it faced the street, and apparently had not been used for a very long time. Ancient dust lay thickly on the faded chenille bedspread, with its thin fringe showing gaps like missing teeth. It took me a moment to realize that what was different about this room was that it was completely devoid of clutter. It looked like the door had been closed on it thirty years ago and never opened again. It was the one room that only needed to be cleaned before I could move in.

I was finished. Although the house could be wonderful it was more than I could possibly take on. There would be years of work for me here, even months for a full-time restoration team. I started down the stairs, then realized I should probably turn off the lights. I backtracked, turning the lights off in reverse order.

That was when the first unusual thing happened.

As I was turning off the light in the second bedroom, the one with all the shelving, from where I stood in the doorway and in my peripheral vision, the watercolors in the trays on the desk were wet and new, shining under the overhead light. Since I was the only one upstairs, it startled me enough that I jumped. When I turned to look at the paints closer, they were as cracked and dry as they had been before.

Unfortunately, I dismissed that first warning of what was to come. I decided it was only a reflection of the overhead light. After all, the old woman seemed to live downstairs. No one else was upstairs with me. How could those paints have possibly looked like they were new and being used?

I went downstairs. Paula and I briefly toured the dining room, that had a cot and portable toilet in the corner, then entered the kitchen. She pointed out that the cabinets had been replaced recently, but the smell of dead mice and rotted food permeated the room and the wallpaper above the electric range was streaked and shiny with grease. A small breakfast room adjoined the kitchen, its table and chairs stacked high with even more junk.

Paula briefly showed me the small bathroom that opened off the kitchen. In the interest of convenience, a clothing rod had been installed above the toilet and it looked like most of Miss Addie's clothes were hanging on it. I was sure she did not go up the stairs any more.

After a brief look at the basement and garage, we rejoined Miss Addie in the living room, still in the chair with the dog lying at her feet, growling at us. By then, I was getting used to the odors - they did not seem as bad as they had at first. Paula wrapped up the visit. Miss Addie did not get up as we left. In fact she barely acknowledged our departure, and Paula closed the front door behind us.

"It could be a wonderful home," she chirped with enthusiasm, but avoided my gaze, "so many extras you won't find anywhere else in this price range - classic Colonial Revival, hardwood floors throughout, a wood-burning fireplace, forced-air heat, mature landscaping, two blocks to the bus line, and the detached garage with a workshop..."

"Its filthy and disgusting," I interrupted.

"...and the price has been significantly reduced."

"No doubt!" I snorted with a sarcastic laugh.

"Don't you think this is a wonderful old neighborhood?" she continued, unfazed. "So close to the college, the library, and shopping. With some elbow grease, you can make it beautiful again and it would be a good, solid investment for you. You would be buying the worst house in the neighborhood - an immediate equity builder for an experienced rehabber like you."

I had to admire her optimism, but until now, all I had really done was paint and replace carpet. This was way beyond that.

"I don't think so, Paula."

"It may not last long at this price," she continued. "Think it over. We could make a low offer to start and then negotiate our way up from there."

She did not stop talking as I got into my car, started the engine, and drove away. "Let me know," she called after me.

Back at home, and with the watercolors incident completely forgotten, I could not get the house out of my mind. I could not stop thinking about what I could do with it if it were mine. It was solidly Colonial Revival and the "modernization projects" that Miss Addie had inflicted on it would not be that hard to strip away. I was sure the hardwood floors could be beautiful if sanded and varnished, especially if they had been protected under all that carpeting for the last twenty to thirty years. Since it was pre-war construction, built in the thirties, the walls under all those layers of old wallpaper would be plaster and lath. The woodwork, however grimy, was still beautiful and the paneled doors looked like they still had the original hardware. Most likely, a degreasing wash, a light hand sanding, and a coat of primer and fresh paint was all that the woodwork really needed.

So, after a series of sleepless nights and distracted days at work, I called Paula and asked her to make an offer. After a few more days of negotiation, with Miss Addie stubbornly sticking to her original asking price and ceding almost nothing, I agreed to a price higher than I ever should have paid. In forty-five days the house would be mine.

Chapter Four

With the house under contract, Miss Addie came apart completely. It should have been no surprise - there had been plenty of clues. What was shocking was the speed of her descent into complete madness.

Almost as soon as she accepted my offer and the closing date was set, she started dragging her heels at every step of the process. At first, she said she had the legal abstract to the property, which was still required in Missouri. Simply updating the existing abstract, instead of having to start from scratch and researching every transaction on the property back to the Louisiana Purchase, would provide a substantial savings for her. The abstract company delayed their work twice while she looked for the document among her papers. Only when the work could no longer be delayed, and in fact she would be charged the additional fees even if she had it, did she produce the document - making me suspect she had it in hand all along.

There were other annoying delays. My bank required a routine home inspection. Addie only had to give the inspector access to the inside of the house, but she would telephone Paula moments before the inspector's appointed time, saying she had another engagement and it would have to be rescheduled. After using that tactic twice, Paula insisted she would meet the inspector at the house and let him in. Addie resisted, but finally agreed she would leave a key hidden on the porch, which in fact she never did. As soon as she could get to a pay telephone, Paula called Addie's attorney and asked him to explain to his client that non-performance could void our contract. Addie was home and gave the inspector access the next morning. Still, at every step of the process, she was sly and cunning in working the system to her advantage - all with the irrational objective of delaying the closing.

I would have been more patient with these delays except that the house I was living in sold almost immediately. As soon as I agreed to buy Miss Addie's house, Paula listed my house. I had spent the last two years remodeling the two bedroom ranch and bringing it up to date. I had built up a significant equity that I would use for a down payment. Before she showed it, I asked Paula to walk through the house with me to point out anything that needed to be done. She gave me a short list that I could clear the following weekend. It did not matter, the house was under contract the next day.

Paula wisely put a condition in the contract that the sale of my house would be delayed until three days after I closed on Miss Addie's house. A targeted closing date, about thirty days in the future, was discussed verbally with my buyers, but thankfully was never put in the contract. In the end, the closing on Miss Addie's house was postponed twice. The first time because the management of the apartment she planned to buy in a new high-rise condominium failed to approve her application - primarily because they had a strict no-pets policy. The second time because she was hospitalized, with vague symptoms, the day before we would sign the papers. Even her own attorney was exasperated with her by then.

I offered to withdraw from the contract, but Miss Addie grew venomous at that, declaring I would not get "one red penny" of my deposit back - she was keeping it all just for the aggravation I caused her. She had no legal grounds to do that, as her attorney sternly warned her, but the situation was getting ugly fast. I told Paula I still wanted the house, but I was increasingly uneasy at how the process was going.

Finally, everything was in place and the closing date was set. One of the final requirements in the process was for Paula and me to walk through the house with Miss Addie's agent, assuring everything was as agreed. Her attorney would go by the house an hour before we were due to arrive, take Miss Addie out to a late lunch and bring her from the restaurant to the title company to sign the papers.

Even the walk-through raised concerns. Although the contract had always stated that I would take possession of the house, including the seller's keys, at the closing, it looked like she had packed nothing. If anything, there was even more clutter than there had been the first time I was in the house. By contrast, everything I owned was already in packing boxes at my old house, ready to start the move that evening. My buyers were ready to move in as soon as I was out. They were similarly packed and waiting to leave their apartment. It all hinged now on Miss Addie being out of the house so I could start moving in.

The closing stalled momentarily while the attorneys held a side discussion determining if Miss Addie was sane enough to sign the contract. When they returned to the table from the corner of the room, my attorney asked Miss Addie outright if she understood the contract gave me immediate possession of the house.

Miss Addie chose that moment to be confident. She raised a single eyebrow of disdain, opened her purse, took out an unfiltered cigarette, rapped it sharply to compress the tobacco, then leaned forward to her attorney, assuming he would light it for her. It was like watching some deranged old film star.

She pulled in a long, chest-full of smoke, picked an invisible tobacco shaving from her tongue with a gloved finger, leaned back with the hand holding the cigarette dramatically in the air, exhaled, and answered calmly, "Yes, of course. Why on earth would you ask me something as preposterous as that?"

"Because you haven't packed a single thing!" Paula cried out, unable to stop herself. "You haven't done anything to get out of the house and you are supposed to hand over the keys right now, right here, goddamn it."

"Oh, that," Miss Addie replied, waving it away with her cigarette hand. "I hired a woman to come and help me pack. She will start this evening - once I am sure I have my money. She is a strong, Negro woman. It surely can't take her very long. I will be out in a week or so."

"Are you kidding me?" Paula shouted, coming out of her chair and leaning across the table with a finger in Addie's face. "It is 'possession at closing,' lady. It always has been. My client is packed and ready to move right now. The sale of his house is scheduled for tomorrow. His buyers are packed and ready to move, too. They can't stay another day in their apartment. You have put this off more than two months now. Do you have any idea how serious this is?"

Miss Addie looked at me then, almost coquettishly. "I don't care if you want to move in tonight. You understand that people will talk, though."

I couldn't even speak. My attorney was talking over Paula and Miss Addie's attorney was assuring him everything would be alright. In the end, they negotiated that Miss Addie could have seven more days, exactly 168 hours starting right then, to vacate the premises. I would stay in a hotel and the moving company would hold my entire household in storage. The entire cost of it would be deducted from the sale.

"And just exactly how much is this bull crap going to cost me?" Miss Addie objected, glaring at my attorney.

"It's going to cost as much as it costs, that's how much," her attorney shouted at her. "Shut your stupid mouth! You are lucky no one is suing you over this - and he still could."

Even with her own attorney's ultimatum, my week at the hotel stretched into two, and then into three. Paula was in daily contact, seeing if she could offer any assistance to speed things along. Miss Addie employed every possible delaying tactic and alternated playing the pitiful widow about to be evicted from her home and the shrewd negotiator. Paula gave me a daily report of what Miss Addie said:

"You wouldn't throw an old lady like me out in the street would you?"

"I found a new place, just an apartment really, and only temporary you understand, but it has to be totally redecorated before I can even consider moving in. Surely no one would begrudge me a little more time until the painters finish, would they? I simply will not survive if I have to breathe those poisonous paint fumes."

"I still say he can move on in. That offer is still on the table. I don't need all that much room, really. Just the dining room and kitchen. He can have the rest of the house. Is that being so unreasonable?"

"I want to officially invite him to stay with me for a period of no more than six months as my house guest. That way I can introduce him to the house and show him what he needs to do to be able to live here."

After a time though, Addie fell into complete silence. Her telephone went unanswered and she did not come to the door when Paula when by the house. The mail was piling up in the box, which normally would indicate Addie was gone, but Paula could hear the dog on the other side of the door, scratching and growling when she knocked. Paula always shouted through the door that she would be back.

Then the day came when the attorney frantically called Paula to tell her that the funds being held in escrow had somehow been released to Addie, after all. Had the check been deposited to Addie's account, it could have been readily retrieved, but she had cashed the check, carrying the entire amount out of the bank in large bills. With that, both attorneys agreed that the sheriff needed to be involved. Paula called me and I left work early. I didn't want to go, but the sheriff said that, as the new owner he needed me present when the house was entered.

We stood on the porch, the two lawyers, Paula, and me, as the sheriff pounded on the front door, calling out to Addie repeatedly and warning her that if she did not open the door he had the authority to break it down. Actually, he had a locksmith standing ready to drill the lock if the door was not opened. We heard the dog barking and someone moving around inside. The locksmith was preparing his tools when Addie opened the door only wide enough to show her face - or actually just the left side of it between the door and the door frame. A moving van was parked at the curb, with a crew ready to start packing the contents of the house as soon as we gained admission.

"You can't really mean to evict me from my home," she said pitifully in a small, defeated voice. "I have nowhere else to go."

"You sold this house," the sheriff replied. "It's not yours anymore. You have the money. You can't stay here now. I have…"

"Adeline, you listen to me now," her attorney cut in with authority. "You have to stop this. These people are here to help you. I will help you, but you have to let us in."

She considered what he said. "Give me just a moment," she said and quietly closed the door. "You have one minute!" the sheriff yelled after her.

She came back soon enough, slid the security chain, and opened the door. None of us were prepared for what we would find inside.

Addie had used the weeks since the closing to barricade herself inside the house. The bundles of magazines and newspapers had been moved around to block every window and door, stacked at least two bundles thick. The only light inside was from the overhead fixture. It took a moment for my eyes to adjust to the darkness, but I could see that the floor was completely awash in old newspapers. When the stacks against the windows and doors were finished, she must have unbound the remaining bundles and sifted them around the rooms, like drifts of stained snow, almost knee deep in the corners and against the walls.

Addie was wearing the same outfit she had worn to the closing, making me wonder if she had changed out of it since then, but the diamond earrings she wore looked real this time. She went to the armchair she had dragged to the middle of the living room, turned as if to sit, but remained standing with her hands in the pockets of the coat - facing us, silent and defeated. Even if she was completely deranged, I felt a little sorry for her. Hopefully the sheriff and her attorney could help her now.

Paula was the first to see the coffee table. Her hand went to her mouth, but she was unable to stifle a horrified scream.

Completely cleared of clutter, what was now on the table was carefully arranged. The terrier lay in the middle with his belongings around him. Miss Addie must have strangled him and laid him there in the final moments before she opened the door to us the second time.

Following Paula's gaze, Addie looked sorrowfully at the table, "Poor Roy Boy!" she said, her voice breaking. "He could not have withstood leaving the only home he's ever known."

Paula started toward the front door, but Addie's continued words stopped her. We were all stunned, momentarily frozen by what we were seeing and hearing. The unblinking Miss Addie kept talking, seeming to gather strength as she did.

"This house is evil. I always knew that - that it is filled with evil. It destroys everything. I told Roy Boy nothing can get rid of it. Nothing can ever save us from them. I have lived with it too long. Too long. Nothing can save us now, nothing at all." She paused a moment, hesitating. "Mother knew how to be free. Yes she did. She knew exactly what to do."

I was a few seconds behind in recognizing that the coffee table was now a funeral pyre for the dog and the scattered newspapers were the fuel for the fire that would consume it. Her attorney lunged forward, grabbing Addie's arm at the wrist as she brought her hand from her coat pocket. The cigarette lighter in it was already lit with a flame that was like a torch in the darkened room. In the light, Addie's face contorted in fury and she screamed and fought, kicking and trying to wrench her hand free from him. Then she stopped fighting and simply let go of the lighter. It fell to the floor, still flaming, and immediately caught the crumpled paper scattered there. For a moment it looked like the entire place would go up - and with all of us in it. Addie reached in the other pocket of the old fur coat, brought out a wad of hundred dollar bills and threw it at her lawyer, screaming at him to take it all. The money was as evil as everything else was.

Springing into action, her attorney tore off his overcoat and threw it on the floor, smothering the flames. At the same time, with one swift motion and Addie clawing and fighting him like a wild animal, the sheriff pulled both her hands behind her back and locked them in his handcuffs. Then he pulled his two-way radio from his belt and called for backup and an ambulance.

Shaken, we waited outside on the porch. Until the ambulance arrived and the paramedics sedated her, Addie fought against the handcuffs, kicked at the sheriff, and ranted and raved that she be let go and that only fire would cleanse her and remove the curse of evil that was on us all. A few neighbors came out onto their porches to see what was going on, but not one of them ventured closer.

After the ambulance took Addie away, her attorney, still as shaken as the rest of us, rambled as he tried to explain that Addie had likely dealt with too much in her lifetime; losing her father as a young girl, and then her mother, and then her husband. But losing their business and whatever social position she thought she had had been too much. It was too bad that she never had any children. She had no family left. They could be a comfort to her now.

Then, as if he had said too much, he stopped. He only added that he would make sure she got the care she needed. He went back inside to pick up the scattered hundred-dollar bills. With us watching, he combined it with the still-bundled bills from Addie's purse, counted it and determined it was all there. He said it was all she had left. Addie had long since spent through all of her husband's life insurance.

He put the dead terrier in an empty cardboard box, came back outside, and motioned to the moving crew that they could begin packing Miss Addie's things and taking them away. The house was finally mine.

Chapter Five

It took almost a week to clear out the house. A construction dumpster was brought in and the crew started by removing everything that was clearly trash. Just doing that filled the dumpster four times. Miss Addie's personal effects were then packed for storage. It was possible, but doubtful, that she might be released from the hospital to live on her own at some future date. The day finally came when the house and the garage were empty. I could take possession of my house.

When it was empty, the house seemed even filthier, if that was possible. I had the carpet cleaned, but it still stank. From experience I knew the foul odors would not go away until the carpet was removed and the floors underneath were sanded and varnished. All the layers of wallpaper would have to be removed and the old plaster ceilings and walls would have to be sealed, primed, and painted. I was beginning to realize that it would take years. Just dealing with the odor Roy Boy left on the staircase was going to require replacing the bottom stair tread and riser, and possibly the supporting framework underneath. Until I could do these things correctly, I at least had to get the house clean enough that I could move in.

Fortunately, the wood floors on the second floor were better. With the worn rugs gone, much of the floor was still in original condition, with only the exposed perimeters around the rugs darkened and gummy with age. A weekend with a petroleum-based floor stripper, that could only be used when all the windows were open, removed most of the grime. The outlines of the old rugs were still visible, but I temporarily sealed the floors with an industrial-strength sealer. It was not perfect, but it was clean enough I could put down my own rugs and live with it.

I had a surprising amount of help on moving day, too much help it seemed at first until we realized half of the crew would need to clean before anything could be moved in. Two friends volunteered to take down the old window blinds and wash them outside with a bucket and hose. Three guys, equipped with buckets, bleach, scrub brushes, and brooms headed downstairs to scrub the basement walls and floor. Another team, wearing bandannas over their mouths and noses, concentrated on washing the insides of the kitchen cabinets with disinfectant. Midway through that project, there was a shriek when one of them realized that the crud she was trying to pry off the floor in the back corner of the refrigerator alcove was the remains of a long-dead mouse. She wouldn't even go back in the kitchen after that.

I saw more than one exchange of disbelieving looks that day - why would anyone leave a perfectly good house that he just remodeled for this? I ordered lots of pizza for lunch, but no one had much appetite.

At the end of the day, everyone went home exhausted and dirty, but all my furniture was stacked in two upstairs rooms, the windows had all been washed, the old drapes were on the trash pile, the carpets had been vacuumed - twice - and the large appliances were plugged in and operating.

I staggered upstairs and collapsed in bed, exhausted. I was not used to climbing stairs and I must have been up and down them at least a hundred times that day. My body ached badly, but I soon fell into a deep sleep. I did not stir until there was a loud crash and the sound of glass shattering into a million pieces. It came from somewhere inside the house - on the second floor. I turned quietly under the sheets to look at the lighted dial of the alarm clock. It showed 3:05 A.M.

What had happened? Did someone throw a rock through my windows? Was someone inside the house - and now on the second floor?

I lay silent, almost unable to breathe. Should I jump out of bed to turn on the overhead light? In the heavy silence, I listened for footsteps. Two floors below, the furnace kicked on with a "whoosh" as the gas ignited under the heating plate. Otherwise, the house was engulfed in complete silence. There was not even a sound outside - it was windless and completely still.

I could not call anyone for help. My telephones had not been installed yet. The only telephone was in the kitchen - an ancient one with a rotary dial. I was not sure if it even worked.

I thought I heard a mouse scamper across the attic floor above me. Far away, a dog barked in the silence. I waited for an eternity, listening to my heart pounding in my ears, unsure if I should stay, cowering in my bed, or get up and confront the intruder who might be unaware I was in the house and might leave on his own.

After what seemed like an hour, I looked at the clock again to see that only ten minutes had passed. I reasoned with myself that no intruder could have maintained complete silence for that long. I would have heard his breathing, sensed even his slightest move at such close range, and on top of that all the floors squeaked. No one could move around without me hearing. I lay, listening breathlessly, for almost an hour before I fell asleep again.

The next morning the only thing out of place was a window sash on the sun porch. It was on the floor, leaning against the wall. It might have fallen inward, but not one pane of glass was broken. In spite of the shattering noise that had wakened me, I could find no broken glass anywhere - inside the house or out.

Examining the sash more closely, it was possible it could have fallen but stayed in an upright position. That would explain the crash I heard, but not the sound of glass shattering. I picked it up and, with some difficulty, forced it back into the frame. It was possible the latch had not been set correctly after the windows were washed, but how would it have fallen inward on a windless night - and especially when it fit so snugly that I could not pull it back out now? I was starting to wonder if I had just dreamed it all.

I spent most of Sunday morning lining the kitchen cabinets with new shelf paper and started unpacking the boxes marked "kitchen." With all the furniture upstairs, the house was large and empty around me, echoing in spite of the carpeted floors. I set a goal of unpacking half the boxes before I stopped for lunch. At two o'clock, with my stomach growling, I finally washed my hands and changed clothes to go out for lunch.

As I walked out the back door, I realized I only had my car keys, not the keys for the house. They were probably on my bedside table where I had put them after locking up last night. When I turned to go back inside, the door slammed shut in my face.

Had the wind somehow caught it? With only a gentle spring breeze it did not seem likely. Some of the upstairs windows were open to air the bedrooms, but to blow this heavy door shut would require a strong draft. The slamming door had almost pushed me out of the way. I tried the door knob, but it was locked. I was locked out.

I went around to try the front door, which was also locked, and checked the downstairs windows. Every one of them was also locked. Prowling around the house would look suspicious if anyone saw me, but there was no one around. It looked like all the neighbors were away, or inside their houses in spite of the mild afternoon.

I had no ladder tall enough to reach the second story windows, but maybe one had been left behind. I went to the garage only to find all its doors were locked too. My car was parked inside the locked garage.

Not sure what to do, I sat down on the back steps only to realize that my wallet was not in the back pocket of my jeans. Had it fallen out? I was sure I remembered putting my wallet in that pocket when I changed clothes - I always did. Maybe in my hurry to leave I had missed my pocket and did not hear it fall on the floor.

I felt a rising panic. After all, I had no money, no identification, and the key ring I was holding opened none of the locks on the house. How could I explain what I was doing if someone called the police?

I decided I had to break a window, but I could not find a rock or anything else big enough. Finally, I wrapped my jacket around my fist and turning my face away, punched out a pane of glass in a window on the back of the house. I reached through to unlock the window, pushed up the lower sash, hoisted myself up, and tumbled forward into the breakfast room.

As I started up the stairs, I spotted the house keys on the living room mantle. In preparation for the carpet cleaners' return on Monday, the living room and dining room were completely empty, so the keys were conspicuous. It was an odd place for me to leave the keys, exactly in the center of the mantle. Something about it did not seem quite right, but I must have left them there after locking up last night. My wallet, as I suspected, was on the bedroom floor by the dresser. I told myself I needed to be more careful about these things, starting immediately.

So, when I came back after lunch, I made a point of taking my billfold and keys upstairs. From now on, I would put them on the desk in my bedroom the moment I came home. From now on, that would be where I kept them. I stopped half-way up the stairs when I saw what I had missed earlier.

The thick living room carpet, vacuumed the last thing yesterday, showed only one set of footprints to the mantle. There were no footprints anywhere else in the living room. I could see many footprints through the entry area and up the stairs, but there were none beyond that. When I went to the mantle to get the keys it made a set of footprints on the carpet - the only ones showing now. There was no way I could have walked across the freshly vacuumed carpet to the put the keys on the mantle last night without leaving another set of footprints.

I felt the hair rise on the back of my neck. I had the eerie feeling someone was watching me. Someone else was in the house, upstairs, and possibly even waiting for me just around the corner of the landing. I had to get a mirror for that landing - so that I could see around the blind corner. I stood in silence on the stairs, listening and waiting. I thought I heard the faint exhaling of breath, but it was only the echo of my own breathing in the empty room.

Eventually I decided it was one of my friends playing a practical joke on me. One of them must have gone out yesterday while everyone was busy, had a copy of the key made, then came back and moved my keys after I went to bed. That might even explain the crash I heard. They could have used a long pole, standing at the base of the stairs where they would leave no footprints, to put the keys on the mantle. That had to be it. If so, they would say something about it eventually. It made me feel better about the odd things that had happened, and helped me summon the courage to go on around the corner of the landing and up the stairs.

The rest of the day passed quietly. I finished unpacking the kitchen boxes, connected my washing machine and did several loads of laundry. I unpacked the rest of my clothing boxes and organized the bedroom closet. When I went to bed that night, completely exhausted, nothing interrupted my sleep.

Weeks passed without another incident - or at least without me noticing. It was an extremely busy time at work, made more so by a week-long business trip. As if I didn't have enough to do, I offered to host the annual Easter dinner for my family. It would give me a chance to show what I had done with the house so far and I could also thank those who helped me with the move.

The worst of the odors were fading, although there were remnants of the chamber pot, the terrier, tobacco smoke, and old medicines when the house had been shut up all day. When I could, I left some windows open to air the rooms. I hoped it would be better when the family came.

Easter was sunny and warm. I served lunch buffet style and everyone spread out in the living and dining rooms with their plates. The rooms were brighter without the old, heavy drapes and the lilac bushes were in bloom, filling the house with their heavy fragrance. After lunch, we gathered on the front porch for photographs. I had a new 35 millimeter camera. The camera had a viewfinder that looked through the lens so you saw exactly what you photographed. It was almost impossible to take a bad picture with that camera.

After taking pictures, I took everyone on a tour through the house and described my plans. By then, I had paint chips and wallpaper samples taped on the walls of each room, helping show what would be done. Everyone seemed to be able to visualize what it would look like eventually, or were at least polite enough to nod and smile in approval.

As she was leaving, I promised my mother's cousin, Edie, a copy of the best group photo, but it was to be several weeks before I remembered to take the roll of film to be developed.

I thumbed through the prints at the photo shop in the mall. The roll of film had 24 exposures and the family photographs were at the end of the roll. I selected the best one and had a reprint made for Edie. On the way home, I addressed an envelope to her, enclosed the photo with a brief note, and mailed it at the post office. She called me as soon as she got it, two days later.

"Thanks for the photograph, it turned out real nice didn't it?" she began in her chatty way.

"You're welcome, and yes it did," I said. In talks with Edie, you had to jump right in. She never even paused to take a breath.

"I didn't remember seeing your brother Robert's daughter, Jennifer, there," she said.

"She wasn't," I said. "They couldn't make it in from Kansas City that weekend with his new job and all."

"Well, she is certainly in the picture," Edie insisted.

"I don't think so, maybe it was Anne," I replied. Anne was another niece who lived in town. The two were close in age and were wearing their hair in the same style.

"Young man," Edie said peevishly, "I don't think I have gone around the bend just yet. I can see Anne standing right beside your mother on the porch. What I am talking about is Jennifer is looking out of the upstairs window."

How had I missed it? I told her to hang on a minute, dropped the phone and ran to my desk, yanked open the drawer and tore through the packet of photographs. I found the one of the smiling group I had copied for Edie and returned to the telephone.

"Edie," I said, "where do you see Jennifer?" When I picked out the best photo at the photo shop I was mainly looking for one where everyone was smiling and no one had their eyes closed.

"Like I told you, she is looking out of the window upstairs."

Edie's print had been enlarged, but I looked carefully at the upstairs windows in my smaller versions, still not seeing anything. "Tell me exactly which window."

"Well, I guess it's the bedroom right over the dining room, if I remember right," she said, curious now. "Can't you see it?"

I looked at the photos carefully. In one, the glass reflected the light, and in the reflection I could make out the roof of the house across the street and the trees beyond it.

"Look in the corner of the window on the right hand side," she said. "It is just as plain as day on mine."

I stared at the lower window sash of that window, and could just make out a shape in the reflection. Before my eyes, the smear seemed to pull together into a shadowy and somber face, shoulders and long hair, as if someone was leaning forward to look at the camera. But as quickly as it had formed, it faded.

"I want to have a look at your photograph," I said.

"Who do you think it could have been?" she asked.

"I think it's just a reflection, but I want to see yours," I said. She said to come over any time and we said goodbye.

As soon as I could, I drove to her house and looked at her reprint. The print had a strangely high definition. I could make out the individual flowers in the print of my great aunt's dress, the thin gold chain my mother wore, and even individual blades of grass at our feet. The picture was strangely clear.

And clearly, in the second floor window, there was a young girl. She wore a plain white blouse and her thin face was pale, with solemn dark eyes that stared straight into the camera. Long honey-colored hair was brushed back behind her shoulders. I understood Edie's confusion, she did look a little like the niece who was in Kansas City that afternoon.

"It must be a double exposure of some kind, Edie," I said,

40

grasping at some type of explanation. "It's a new camera and I have been having some trouble using it."

She looked at me, and behind the bifocals her eyes showed her doubt. Her husband had used my camera to take the pictures of the group. He was somewhat of a camera buff and took excellent photographs.

"Let me have another print made for you," I offered.

Back at home, I took Edie's print outside to the spot where the picture was taken. Looking up from there, I could see nothing in the windows. It was later in the day and the light did not reflect in the same way off the house across the street.

It was the room that had looked untouched when I first looked at the house. While every other room in the house had been piled high with Miss Addie's hoarded junk, this room looked like it had been abandoned for years - sealed off even. I went inside to see if something in the room might have looked like a girl in the photograph.

It was set up as a guest room, although it had not been used for that purpose. The space between the two front windows was wide enough for the bed and the night tables were place directly beneath the two windows. The lamps I had ordered for the tables had not been delivered so the tables were as bare now as they would have been on Easter. It would not have been possible for anyone to sit at the window without moving a night table. Furthermore, no one was in the house when we were all on the porch. I looked at the photograph again and accounted for everyone who was there that day. We were all on the porch and included in the photograph.

I tried to remember if I had seen the room that day during lunch. I had made one quick trip upstairs shortly before everyone had arrived and again when we toured the house. The weather had been warm so no one would have worn a coat or jacket that might have draped on the headboard beside the window. The best explanation I could come up with was that my sister-in-law might have changed her baby just before we went out to the porch, and left the diaper bag on the night table. If it was there when the picture was taken, it, along with the reflections on the glass, could have ended up looking like the girl in Edie's print.

But was that possible in only one photograph?

The new print I ordered for Edie was not as clear. The window was blurred the same as it was on the smaller prints. I stopped at her house on the way home and gave her the print. I had not called ahead and she was surprised by my visit.

"That was just about the strangest thing I ever saw. I can't understand it at all," she said, patting at the rollers under the scarf on her head. "I'd invite you in for a while, but we're going to a program at church tonight."

I politely declined her indirect invitation, saying I still had a lot to do at home.

"Well, thank you for the picture," she said. "You sure do have a nice house. I'm so proud of you for it."

I waved as I backed down her drive. She stood on the porch of her tidy brick bungalow, waving and smiling, and looking around to see if any of her neighbors were looking at her on her front porch with her hair in rollers.

I took the print home and put it in my photograph box. Before closing the envelope, I looked again at the strange apparition in the window. The image of the girl was so clear. Could it really have been outside reflections against the darkness of the room? Had a tree shifted just as the eye of the camera had opened with its reflection creating the illusion of someone sitting in the window? But I could even see the color of the girl's eyes in the photo. Could it really have been that clear if it had been only an illusion?

I put the photograph away and shut it out of my mind. After years of living alone I had learned not to fill my head with such things. Reading a book about ghosts can be thrilling, but let a stair tread creak back into place in the middle of the night and the mind jumps to the worst possible explanation. No, if I was going to live alone, I did not need to fill my subconscious mind with a strange girl's face staring from a vacant bedroom's window.

Time was going by quickly. Work at the office settled down - it was generally slower during the summer months. Without overtime, I was able to resume my projects at home with renewed vigor and I began the first remodeling project - stripping the thick layers of old wallpaper off the dining room and living room walls.

I started with the living room. The process was tedious. It required soaking the old wallpaper with a solvent I bought at the paint store. Wearing rubber gloves, I dipped an old towel in a bucket of the solution and then blotted it against the wall until the paper was soaked through. After an hour of soaking, vigorous scraping would remove a layer of paper. I had to soak and scrape again and again until I finally reached the plaster wall. I counted six layers of paper on the living room walls, and it looked like the dining room had more.

There would be moments of familiarity when I peeled away a layer to reveal an older layer underneath. This familiarity grew stronger with the older layers. But I had been in old houses like this most of my life and told myself I was remembering the same patterns from one of those. The first time I revealed the oldest layer, I had a sudden mental image of the entire room. It was like a quick mental snapshot with full detail - down to the curtains on the windows and even the magazines on the sofa table. For a moment it was like I was in a three-dimensional projection of the room as it had been.

But mostly, I slogged on. The wet paper and old paste liquefied and formed a putty, coating my gloves and running down my arms. I worked on it all weekend. During the week, if I started as soon as I arrived home and worked until bedtime, I could clear another section about two feet wide and two feet high. The progress was slow - too slow.

Roughly calculating the area of remaining wall surface and how much area I could strip at a time, I estimated it would be mid-October before I finished the living room, the entry area, and the staircase. Without ever having done this before, I had underestimated the task, stupidity believing I could have all the wallpaper in the entire house stripped by the end of July - and the walls and woodwork in all the rooms painted by Christmas. I was falling farther and farther behind my schedule, but all I could do about it was keep plodding along - four soggy square feet at a time.

Chapter Six

By coincidence, that summer I hired a new bookkeeper who had remodeled an old house before her divorce. We ended up talking more about houses than her job qualifications during her interview and she suggested a wallpaper stripping method she had used herself. Before she left, she wrote the recipe on my notepad. Of twenty applicants, she was the one I hired.

That weekend I attacked the remaining wallpaper with unexpected gusto. The main ingredient of her recipe had been difficult to locate, but after calling several old-fashioned hardware stores I found a supply that would last me through the rest of the project. The new solution cut the soaking time in half and long strips of wet paper peeled away after just one application.

I worked on it late Friday night and was up and at it again before daylight the next morning. By Saturday evening I had worked my way around the remaining walls of the living room. I should have quit there, but I wanted to get a start on the staircase before I stopped for the day.

The landing was going to be more difficult. The ceiling there was higher and I could not reach it with the step stool I had been using for the living room. I was only going to work on it for a little while so, instead of getting the step ladder from the garage, I dragged one of the dining room chairs to the landing. When I stood on it, I could just barely reach the top of the wall.

By trial and error, I had learned to start soaking at the top and work my way down. Standing on the chair and reaching high, I sponged the wet towel against the paper until nothing more could be squeezed out. I stepped down off the chair, dipped the towel in the bucket, and stepped back up on the chair. The process was slow, and the house was hot. There was only a slight breeze on the staircase from the open windows. A fan would have helped, but also worked against me by drying the paper I was trying to get as wet as possible. I promised myself I would stop as soon as I finished the square I had started.

I stepped down from the chair again, swished the towel around in the brown water and tried not to breathe in the acrid fumes. I stepped back up on the chair. As I reached for the top of the wall, the chair tipped and I was falling backwards down the staircase. I tried to grab something - anything - but caught only flat walls and air. I was going to fall backwards down the staircase.

In the final split second I jumped forward off the chair and, as it tumbled on down the staircase, I came down hard on my hands and knees. With a splintering of old wood, the chair crashed into the newel post at the base of the steps.

I started down the stairs. The chair, part of my dining room set, now lay in pieces. It could never be replaced. Why was I so lazy and stupid? Why hadn't I taken the extra moments to get my step ladder from the garage?

With my first step, something was not right. I looked down and moaned in shock. The entire heel pad of my left foot was dragging behind my foot like a bloody lump of raw chicken, hanging only by a small flap of skin at the back. My foot must have come down hard on one of the tumbling chair legs as I jumped in the opposite direction, ripping the heel pad almost completely off my foot. I was standing on the raw flesh and bone underneath with blood soaking the carpet.

The sight of blood, especially my own, has always made me feel faint. Fighting away the blackness that was gathering around the edges of my vision, I sat on the top step and simply pushed the near-severed heel back to where it should be on my foot and held it in place. That almost stopped the flow of blood, but it was all over my hands now too - more blood than I had ever seen. I knew I was going to pass out. I bent forward, putting my head between my knees to stop the spinning.

I needed help. I had to get help. I had to figure out what to do. The telephone was in the kitchen. I had to get to the telephone. Somehow, I managed to go down the staircase, sliding down one step at a time on my rump while holding my bleeding foot together. I left a trail that looked like someone had been murdered on the landing and the body dragged down the stairs. At the bottom I held onto the newel post and stood and, holding my injured foot with my right hand, made my way around the pile of broken chair pieces lying there and hopped to the kitchen, using my left hand for balance and leaving smears of blood on the walls.

Fighting with alternating urges to vomit and to faint, I bound my foot tightly with a dish towel from the kitchen sink. It seemed to help, even though blood soaked through it immediately.

I found the telephone directory, a small miracle in itself, and called my doctor at home. He asked if I needed an ambulance. It was only three blocks to the hospital, and I decided I could get there quicker by driving myself. He would meet me at the emergency room as soon as he could get there. He said he would call ahead so they would meet me at the entrance.

I wrapped a second towel around my foot, then ripped up another and used the strips to tie the towel in place. I found my car keys and without changing clothes went to the car. At the only stop light between the house and the hospital, I fought to stay conscious and prayed for the light to change.

I drove directly to the emergency room entrance. A nurse was waiting for me at the door, scolding me for driving myself. She made me leave my car where it was and sit in the wheelchair. She wheeled me inside and then helped me get onto a table in the emergency room. She gave me a tetanus shot and checked me for shock.

The doctor came in and had me lie on my stomach facing away from him. He removed the wrapping from my foot, complimenting me on my work.

"Boy Scouts' first aid training, I guess," I joked through clenched teeth. With the shock of the impact wearing off, my foot was throbbing red hot. If I let myself scream or cry I would not be able to stop. He gently examined the wound, which was beginning to clot, gluing the heel pad back to my foot.

"You say this was all hanging backward?" he asked.

"Yes, only attached by that flap of skin at the back," I said. "Am I going to lose it?"

He looked at the skin that had remained attached.

"No," he finally said. "The pad is intact, torn away in one piece, but you still have enough blood vessels coming from the back of the heel to supply the pad. In actuality, the callous part of the heel has little blood supply and very little feeling, although I am sure you don't agree right now. Most of your pain is from the damage to the exposed flesh underneath which will heal in time. Eventually, the soft tissue will generate a new pad and what you have damaged tonight will peel away. That will take several months to complete.

The best thing to do now is to stitch it back into place to protect the damaged flesh underneath."

All the time he was talking, I was aware he was working behind me.

"This will hurt a bit," he said. The nurse came around to take my hands in hers and held tight.

What followed felt like liquid fire from my foot shooting up my leg into my belly. He peeled back the pad and doused the raw flesh underneath with saline to clean it and then with antiseptic. I bit my lips together to keep from screaming out at the pain. Two tears ran down my cheeks and the nurse wiped them away.

With the wound cleaned, I could feel him push the pad back into place. With the nurse assisting, he began stitching. Forty-eight stitches later he put a heavy bandage on my foot, gave me a shot of antibiotics, and wrote out a prescription for a pain killer and a crutch that were filled from the hospital's pharmacy. He told me to come by his office in two days to have the dressing changed.

"Try not to walk directly on it, don't get it wet, and for heaven's sake don't wear a shoe on that foot." As if I could get a shoe on over the cast-like bandage.

I went home, let myself in, set the bottles of medicine on the kitchen counter, and went on through to the living room. The shattered chair still lay at the bottom of the stairs, ruined.

Leaning on the crutch, I hopped up the staircase on my right foot, picked up the wet towel and the scraper and looked at the blood trail on the carpet. A little blood goes a long way. It looked like someone had been murdered on my stairs. Even though it was late, I was too keyed up to go to bed, so I refilled the bucket with cold water and, over the next hour, washed most of the blood from the carpet and off the walls.

I could not understand how I had fallen. I placed another dining chair on the landing in exactly the same place. The marks were still visible in the carpet - just one set of four dents, signifying the chair had not moved at all while I got on and off it. It was at least two feet from the chair to the edge of the landing. Had I somehow pushed it backwards that far without realizing it? I shoved the chair toward the edge now, but it did not slide easily on the carpet. In fact, it took a strong and deliberate shove to move it more than an inch, and then it left a trail in the nap of the carpet. There were no other marks like that from before.

It took some effort to push it all the way to the edge. Careful to keep my balance, I leaned over to put some weight on it. Even though it looked like the back legs were on solid footing, they really only rested on the nap of the carpet. It tipped backwards easily, but this time I caught the chair before it rolled on down the staircase.

Even though the tracks on the carpet said differently, the only possible explanation was that in climbing on and off the chair, I had gradually nudged it to the edge without realizing it. I was fortunate I had jumped off rather than tumbling down the staircase with it. My torn foot was nothing compared to the injuries I could have suffered falling down the stairs along with the chair and its four pointed legs. I really could have been killed.

Finally deciding it was time to call it a night, I took two more of the pills and went to bed, propping up my injured foot high on two pillows. As the drug took effect, the throbbing in my injured heel began to subside and I relaxed.

I felt myself sliding sideways into heavy sleep. As I lost the last remnants of consciousness, I thought I heard something down the hall. There was taunting laughter and the chant of a nursery rhyme, familiar, but something that I could not quite remember. I tried to listen, but I was drifting down deeper and deeper into the drug. Finally, a door slammed somewhere and the chanting stopped, and I let myself go into a deep and welcome sleep.

With the thick bandage on my foot, I almost had to learn to walk again. Determined not to rely on the crutch I worked out a limping gate, walking normally on my right foot, while only placing my weight on the ball and toes of my left foot with the injured heel lifted slightly off the ground. Even though I gave up my running routine and tried to keep walking to a minimum, the calf muscles of my left leg were continually sore. It woke me every night, drawing up in a tight cramp that only went away when I stood and fully extended the leg.

I saw the doctor every week for months. The bandage was changed and the wound was debrided - a fancy word he used that meant slicing away the dead skin. The first few times I could not look, but finally I forced myself to watch. I gasped in revulsion.

The heel pad had turned completely black and a sickly sweet

odor emanated from the wound. Every week, the doctor used a scalpel to trim the heel pad and took out a few more of the stitches. The day I finally looked, I was shocked at the size of the stitches, each the size of a dime and crisscrossing the scar line that ran almost all the way around the heel.

When I gasped, he looked up and said reassuringly, "This is healing nicely." He explained why the dead parts needed to be trimmed away, and showed me the new, bright pink flesh the trimming revealed.

"The heel is generating a new pad from underneath that will ultimately replace the old one. For now, the old skin protects the new growth and helps it form in the correct directions. If you had lost the pad entirely, we most likely would have to do a series of operations to correctly shape the growth of the heel, but this way when the old pad has completely died and has been scraped away, as I am doing now, the new one should almost exactly replace it."

Watching him work, I was surprised that there were parts of the heel where I had no feeling whatsoever. Some of the scraping and trimming nearly put me over the edge with its tickling pain, but on other areas I could watch him deeply trim away the old flesh as though it was another person's foot and I was merely an outside observer. He told me I had some nerve damage and while the feeling might return eventually, there might also be patches where I would feel nothing: heat, cold, pain, or even pressure.

I still needed pain killers, especially on the nights after seeing the doctor, but he had changed the prescription to a milder drug. I often woke to hear the same chant I had heard the night of the accident. At first, I stumbled out of bed to find the source. Maybe I had left the radio on or children were playing outside under the street light, but everything was turned off and the street was always deserted.

I had almost convinced myself it was drug-induced - sort of a recurring hallucination that came as I drifted off to sleep. But one night when I was back in bed after searching and finding nothing, I realized that the door to the guest bedroom was closed, even though I distinctly remembered it was open when I went to bed. The windows were open that night and I propped it open to keep it from blowing shut during the night. When I went back to look, the rubber doorstop wedge was deliberately pushed aside. It was the slamming door that had jarred me from sleep. Unlike the shadowy woman who walked through my bedroom in the middle of the night and seemed unaware of my presence, if this was being caused by the girl in the photograph, she knew who I was and was taunting me. Like the child she was, she could be using bad behavior to get a reaction.

My foot was throbbing, so I sat on the chair in the guest bedroom and tried to remember the words I had heard. Rubbing the bandage to relieve the maddening itch underneath, it seemed that the words 'Marching through the town' were part of it.

I vaguely remembered a book of nursery rhymes my mother used to read aloud. Maybe what I was hearing in the dream was one of those. If I had that book, maybe I could find the rhyme.

I called my mother the next morning, but with her children all grown, she no longer had the book. She was curious why I wanted it, but I told her I had a meeting in a few minutes and had to go. For a few days, as soon as I was off work, I went to all the bookstores in town, going through all the books of nursery rhymes, with the explanation that I was looking for a birthday gift for my niece. I read at least two dozen of the books, even one that claimed to be the "complete" edition of classic children's nursery rhymes, but could find nothing even close to the phrase I was looking for.

I went to the public library as soon as it opened on Saturday morning and asked the librarian for any and all books of nursery rhymes they had. With a blank face she asked the ages of my children and stared in silence when I told her I wanted to read them for myself.

"I was looking for a specific one I have been trying to remember," I said. "You know how something gets stuck in your mind . . . You know, "Marching through the town" or something like that?"

She looked at me for a long moment as if nothing like that ever happened to her - getting something stuck in her mind - then went to a back counter, thumbed through a shelf, produced a thick and battered catalog, and consulted it for several more minutes.

"Most of the rhymes in children's books today have been sanitized from their original versions," she said without looking up. "Especially after the turn of the century. None of the books in the children's department last more than four or five years, so all you would find in that department are the current versions."

I thanked her, thinking she was finished, but she held up a hand to silence me, still looking through the binder. I waited until she spoke again.

"Yes, just as I thought! We do have a book in the adult section on the fantastic origins of children's games which may be of interest to you." She made a note of the reference number, handed it to me, and said it would be on the second floor, in the section of old reference books in the back corner. She just waved me off when I thanked her again. I think I was starting to annoy her.

I found the section and eventually found the book, which was filed out of order. It was an old, worn volume, with the gold lettering almost gone from the spine. The title was barely legible; *A Study of the Macabre Origins of Children's Rhymes.*

I opened this book and I was immediately intrigued with the older style printing and the hand-sewn binding. The paper was thick and yellowed and showed the accumulated stain from many hands at the edges of the pages. A musty smell arose as I thumbed through it.

The book was a collection of essays about the chilling origins of many children's nursery rhymes. One explained that *Ring Around the Rosie* originated when bubonic, or the "Great Plague," swept through London in 1665. The phrase "Ashes, ashes we all fall down" was a nod to the mass cremations of dead too numerous to bury - hardly a pleasant thing for children to be chanting.

Another passage said that *Mary, Mary, Quite Contrary*, mocked Mary Tudor, who was also called "Bloody Mary." She was the daughter of Henry VIII, who sought to return England to Catholicism when she took his throne. "Silver bells, cockle shells, and pretty maids all in a row," in this rhyme referred to various torture devices she used on the Protestants who would not convert.

Intrigued, I took the book to a table and read half a dozen more of these similar chilling descriptions, but none of them compared to finding the rhyme I had been trying to remember. As I thumbed through the remaining pages, what I was looking for all but leapt off the page:

> *Goosey goosey gander,*
> *whither shall I wander?*
> *Upstairs and downstairs*
> *and in my lady's chamber.*
>
> *There I met an old man*
> *who wouldn't say his prayers,*
> *so I took him by his left leg*

and threw him down the stairs.

Even this toned-down version was gruesome, and no doubt why it was not included in the children's books sold in modern bookstores. The essayist explained that when Cromwell eradicated the Catholic Church from England, this rhyme was actually a taunt against Cromwell's soldiers, who goose-stepped through the countryside looking for the last hold-outs of the Catholic Church.

In that reign of terror, the landed gentry who did not convert hid their beloved parish priests in concealed rooms and worshiped at home. When Cromwell's soldiers raided an estate, they marched up and down the stairs, and even into the lady's chamber. When the hidden room was found and the priest exposed, he was forced - to his eternal damnation - to not only recite Protestant prayers, but in English instead of Latin. If he refused, they threw him down the stairs, usually fatal for the aged priest, while the soldiers laughed.

The essay concluded with what was thought to be the original and complete version of this rhyme. Reading the last two verses sent a chill down my spine:

Old father Long-Legs
can't say his prayers,
take him by the left leg,
and throw him downstairs

The stairs went crack,
he nearly broke his back.
and all the little ducks went,
quack, quack, quack!

I knew these were the words I had been hearing at home. Even sitting in the library, I could hear the voice reciting those last lines and the taunting laughter that echoed down my hallway.

I closed the book for a moment, marking the page with my finger, and tried to stop trembling. I glanced around. I was the only person on the second floor. I read the entire essay again, but it offered no further explanation for my situation. The old man represented the clergy, but I was not even Catholic - in fact I barely went to church. I didn't know a word of Latin, so when I prayed I definitely prayed in English. Sure, I owned the house, but I was definitely not landed gentry. Why was this rhyme being used against me?

Until that moment I had never really believed in anything

remotely like this. I always said that when you were dead, you were dead - end of story. But I was beginning to grasp that there was someone or something in my house, possibly taking the form of a young girl, that wanted to harm me. Did it want to grab me by the left leg and throw me down the stairs? It had nearly succeeded. What had I done to summon this kind of animosity?

Until the librarian flashed the lights and then came upstairs to tell me it was closing time, I spent the rest of the day browsing through the other books in the section. I had eaten nothing all day, so I decided to go to a cafeteria I liked. Not wanting to go home, I lingered over dinner, then drove aimlessly around town until long after dark.

Finally, I drove home and parked the car in the garage. Immediately I wondered how I could have been so stupid to come home so late, when the house was completely dark. I crossed the small yard and opened the storm door. When I stuck the key in the lock, the door swung open slightly on its hinges. I was positive it was locked when I left for the library.

With an eerie creak of the hinges, I pushed the door open enough to reach inside for the light switch. Through the door's window I saw the harsh overhead light flooding the landing and stairwell and casting a rectangle of light into the dark kitchen. From inside the house, I heard the telephone ring four times and stop. I stood silently listening for any other sound inside the darkened house.

After what seemed like an eternity I pushed the door all the way open. If someone was in the house, he was silent. Instead of going up the short flight of stairs to the kitchen, I decided to search the basement first. I threw open the doors to the small pantry in front of me, but there was nothing except a jumble of canned foods, cooking pots, paper supplies and, for some reason, the hammer I had misplaced months ago on the shelf that was at eye level - unseen until now, even though I used the pantry almost every day.

Taking the hammer with me, I snapped on the basement lights and crept down the stairs, checking behind the furnace, the storage cabinets under the staircase and even the old coal chute swathed in cobwebs. No one was in the basement.

I made my way through the house. I checked behind the living room sofa, underneath the dining room buffet, and behind the door in the half bath downstairs. I left all the lights on in each room as I went. Up the staircase, I looked carefully in the new mirror on the landing before making the blind turn, making sure nothing was around the corner on the stairs.

On the second floor I proceeded through the bedrooms one by one, always keeping an eye on the central hall. I had heard stories about intruders going from one room to another while a house was being searched, hiding in a previously-checked closet.

I wondered if my imagination was running away with me until I reminded myself that I was certain I had locked the door as I left for the library that morning.

Finally, I approached the guest bedroom. My search had revealed nothing and every light in the house was on. I looked under the bed, lifting the bed skirt cautiously to peer underneath. The closet was the last hidden space and as I stood in front of the door I realized I should have called the police rather than foolishly searching the house myself. Other than a hammer, I was completely unarmed. What was I planning to do anyway if I found someone - smack them with my hammer? And then what? I could not run. Was it too late to turn and walk from the room and leave the house? Whoever was inside the closet would have heard my search until now and realized I was hesitating at the last moment. Realizing my fear, whoever was there would have the upper hand in what followed. I felt the hair on the back of my neck rising as the adrenalin rushed through my veins.

I held my breath, gathered my courage, and yanked the door open. A movement to the right caught my eye and I yelled and gave a hard, slicing blow with the hammer, catching only a wisp of something soft. I pulled back my hammer, ready to strike again, but other than a jacket swinging on its hanger, the closet was empty.

I almost collapsed in relief; there was no intruder. I limped through the house turning off lights and rechecking locks, getting the house ready for the night. I decided I must have left the door unlocked when I left for the library, even if I was sure I remembered locking it.

I went to bed that night without taking any medication. I lay in bed trying to calm my thoughts for sleep. I had stayed too long at the library and my foot hurt in a different way tonight, not sharply focusing along the scar line, but in a diffused pain across the entire heel.

After an hour I decided I wasn't going to be able to sleep

without the pills and got out of bed. I limped down the hall to the linen closet to get the bottle. I took two, then I stood, listening at the door to the guest bedroom. There was total silence.

I opened the door and looked around the room. A shaft of moonlight came through the windows, shining on the bed. The rest of the room was in shadows.

I went in and settled in the chair in the opposite corner, massaging my aching foot through the bandage. I leaned back and tried to clear my racing mind. What was in this room? What was here that wanted to harm me? Was it the child in the photograph - a lost soul? I tried to relax my mind and to reach out to what was here, but could not. There was nothing here now.

I went back to bed, wondering if there was someone I could call for help, but from that night on I was not bothered in that way again. I bought some children's books and left them opened on the dresser. At night I started stopping at the door to silently communicate a 'good night' to her. I wondered at my own sanity in doing this, but it seemed to quiet the activity in the guest room at night. For the next two years, other than waking for the occasional 3:05 A.M. appearance, my sleep was undisturbed.

Chapter Seven

For a long time, it seemed like the more I did to the house, the worse things got.

An experienced home renovator will tell you, sometimes quite poetically, to take one room, make it your own, and then allow the house to reveal itself to you. Good advice, except my house was buried under so many layers of grime and bad remodeling projects that approach was not possible. At last, I had to admit that the house was uninhabitable, and living in it during the project was not only counterproductive, but probably dangerous to my health as well. I packed everything I owned, put it in storage, and camped out on a mattress and springs in the breakfast room, cordoned off behind a double barrier of plastic sheeting.

After my foot healed, the first year was consumed with stripping away everything that was wrong. I taught myself to use a steam-powered wallpaper remover, which was faster, and the day finally came when all the ceilings and walls in every room were bare plaster. I opened a bottle of wine that night, walked through the echoing and empty rooms, and raised a solitary glass to the results and to myself for finally reaching that milestone.

Next, I pulled up the old wall-to-wall carpet, leaving a small mountain at the curb for the trash man. A heavyweight, drum-type floor sander became my next best friend. I laid a small, temporary floor of salvaged wood in the dining room and practiced on it until I was confident with the machine. The dust the sander raised permeated everything, but the dark and crackled layers of old wax and varnish disappeared almost magically, revealing beautiful, top-grade oak floors underneath.

When the varnish was dry, the floors were covered and taped so that reclamation of the woodwork could begin. All of the battered first-floor doors were sent out to be professionally stripped and primed for paint. The final cost of that ran too far over my budget, so the second floor became another do-it-yourself project. One door at a time was taken down, numbered, and carried to the garage to be sanded smooth and primed for painting.

Not counting the sleeping porch, there were twenty-six windows in the house, each one double-hung with an upper and lower sash on concealed counterweights. In keeping with the Classic New England style, every sash had six panes of glass held in place by wood muntin bars. Each muntin had to be hand sanded precisely without scratching the glass. Sanding and preparing a single window for paint took an entire Saturday of work. The baseboards, door facings, and crown moldings were next. I hired a finish carpenter to duplicate the crown molding that was mysteriously missing from the living room.

When I started on the second floor doors, my first step was to take off all the hardware, mark it, and set it aside. Through the years, someone had decided to paint the hardware the same as the doors, and now the chipped paint was so thick that the fine detailing in the metal was barely visible. At first, I planned to strip the hardware to the bare metal, spray it with primer, and then paint it with enamel paint that matched the painted wood. When I stripped the first lock plate, I was delighted to discover that it was solid brass, in keeping with the dining room chandelier.

By itself, the chandelier had been the kind of surprise that a renovator brags about. It was sticky brown with accumulated grime, most of it nicotine from Miss Addie's chain-smoking. Instead of trying to clean it in place, I disconnected the wiring and took it down. Realizing only then that the chandelier was solid brass, it simply took a couple of cleanings with brass polish for it to gleam again.

The cloudy brown crud on its glass hurricane globes was more stubborn and could not be scrubbed away until they were soaked overnight. The next morning I washed and rinsed them and was amazed there was not one nick or chip. I also realized they were full-lead crystal instead of plain glass. Someone had spent some money on the fixture. When I screwed in the correct light bulbs and the fixture was back in place, it was like the house breathed a sigh of relief.

Over a three-day weekend, I stripped and refinished all the staircase treads. Then, each spindle of the balustrade was sanded and tightened. Furniture stripper and fine steel wool removed the gummy black residue from the bannister rail, revealing fine, tightly-grained mahogany.

Eighteen months into the project, the day came when I finally had a blank slate. I was ready to begin.

Like a reluctant lover at first, she (and I had started thinking of my house in the feminine sense by then) gradually revealed herself to me. Along with all the grit, sweat, blood, and even tears, there had been wonderful surprises. As the layers of neglect and abuse began falling away, she more generously shared her delights: the deep window sills in the living room that were wide enough to hold a candle at Christmas time, the finely grained wood panels of the front door, the dovetail joints in the drawers of the built-in dresser in the master bedroom's walk-in closet, and even the packet of forgotten photographs behind one of those drawers.

Over a rainy weekend, at the end of the demolition phase - and on a whim - I pulled up the old kitchen linoleum. There turned out to be two layers of it, the top was a hideous "place and press" type that was probably put down in the 1960s, then a sturdy layer of serviceable gray linoleum suited to a hospital or industrial kitchen. After the old linoleum was carried to the curb, I scraped away the old asphalt backing that remained on the floor and finally sanded the wood with the floor sander.

The wood floor underneath was only an underlayment of C-grade, six-inch-wide, tongue and groove, pine subflooring laid down with no concern for matching the grains. The planks were peppered with knots, blemishes, and uneven colorings. They had never been sanded and there were still circular saw marks on some of the boards. Others looked like they had been scraped and leveled by hand before the linoleum was laid. They needed to be sanded before any new flooring could be laid over them. The plank floor would never be completely smooth, but I still ran the sander over it, taking off the rough spots.

I had only intended to prepare this subfloor before putting down the underlayment for the ceramic floor tile I had on order for the sleek, modern kitchen I had planned. But looking at the freshly-sanded wood, it was like the house spoke to me, telling me what she wanted. I wasn't sure if it would work, but I sanded the floor again, using only fine sand paper - leaving some of the saw marks and scrapes. Then I gave it three coats of satin varnish. The soft highlights of the finished wood ranged from dark gray where the more porous planks had absorbed the asphalt backing, to warm golden tones, and even some shades of mahogany red.

Because of the floor, my plans for the kitchen changed to what my decorator friend, Pamela, said was "Old Charleston" the first time she saw it. I made sketches and came up with a new design that included glass doors on new upper cabinets, a farmhouse style sink, a center island of painted bead board paneling, and even an old-fashioned gas range set into a new alcove of used brick that looked like an Old South kitchen fireplace. The plan came as one complete idea - as clearly as if I had been handed a set of color photographs - and it was all based on the floor that had been there all along, under two layers of old linoleum.

It was the same with the new French doors that flanked the living room mantle. It was really a simple project; the most difficult part was taking out the windows and cutting the openings down to floor level. My carpenter installed two ready-made, pre-hung doors. Each door had fifteen panes of glass and looked like they had always been there. They also gave direct access to the back yard from the living room. That idea came to me early one morning - again, complete and as a finished picture - when I paused in the living room as I was leaving for work, and from that angle I saw that the doors would be better than windows.

When I started, my plan was to return the house to its original condition. I even saved pieces of the first wallpapers, carefully labeled by room, hoping to match them as closely as possible when it was time to order new.

But over time, I recognized that the house was actually a faithful and true Colonial reproduction, instead of the 1930s modern version of the Colonial Revival style. Simply returning the house to its original appearance would do her a disservice. She deserved better than that. I started a portfolio of articles on Colonial architecture and interiors, paint colors, and even an article on the period's paint-making methods. In the end, all of the walls, except the kitchen and breakfast room, were painted in the colors of Colonial Williamsburg and Mount Vernon. With the decorating phase underway, I began scouting out estate sales and auctions for antiques or reproductions that were in keeping with the period.

After three years of work, when the inside work was almost complete, Pamela found a reproduction of an early, hand-painted wallpaper that she insisted was perfect for my dining room. The dining room walls were already painted Federal blue, but when I saw the paper I agreed. It came dearly, even with her decorator's discount. My carpenter returned to construct a paneled wainscot topped with a deep chair rail. I painted all the dining room woodwork, including the new wainscot, a crisp linen-white. With everything else in place, the new wallpaper was hung. From the first strip, it was as if it had always been there.

As a surprise - and a delayed house-warming present, Pamela sewed a set of Federal-style headers - a swag and jabots - for each dining room window from a bolt of raw silk she had left over from a decorating job. The fabric exactly matched the background of the new wallpaper. She lined the pleated jabots with another remnant of a slightly darker satin-striped fabric. I helped her put up the new draperies, and with that, the interior of the house was finished.

Over time, I had recognized that Pamela, so enthusiastic about the project, would not be left in my house alone. She was reluctant to go upstairs, even if I was with her. We never talked about it, but when she shivered the first time she was in the master bedroom, I knew she sensed something there. I had been asking her advice about shelves I wanted to put in the closet when I realized she had looked over her shoulder at my desk in the corner the third time. I pretended I had not seen, and she made excuses to leave when it started getting dark. No matter how many lights I turned on, she was always out of the house by dusk.

With the dining room finished, the house was bright, sunny, inviting and cheerful. It was almost impossible to recall how awful it had been the first time I saw it. Nothing else had happened since my accident on the stairs and even though I still had a slight limp sometimes, I told myself that whatever was leftover from whatever had happened was long gone now. Even the air inside the house was relaxed now.

When the inside was finished, the house almost seemed to sing. Then, like an impatient mistress who is never satisfied, she reminded me it was time to start on the exterior.

Chapter Eight

I was well into the exterior restoration work when Eva parked at the curb that spring morning.

Scraping through the layers of paint on the siding and trim verified the house had always been white, although the color of the shutters had varied. They were working shutters, mounted on hinges so they could be closed over the windows and latched. The hinges had rusted in the open position and likely had been that way for years. My carpenter was working them over, one pair at a time. I would paint them before he put them back up.

Even before I started stripping and priming the wood trim, the paint colors were already decided. Inspired by a trip to Charleston, Pamela suggested a palette of pale yellow for the siding, white for the trim, and a glossy black for the shutters. She said the front door would "pop" if it was painted a deep cranberry red. On her suggestion, I ordered the paint from a company in South Carolina that specialized in replicating colors for historic properties. If Eva had stayed longer, I would have brought out the file to show her the exterior plans.

After Eva left, I worked until it was almost dark. I was encouraged by how much I accomplished that day and planned to work most of Sunday, too. I wanted to have everything ready and primed for paint by fall. It would be even better if I could have the painting finished and all the shutters back on the house for the Christmas season.

After a hot shower and change of clothes, I warmed up dinner in my new microwave oven. It was set back into its own niche in the new kitchen fireplace. There was a second niche directly below it where I kept several sticks of firewood, even though there had never been, and never would be, a fire in the kitchen fireplace. The tall, open hearth itself was entirely taken up with a six-burner gas range. When the old Colonial Hotel downtown closed and the furnishings and equipment were auctioned off, Pamela bought the range. She insisted it was perfect for me. Completely refurbished, it cooked beautifully, but I preferred the microwave for a quick warming of leftovers.

I poured myself a glass of wine and when the microwave's beeper sounded, I took out my plate, pulled open a drawer in the island for a fork and napkin, and carried my dinner and a glass of wine upstairs. I had turned the extra bedroom, the one that had the dried-up watercolors in it the first time I saw the house, into a small den. Bookcases now lined the walls and, on Pamela's advice, an oversized sofa and an antique armoire that served as a television cabinet were squeezed into the small space. It made a cozy area and I liked to relax there and watch television when I had dinner alone.

I usually watched the British television comedies the local public broadcast station aired on Saturday evenings. During a commercial break, or actually a break where they asked for donations to continue their programming, I carried the dishes back downstairs, put them in the dishwasher and poured myself a second glass of wine. Before going back upstairs, I checked that the doors were locked and the lights were on their night settings. That way, I would not have to come downstairs again when I wanted to go to bed.

On Saturday evenings, the station ran four comedies in a row - thirty minutes each. I must have dozed off during the third, because when I woke with a start, the fourth show was well underway. I was slumped down on the sofa so I pushed myself to more of an upright position, then swung my legs up and around to stretch out sideways, picked up my wine glass from the end table, finished the last sip, and settled back to watch the rest of the show. I would go to bed as soon as it was over.

I had seen this show before and the series was a personal favorite - set in a London department store with a motley crew of retail clerks and inept management. I easily picked up where it was, there was about twenty minutes left.

Along with the show's dialogue and recorded laugh track, I was hearing a sort of prolonged squeal or squeak. I knew that the station recorded the shows from a weekly network feed and then played them during the scheduled time slot. They really needed more up-to-date equipment and there were regular issues with the audio on these shows. I got off the sofa to see if fine-tuning the station would help.

The television cabinet was by the door to the hall and until I was standing in front of it, I did not realize the noise was actually coming from outside the den. Annoyed, I stepped out into the hall, turning my ear toward the noise to determine where it was coming from. It was not continuous. It started and stopped, sometimes with a few seconds of the squeal followed by a second or two of silence. Over the television it was hard to tell where it was coming from, so I pulled the den's door closed behind me and stood, listening.

The rest of the house was silent, then it started again, coming from the guest bedroom. It must be a branch or something outside rubbing against one of the windows. I entered the room, turning on the overhead light. In the silence, I inspected all four windows, even raising the blinds, but there was nothing rubbing the glass. I was checking the last window when the noise came again, clearly from inside the room and behind me. I turned and saw nothing. I quietly knelt on the floor and lifted the bed skirt to look underneath, half-expecting to see a hidden squirrel or worse, but nothing was there. While I was kneeling, the squeak came again - from the direction of the dresser, set between the door to the hall and the closet door.

Still kneeling, I straightened up, looking across the bed at the dresser. Had a mouse or something gotten itself trapped in one of the dresser drawers? There were dust panels between the drawers, so it would be almost impossible for anything to have crawled up inside. Except for a few guest towels, the dresser was empty. Wary now, I stood and walked to the dresser.

The room was completely silent. I listened carefully, both hoping and dreading, to hear the tell-tale scratching from inside the dresser. If any came, I would figure out which drawer it was, find something to cover the top while I pulled it out, and carry the drawer outside to release the mouse or whatever it was.

As I stood listening, the sound came again - but from the framed mirror hung on the wall above the dresser. Still partly bent forward, I looked up at the mirror in front of me.

The mirror was completely fogged up - like a cold bathroom mirror after a hot shower. However the "fog" on the mirror was a misty red, like the glass had been dusted with red spray paint. Not believing what I was seeing, I leaned forward to inspect it more closely. Was someone playing a trick on me? The doors were unlocked all day while I was working outside, but would someone have come into the house, taped off the mirror (since there was no red mist on the frame,) dusted it with red spray paint and then left it for me to find? How was this possible?

Standing with my face not six inches from the glass now, I saw that four letters had been written in the mist - the way a child would write with a finger on a steamed up car window.

From left to right were the letters Y, b, b, and then an upside down capital V.

What on earth? I reached out with my right hand, to wipe the fog away, but the glass was dry and nothing came off on my hand.

I leaned forward, with my face just inches from the glass, trying to figure out what it was and how it got there. The squeal came again, as an unseen finger added a cross bar to the upside down capital V from right to left.

Y b b A

What was that supposed to mean? I wiped the mirror again and held my hand out to the light. Even though something had just marked through the liquid red mist on the mirror, there was nothing on my hand. My side of the mirror was dry. The paint seemed to be on the back side of the mirror. I could still see myself and the room behind me reflected in the mirror. That meant the paint had to be between the glass and the silvered back, if that was possible.

When I looked back, the mirror was completely clear and where my own reflection should be, a girl stared back at me, with eyes sunken deep in dark sockets, thin parchment skin stretched tightly over bone, and cracked and dried lips pulled back from yellowed and rotted teeth.

I jumped back with a shout, stumbling and falling over the end of the bed to crash, flat on my back, on the floor. Gasping for breath, I immediately rolled onto my hands and knees to face the mirror. Scrambling back across the bed, it only showed my reflection now. I pressed my face as closely as I dared, foolishly trying to look inside the mirror - up and down and beyond the sides. I was sure it was the same girl in my cousin Edie's photograph and I was angry.

"You can't do this!" I yelled at the glass. "You can't be here. Get out of my house, you little brat!"

In response, there was silence. I listened, with my heart hammering in my ears. The only other sound was the muffled television behind the closed den door. She was behind another mirror now - waiting for me - and this was going to stop! I would break every mirror in the house if I had to.

I tore through the house, examining the bathroom mirror, the mirror in the master bedroom, the full-length mirror in the closet, the mirror on the landing, and the powder room mirror downstairs. I even flung open the front door, to see if she might show herself in the glass of the storm door with the black night behind it. I checked all the windows, and even the glass on the fireplace doors. All I saw in any of them was my own reflection looking back at me.

Then came the faint, echoing laughter I had not heard for years. I raced back upstairs and ran into the guest room, but there was nothing there. She was playing with me.

"Get the hell out of my house!" I shouted again. "I don't want you here. You are not welcome. You can't stay here. This is my house - not yours. GET OUT!"

Something drew my attention back to the mirror. Again it was coated with red, and this time the writing completely filled the glass, with the letters - now in reverse - repeated over and over:

AddYAddYAddYAddYAd...

The red looked different this time - liquid and wet. I swiped at the glass with my hand. It smeared and my palm was coated with it. But it was not paint. It was thinner and had a faint odor of copper. It was blood.

I looked from my hand back to the mirror, and the letters had separated themselves. It said AddY over and over. Addy. Addie. Miss Addie. Eva's sister, Adeline. The sisters had once shared this room. After that it had been Miss Addie's alone. Now I understood.

I knew the sullen, skull face that glared at me from behind the mirror could not be Miss Addie. She was in an assisted living facility across town. But whatever this was, it wanted Addie back.

Miss Addie had not wanted this. They may have been on friendlier terms when Addie was young, but as a woman she had closed this room off - kept the door locked and never entered. She never even came upstairs.

But it had not let Miss Addie alone. Angry and jealous that Addie grew up it reacted as a child would, and without mercy. Over the decades, the mental torture had slowly driven Addie insane. It eventually made her crazy enough to try to burn down the house with all of us in it. What had she said back then? That fire was the only solution? The only way to get rid of them? The only way out? I was beginning to understand.

I also understood that whatever this was, it was completely evil, and it lived in my guest room.

Chapter Nine

For a time I considered trying to contact Eva. From Mrs. Poindexter, an elderly neighbor who liked to gossip when she caught me outside, I knew that Miss Addie was too far gone now to make sense even if I was allowed to visit. The girl in the mirror appeared the night of Eva's visit. That made me think that Eva might have some insight on what was happening now.

All I had to go on was her first name and that she lived in San Francisco, but I also knew where her sister was. I called the care facility and said that I lived in Miss Addie's old house. Yes, I understood she could not have visitors, but her sister had come by to visit when she was in town. Then I lied and said that she left behind something of value. I only needed a telephone number to contact her so I could return it.

The woman who answered the telephone flatly refused. I asked to speak to her supervisor, who, when she finally came to the phone, was rude and huffy and told me they did not release personal information. When I explained again I had something to return, she asked, with thinly veiled sarcasm, how I would like for them to be giving out my telephone number to any Tom, Dick, or Harry who just happened to call and ask for it. Then she slammed the telephone down, hanging up on me.

Not to be dissuaded, I went to the mall that Saturday, bought a woman's brooch set with cubic zirconium that looked much more expensive than it was, took it out of the box, and drove over to Miss Addie's nursing home.

A sturdy-looking woman with a face like a bulldog came from the room behind the front desk. She was dressed in a proper nurse's uniform, complete with white stockings, white shoes, and a white nurse's cap. She also wore a black plastic name badge. It simply said "Nurse Jones."

"Yes?" she asked, clearly annoyed with my presence.

I explained that I had called earlier that week, and producing the brooch, said, "It must have fallen off Miss Eva's jacket when she was at my house."

I had her attention. If the diamonds were real, it certainly looked like something Eva would have worn.

"You can leave it with us and we will see that it is returned to Mrs. Song."

I had a last name! Eva Song. It only took me a moment to realize that it was probably an Asian surname, and likely a common one in San Francisco.

"I would prefer to give it back to her myself," I said, and the woman's eyes narrowed to slits at the implied accusation of dishonesty. "How about if I leave my telephone number - she already has my name and address, of course, since I live in her parent's house now - and she can contact me at her convenience?"

Nurse Jones grudgingly slid a dog-eared memo pad across the counter at me - a promotional give-away from a pharmaceuticals company - and I wrote my name and telephone number, then added my address. "Would you please see that Mrs. Song receives this information the next time she contacts Miss Addie?"

She examined the pad, tore off the page, and pinned it to the pegboard, in full view of anyone at the front desk - so much for protecting my address and telephone number!

"And how is Miss Addie?" I asked. "Any improvement? Any change?" Nurse Jones just glared at me. "Such a sad case. Well, please give her my greetings, and thank you so much for your help. I hope to hear from Eva, ummm, from Mrs. Song, soon."

I went back to the mall on my way home and returned the brooch. When the clerk asked if "She" didn't like it, I just shrugged my shoulders and stuck out my hands, like "I give up!" She gave me a sympathetic smile and processed the refund.

Unless Eva had reverted to her maiden name, or used the hyphenated last name of Montrose-Song, it would be like searching for the proverbial needle in the haystack. If she did not contact me first, I was going to have to find her among the hundreds, if not thousands, of other Songs in the San Francisco telephone directory. I hoped she did not have an unlisted telephone number.

Chapter Ten

A few weeks later, Pamela called me. She had been shopping with a client in Kansas City over the weekend, specifically in the shops in Westport, and said I needed to look at a pair of French chairs she found there. The shop owner was a colleague and Pamela had the chairs on hold under her name until I could look at them.

"They would be perfect in your living room," she said. She then lowered her voice to a whisper to add, "I am sure they are period - although they come without provenance, so the price is very affordable. Don't even look at the upholstery, they will need to be recovered for sure, but I have a fabulous fabric in mind and our upholsterer is in a lull so he could get on them right away."

I chuckled at her eagerness and promised I would drive up and have a look that weekend. I asked if she wanted to ride along. She would be attending a commercial design seminar in Atlanta, but gave me the shop's address and said she would call her colleague right away to confirm that I would be there on Saturday to see the chairs. She made me promise to call her, collect, at her hotel as soon as I made my decision.

That Saturday, I drove straight to the shop in Westport and fell in love with the chairs on sight. Pamela was right about them – I knew now that most colonial homes included European furnishings and the chairs would be the perfect complement in my living room. Fortunately, the shop took credit cards and the owner, knowing how anxious Pamela would be, even let me use his telephone so I could leave a message with her hotel's front desk.

I love the Westport area of Kansas City. It was the original frontier-days settlement on the river and was a booming retail area during the 1940s, but eventually fell into disrepair. Lately it was coming back as an upscale shopping, nightlife, and design district. I had not planned to stay overnight, but it was still early in the day so I had a leisurely lunch in one of the restaurants. It was going to be a hot day, especially for late June, but after lunch, I still wandered a while, window shopping.

On impulse, I entered a shop that had a beautifully restored façade and an interesting window display. There were other customers inside, so I did not feel conspicuous or invasive just browsing. One by one the other customers left and the owner, powerfully athletic and prematurely gray, came to greet me. He smiled and extended his hand in welcome, apologizing for neglecting me. It was one of the reasons I loved the area; his kind of service certainly did not happen in the big, impersonal chain stores.

I put out my hand to shake his, saying, "No problem, I've enjoyed looking."

The impact of his hand meeting mine stunned me. I felt like I had been slammed backward, followed with the sensation of falling down a long and telescoping tunnel, then lying on my back under a deep blue sky, and immediately getting up and running along a white stucco colonnade with a painfully bright blue sea beyond it. I was running toward a heavily-carved door that was painted white.

I drew my hand back like I had been stung. He looked at me quizzically, "Are you alright?"

Nothing quite like this had ever happened to me. Was I hallucinating? Was I having a stroke? He was going to think I was crazy. I tried to speak, but my mouth was like cotton. I swallowed, "Maybe... could I have a glass of water. Just a sudden headache, I think."

Thinking that might sound even more alarming, I added, "I really should not drink wine at lunch. Those tannins can really do a number in this hot weather, can't they?"

When he returned with the water moments later, I was fine. I felt like running out the door, but I took the paper cup, drank it, and said I was feeling much better. I thanked him, said I was sorry for the trouble, and that I should go.

He walked with me to the door and held it open for me.

"Are you sure you are alright?" he asked. "You are welcome to sit for a while, or I can call someone if you need me to."

"Well, I live in Springfield, so it would be long-distance," I said, trying to make a joke. "Yes, I am really okay now. Sorry to cause you the trouble."

"What did you see just now?" he asked, looking straight into my eyes and cutting underneath everything else with his directness.

I wanted to feign ignorance, but he continued. "When we shook hands just now, what did you see?"

I shook my head and shrugged. "Nothing," I insisted weakly. I wanted to be away from here.

"A blue sky . . . a long white colonnade . . . running away?"

"Well, I don't really think I was running away," I blurted out. Then I added, "How did you know? How could you know?"

"It just happens, sometimes," he said, holding my eyes with his. "Or it does for me, anyway."

"What is it?" I asked.

He shrugged. "No one really knows. It could be something we both remembered that we didn't know we knew, or something like that."

"Well, that certainly clears things up," I said with more sarcasm than I intended. I was becoming more confused than ever.

"I know this sounds strange, but I would like to talk to you about it - if you are open to that," he said. "I. . . I can close up early and maybe we could have an early dinner - somewhere close."

An early dinner? I looked at my watch. Was it really four-thirty already? I started to refuse, to say I still had a long drive ahead of me, but the need to hear what he wanted to tell me was stronger and pulled me in.

He was wearing dress slacks, a crisp long-sleeve shirt, and a blazer. I was in jeans, loafers without socks, and a polo shirt. I really could use a shower, too.

"I'm not dressed for dinner," I said.

"My shop uniform," he grinned, unbuttoning the blazer. "I know a casual place near here," he said. "You will fit right in. I will be the one who's overdressed." He took off his tie and stuffed it in a pocket.

"I don't even know your name," I said.

"Martin Moore," he said with a grin and stuck his hand out again. This time, nothing happened when our palms met.

"Jack Jackson," I replied and added, "I have never done anything like this."

I should have felt foolish admitting how rigid and un-spontaneous my life was, but there was something basically kind about him and I was completely at ease. After he locked up, we walked to a restaurant in the next block. He was apparently a regular customer - the hostess greeted him by name and asked if he wanted his usual table. As we followed her, most of the other diners greeted Martin or at least nodded or waved at him. I had to admit that he really seemed to be alright, and not the least bit "off." In the safety of the restaurant, I was more relaxed and confident with my decision to have dinner with him. We slid into a booth in the back with soft leather seats. Facing each other, and with high backs behind the booths, it was secluded and private.

The restaurant would not be busy for hours and it was a casual and comfortably-paced meal. Martin told me everything he knew about what we had experienced. He added that our spontaneous shared memory was likely something that had happened in a past lifetime, triggered by our first meeting.

I laughed out loud at that, and was ready to say I didn't believe in all that hocus-pocus until I saw that he was completely sincere. He had absolutely no reason to be telling me anything other than what he believed to be the truth.

"I'm sorry," I said. "I should not have laughed at you."

"It was your honest reaction," he said. "Nothing at all to apologize for. I would only be disappointed if you were not completely honest with me."

Again, it was an unusual thing to say, but it just seemed right. Over the appetizer we tried to describe to each other more fully what we had seen. I remembered more details - that I was wearing a long white garment. It slowed me down, I could not run as fast as I needed to. Martin confirmed that. He had also been running, catching up to me, and was reaching out toward me when it stopped. I had sensed someone running behind me. I knew what he was telling me was true.

We paused when the waiter cleared away the appetizer tray and again when he brought our salads. Martin asked if I would like wine with dinner and when I nodded, since my mouth was full of salad, he ordered a bottle of good cabernet. We paused once again when the waiter returned with two glasses, presented, opened, and then poured the wine.

We had barely resumed our conversation when an attractive, dark-eyed woman stopped beside the table, "Martin!" she declared dramatically. "I thought it was you."

Martin stood to greet her. They kissed lightly, then he introduced her as Clara Carson, his upstairs neighbor. I started to rise, but Clara waved me down, insisting I remain seated. All the same, I extended my hand and she took it in both of hers.

She gave me a long, intense look and asked, "Who is Addie?" then added, "Is there some sort of trouble with her?"

I was shocked. There was no way she could have known anything about it. I had not mentioned Addie to Martin. I had not even thought about her all day.

"Clara is a little bit clairvoyant," Martin said. "She just blurts these things out - kind of like she has a tic or something."

"And if my name was Zelda and I dressed a little more exotic, Martin would not tease me about it one little bit - as if he is any different!" Then looking to Martin and back at me she added in a stage whisper, "or has he not told you about himself yet?"

"Yes," I managed. "We were just discussing something like that."

Clara raised an appreciative and inquisitive eyebrow, something I also did involuntarily. I could almost hear her think, "Oh, really?" Martin chuckled and asked if Clara would join us for a moment.

"I can stay longer than that," Clara said, sitting beside me in the booth so I had to slide over. "It turns out my date was a no-show. Now why didn't I see that one coming? Tell me everything about Addie."

I think it was Martin's turn to wonder if he believed my story. It was good to be able to tell someone. I started at the beginning - seeing the house in the real estate magazine, the terrible condition it was in, how crazy Miss Addie had been - almost setting fire to the place with all of us in it, and the closed-off guest room. I told them about getting locked out the first day, coming home after that to unlocked doors, the shadowy figure that crossed my bedroom at night, and the girl's face in Edie's copy of the photograph.

When I told them about my accident on the stairs, Clara pressed her eyes shut, took my hand, and held it tightly in hers. I described what I thought I heard that night, and the old library book that explained the nursery rhyme. For a moment she closed her eyes and drew in a deep breath and released it slowly.

Then she spoke, "She meant to do so much more. She is a completely amoral being - a child really. Abnormal psychologists will tell you that their child patients are the most ruthless, completely without empathy or compassion."

We paused while the waiter cleared away our dinner plates. I had barely noticed eating my entree. When the waiter asked about dessert, Martin looked to me and when I slightly shook my head, he waved off the dessert menu. However, he did order another bottle of wine and asked for another glass for Clara.

After the wine was poured, I continued, telling them about the remodeling, how well it had gone, how Pamela came into my life and was a good friend, and how she helped guide me through the project. Without fearing they would think I was unbalanced, I told them how the house almost seemed to be a living thing, how ideas like the kitchen, the French doors, and the patio design had come to me as complete thoughts, and how some things that had once belonged in the house had found their way back through me - the silver coffee service, the mirror on the landing, and possibly even the chairs I bought that morning.

"You have been bringing them back home," Clara observed, nodding.

Then I told them about the most recent events. Another sister, Eva, showing up out of the blue and recognizing her mother's wedding silver. I expected a stronger reaction from them over that, but they seemed unimpressed. It was the most significant thing I had to tell them, or so I thought.

I continued, telling them what happened the night after Eva's visit: the unidentified noise I could not find, the writing in the red mist on the mirror, "Addy" written over and over in the bloody mist, and then seeing the girl in the photograph on the other side of the mirror, or rather a mummified version of her.

"You do know that you are clairvoyant, don't you?" Clara asked, as though she had asked me if I had always liked chocolate cake.

"I think what you saw is an earthbound spirit - an angry one that has been in your house a long time. From the way you describe her clothing, it sounds like the turn of the century, before your house was built. Maybe another house was on the same property before yours, and that's why she is there."

I set my wine glass on the table and leaned back against the cushion, "You really think I'm clairvoyant - or psychic?" I asked quietly.

It was something I could never quite admit to myself, let alone to someone else. After all, I worked with accountants, linear thinkers who went from A to B to C, methodically and without variation. Everything was black or white, balanced or out-of-balance. At best, they would think this was sign of mental instability. At worst, it bordered on evil.

"Possibly," Clara agreed. "Some of us are just more observant and notice things that most people miss. Like when I saw you come in here with Martin, I knew from the way you are dressed that you were not expecting to have dinner with him, and since Martin is usually not here until later, he must have closed up early because of you. You both have car keys with you, so you didn't ride here together, and you must have walked here together from his shop. I noticed you have a slight limp, favoring your left foot and also that that shoe slides up and down a little - or rather you step out of it slightly when you walk, so that heel is a little smaller than the other one, and possibly injured in a fairly recent accident. When you said hello to me, you had a hint of an accent, so I know you don't live here in Kansas City, confirmed by the fact that you did not change for dinner."

I was amazed.

"Some people would say all that is clairvoyance," she continued, "but it's mostly careful observation. It's a little like the profiling work I do for the police. I am just able to catch what most people miss."

She paused for my nod of agreement. "That is not what I'm talking about, though. People who are not psychic don't go around seeing the things you've seen and hearing the things you've heard: like the handwriting appearing in a magical red mist on the mirror, only to turn back to see the face of a girl who died eighty years ago."

Clara, intent now on the spirit-girl, was getting impatient with her own explanation. "Have you never experienced anything like that before?"

Really I had not. I wasn't really sure if I believed there was such a thing, this sixth sense or second sight she was describing. I said as much to her.

"Well, think of it this way," she said. "You know what being color-blind is, don't you?"

"Yes, of course."

"And you know there are some people who can't tell the difference between blue and green, or red and green."

"Yes, I know that," I said.

"Well, what if every person on earth, except just a few of us, could not tell the difference between blue and green. Suppose it all just looked blue to most people. Do you think the color green would stop existing?"

"No, I guess not."

"No - and those people who could not see it would never believe the people who could see the color green would they? The majority of people can't see it, so, to the majority, the color green would not exist. And, if over time, they decided the green-seers were lying and evil, and the green-seers were punished, ostracized, and even burned at the stake for seeing green, eventually, they would learn to ignore it, or keep completely quiet about it. Seeing green would be something no one believed possible, since most people could not see it, or would not admit if they did."

I was beginning to understand. "You, Martin, and I are the green-seers. We can see the green. We are clairvoyants, psychics, prophets, soothsayers, or whatever else you want to call it. We have the ability to see things that most of the population of this world cannot."

Clara rose abruptly from the table. For a moment, I was afraid I had offended her, but she said she had to do some things before she went home. Martin rose from his seat to say goodnight. They hugged warmly. I also stood and Clara hugged me tightly to her, holding her cheek against mine.

"I was totally blown away the first time I realized it, too," she said. "It just takes some getting used to - even among friends.

And I'm still not very good at it. If I was, I certainly would not have been stood up tonight, would I?" she said, her eyes crinkling up with laughter.

She tucked her purse under her arm, and stood on tiptoes again to kiss Martin goodnight. She turned back to me, "I will see you again, soon. We can talk more then."

After she was gone, Martin told me about their friendship, how they found each other in college, and what it was like to have a friend he could finally open up to about his abilities. I was amazed how natural I felt with him and Clara, and how I was able to talk about what had happened to me without getting disbelieving looks or worrying about the repercussions. It was warm, relaxed, and comfortable in the booth and our ensuing conversation flowed easily with the wine. We had sipped it slowly, but we finished the third bottle.

"Oh, my God," I exclaimed when I finally looked at my watch. "Is it really that late?" It was past nine-thirty. I would not be home until long after midnight.

"Where are you staying?" he asked.

"I'm not," I said picking up my car keys and scooting toward the aisle. "I only drove up for the day. I really need to get started. I'm driving home tonight."

"Not after at least a bottle of wine each, you're not," he said, laughing gently. "No responsible friend lets a friend drive like that. We are checking you into a hotel."

I nodded, trying to remember where I had parked my car. Surely I had a parking ticket or two by now.

"Or. . ." he continued, "I have a guest room, already made up. And I assure you I am not a mass-murderer."

I blushed a little, realizing he had read my thoughts earlier. Pamela and anyone else from home would have told me to run, to get the heck out of there. They would warn that they would find me - or what was left of me - months from now, buried in an unmarked grave. But I knew Martin was alright. We were going to be friends for a long time. I completely trusted him.

I nodded my consent, but said, "I didn't even bring a toothbrush."

He grinned again, a grin that was becoming more charming,

"You know, you can buy those things right here in Kansas City. We'll stop and pick up what you need at the drug store. But first, I will walk you to your car, and you can wait in it until I come back with mine. You can follow me."

After a quick stop at Walgreen's, I followed his car to his building.

Chapter Eleven

It was an old apartment building from the 1920s, one of hundreds in the area between the Country Club Plaza and downtown. Red brick, with two apartments per floor, it had a wonderful old, black-and-white-tiled lobby at the ground level. I half-expected a silent film star to come strolling down the ornate staircase. There were three floors of apartments above the lobby level. Martin's unit was on the second floor, so he had a wide, private veranda on the front overlooking the tree-lined boulevard. Clara's unit was directly above his. He explained that everyone in the building shared the same gift. It was like they were all drawn in, and once there, stayed.

"We say that we could save money by disconnecting from the electric company - that we generate enough power on our own to keep the lights going," he joked as he unlocked his door.

I was amazed at the size of the place. The apartment had a huge living room with windows and glass doors opening onto the veranda. There was a hall along the inside wall shared with the other apartment. The hall opened onto the dining room, two bedrooms with a bath between, and then the kitchen. There was also a maid's room beyond the kitchen, with a window that overlooked the shared back porch and rear staircase.

Martin had completely decorated his apartment in furniture from the 1920s. It was a favorite period of his, he explained. There was even a working Victrola in a corner of the living room, and a candlestick-style telephone by the sofa. Any modern appliances, like his television and stereo, were concealed from sight.

After the tour, we settled comfortably on the living room sofa that faced the fireplace. He poured us brandy as a night-cap. There were footsteps overhead; Clara was home and also settling down for the night.

"It must be nice having her so close," I said, stifling a yawn. It was wise that I had not tried to drive home.

"Yes. Sometimes, it's a little too close, though."

"Is there anything between you two?" I asked, then apologized immediately. "I'm sorry. I should not have asked that. You just seem so close."

"There was more, at first, but we are just good friends now," he was completely at ease with my question.

He started to say something else, but hesitated, then shook his head with a half-smile.

"What?" I asked.

"Well, it turns out we were born precisely at the same minute on the same day, so we will turn thirty together this fall. Although we don't actually have the same birthday."

Seeing my confusion, he clarified, "Clara was born in California at 3:16 P.M. on the eighteenth. My father was still in the service in 1954, so I was born in Japan and it was already the nineteenth there, but allowing for the time difference, our birth certificates show we were born at the same minute, just on opposite sides of the Pacific Ocean."

My mouth went dry, "What month?" I asked.

"September," he replied. "I thought I already said that."

I knew he would not believe me, so I opened my wallet, took out my driver's license and handed it to him. "I was born September 18th, 1954, in Springfield, at 5:16 P.M."

Allowing for the time differences, the three of us had entered this world at exactly the same minute. There were likely thousands of other babies born that day, but I had never met any of them. The closest I ever came was a schoolmate whose birthday was two days after mine. This was too much to merely be coincidence.

"Clara insists it means we were meant to be together," he said, handing my license back. "She likes to point out that we not only share birthdays, but also our horoscopes, our biorhythms, numerology charts, and a whole lot more. If nothing else, we have the same chronological frame of reference for everything in life - we always have been and always will be exactly the same age for every event in our lives."

Maybe it was also why the two of them had seemed so strangely familiar from the first moment. We were all experiencing this life at exactly the same moment. We could not be any more synchronized.

"When she really gets going, I tease her by saying all it means is that our mothers let our fathers have their way that weekend before Christmas in 1953," he said, chuckling. "If you count backwards, we were all conceived that same weekend."

I hadn't really thought of that, but I had to admit that my parents did seem to have a special glow in the photographs taken the Christmas before I was born. It must have been the same for Martin's parents, and Clara's parents, and a lot of other couples during those baby boom years.

"I guess we can add you to our little group now. Maybe the three of us can get together this fall and celebrate our shared birthday together."

My glass was empty and I declined another. I leaned back into the deep cushions of the sofa, completely relaxed. Even in summer, the room, with its high ceiling, was cool. A nice breeze was coming through the open windows, stirring the sheer curtains. I could have easily fallen asleep where I sat, but Martin stood and gathered the glasses to take to the kitchen.

He pulled a set of towels from a bathroom cabinet, showed me how to work the bathtub and shower faucets - there were eight knobs in all - said I could shower before bed if I wanted, then left me in the bathroom. I only washed my face and brushed my teeth before opening the connecting door to the bedroom. Martin had changed into a loose tee shirt and gym shorts and was turning down the bed. A water pitcher and glass were on the bedside table, beside a small lamp and a stack of books. It looked casual, comfortable and inviting.

"I set out an extra tee shirt and shorts for you too," he said, pointing to the chair. Suddenly shy, I stepped back into the bathroom to change, but left the door open. When I returned, and after determining I needed nothing else, except to fall into bed, he went to the door. "Sleep well. I'm the second door down the hall if you need anything."

I was already in bed by then, and so sleepy I could barely mumble a reply.

Undisturbed, I slept more soundly than I had in weeks. The next thing I heard was Clara's voice in the kitchen. Martin answered, and from the aroma and sounds of things, they were preparing breakfast. The alarm clock by my bed showed it was past eight o'clock. Sunday was well under way.

"Morning, sleepyhead!" Clara chirped when I stepped in the kitchen. Martin, still in his sleepwear, grinned at me as he closed the oven door and set the potholder on the counter. "Coffee?"

I yawned and nodded, sat in the chair Clara pulled out for me at the table, and ran a hand over my head in an unsuccessful attempt of smoothing down my morning hair.

"Sleep well?" Clara asked, bringing the coffee pot to the table along with an oversized ceramic mug. I nodded yes, then shook my head, yawning again, when she asked if I took anything in my coffee.

We chatted like old friends. I offered to help, but breakfast was almost ready. Martin brought an egg casserole from the oven, Clara had a plate of toast and fresh fruit ready, and we filled our plates. Breakfast was unhurried. Martin's shop was closed on Sunday mornings, Clara was skipping church services, and I really only had to drive myself back home before it was time to go to work on Monday morning. We rehashed our discussions of the night before, Clara explaining more about her gifts and Martin saying she was being too modest about it - she worked on one case after another in her consulting work for the Kansas City Police. I was intrigued, and apparently asked all the right questions, because the next time any of us looked at the clock it was almost noon. Martin needed to open his shop and I needed to shower and get on the road.

"We want to come to see your house," Clara said abruptly. "I would like to see if I can do anything to help. Can we drive down some weekend?" By Martin not objecting, I knew they had discussed it before I got up, and he was in agreement.

I was both surprised and pleased by the offer. I really wanted to know them better and to become friends. "Yes, you can. How about next weekend?"

Martin laughed, "Well, I need a little more time. Clara usually watches the shop when I'm away, so I will have to get someone else lined up. How about the weekend after that?"

Chapter Twelve

With our busy schedules, Martin's and Clara's trip kept getting put off. There were frequent telephone calls back and forth, but summer ended and fall passed us by. On a quiet evening in the first week of November, I had settled in front of the television just as the telephone rang. I picked up the extension in the den and it was Martin.

"We are coming down the Friday after Thanksgiving whether you like it or not," he announced without even saying 'hello.'

"Oh really?" I replied, as though I was insulted. I knew he was teasing. He had been sending me books to read. He slipped a card in the last one, "Just set a date and make it happen!"

It was postponed once again, but we finally settled on the second weekend of December. Martin and Clara would drive down after work on Friday, arriving by nine o'clock. Everything was ready and waiting when they arrived. Pamela had been there every evening that week. Although I could have done it myself, she helped me clean the house thoroughly, made sure the silver was polished, the beds were changed, and all the towels were freshly laundered. She made three casseroles I could pop in the oven if we wanted to stay home instead of going out for dinner when the restaurants were sure to be packed. She even made sure the wine rack in the pantry was properly stocked and my wine glasses were spotless.

It was really very generous of her since she had to be out of town again all that weekend. I left work at noon on Friday and she stopped by on her way to the airport with fresh flowers for the dining room table, and smaller, less formal, bouquets for the breakfast table and the guest room. It was really too much, I told her.

"It's your first real weekend to have guests," she said. "And don't worry, I'll be calling in the favor when I need help - like my Christmas party next weekend." Her annual party was legend. I chuckled and said she could put me down for waiter, and cleanup, again.

They arrived exactly on time. As soon as Martin parked the car, Clara and another woman climbed out and greeted me warmly. I had not expected a third person. In reality, since I used the third bedroom as my den, I only had two bedrooms that were actually set up as bedrooms. Martin already said he wanted to sleep in the guest room, and I had planned to sleep on the den sofa and turn my bedroom over to Clara. It was a queen size bed so the two women would just have to share it.

Clara introduced Deanne Delarosa, a large, almost shapeless woman who was so shy with me that she almost seemed socially challenged, and left me wondering how she would play into what was to come.

Since they only had light overnight bags that were easy to carry, I gave them a quick tour, starting with the first floor before we went upstairs. On the second floor, we had a look at the guest bedroom. I said it would be Martin's for the weekend, but Clara shut her eyes, took a deep breath and asked if Deanne and she could have the room instead. She added that the dining room, directly beneath the bedroom, would be ideal for the session. Deanne seemed apprehensive about occupying the room, even for one night, but Clara insisted and Martin said he would trade with them - or sleep in the den if I wanted to stay in my own bed.

I went downstairs while they unpacked and settled. One of Pamela's casseroles was almost ready in the oven. I set the breakfast room table for a casual dinner and was opening the wine when Clara came downstairs. She showed me the thick green tablecloth she brought. I removed the centerpiece from the dining room table, then took out the leaves so it was almost square. Clara spread out the cloth and placed one of my candle holders in the center.

Dinner was as cheerful as it could be with all of us anticipating what was to follow. As soon as the table was cleared, we moved to the dining room. Clara lit the candle and we took our places around the table, one person on each side. We joined hands and Clara began a relaxation exercise, breathing deeply as she gently rolled her head from side to side. We matched our breath with hers, and as the rolling stopped, she began intoning an almost silent chant while we sat with half-bowed heads. If everyone had not been so completely serious, and Deanne had not fixed a serious sideways eye on me, I would have been tempted to giggle at the whole thing.

Clara went into a deep, meditative state and Martin began a quiet dialog with her. He led her into a deeper trance. After a long while, with her eyes almost closed, she raised her face. She was completely relaxed - and receptive. It looked like she wasn't even breathing. I was expecting a more dramatic transformation or some kind of signal that contact had been made. Instead, there was a barely perceptible change in her facial expression.

I consciously cleared my mind as Martin had reminded us to do before we began. For a fleeting moment I thought what I had just witnessed in Clara was like the transformation of death, when life is released from the body. I pushed that thought from my mind and felt a snapping jolt course through our joined hands and then release.

Martin looked around the table for visual confirmation that we were ready. He was our guide for the evening. He began.

"We are here to help you," he said calmly, and in his normal speaking voice that was almost startling in the silent house. "We are here to assist you and to help you find peace. We have a message from Addie. Are you here? Can you hear us?"

He continued in this vein for several minutes, repeating Addie's name often. He would pause momentarily as we waited for an answer. The candle's flame jumped and flickered as it burned, but there was no response.

"Use the rhyme," I whispered to him.

He obliged, "Goosey, goosey, gander march through the town." He repeated the entire verse twice with no response. Across from me Clara sat motionless in her chair, scarcely breathing. My hands, joined with Martin and Deanne were warm from their touch, but there was no special feeling.

He began again and without quite realizing I was doing so, I whispered the verse with him. When we reached the final line, a current ran through our hands and another voice, seeming to come from deep within Clara joined us in the last lines.

"There I met an old man who wouldn't say his prayers. I took him by the left leg, and threw him down the stairs." A childish laugh followed. With a small nod, Martin signaled that we had made contact.

"Addie's friend, are you here?" he asked.

Clara's head snapped up, with wide open eyes and a blank

85

look on her face. Without her lips visibly moving the voice came through her slack mouth, "Yes." It was the voice I remembered.

"We are happy you are with us," he said.

"I like parties," she said. "Mama said I can have a real one on my next birthday."

"Well, this is a party for you," Martin said.

They chatted for a while. Martin put her at ease, asking her about her toys and books, and she described them in detail. He asked her how old she was and she said she was six. She didn't know what year it was and seemed perplexed by the question. When asked, she readily replied that her name was Elizabeth.

He asked if she had a favorite doll, asked about her clothing, and then he asked her what she saw when she looked out the window.

"The windows are higher up than they used to be," she said. She seemed confused.

"What do you mean, Elizabeth?" I knew from my preparatory readings that he would use her name as often as he could to keep her engaged and focused.

"They didn't used to be so far from the ground," She said.

"Why is that, Elizabeth?" Martin asked.

"Because this is not the old house," she was distressed. "I liked the old house, my mama lived with me there."

"Yes, that is right, Elizabeth," Martin said. I wondered where this was going.

"Elizabeth," he said, "I want you to do something for me"

"What?" she asked suspiciously.

"We are playing a game for our party." he said. "I want you to go to the window and tell me what you see."

"No!" she cried out. "I don't want to do it!"

"Elizabeth, we are all going to take a turn, but since this is your party, we want you to have your turn first."

"No, I don't want to! Let someone else do it!" she whined.

"Why not, Elizabeth?" he asked her.

"Because they are out there," she said, on the verge of tears. "I am afraid of them."

"It's alright, Elizabeth. We won't let them hurt you. Don't look out the window. Instead let's talk for a while. Tell me, what is your favorite thing to do?"

Elizabeth was upset and Martin knew he was in danger of losing the contact. She was silent and we all waited.

"I can't do anything," she finally said. "Mama said I have to stay in my room until I am better."

"Are you sick?" Martin asked.

"No, my leg is hurt. I fell down the steps and the doctor came and pulled on it to make it better and he wrapped it up tight and now I have to stay in my room."

"Did you break your leg Elizabeth?"

"Yes, that's why the doctor pulled on it," she said.

"How did he get to your house?"

"He came in his automobile, silly. I watched him from my bed by the window. I cried because I knew he would hurt my leg again. Papa already told me it would have to hurt again to get better."

"Can you tell me what his car looks like Elizabeth?"

"No, but Papa says it's a brand new 1922 Packard Touring car. He said the bastard always has a new car, but Mama said he shouldn't say that word in front of me."

We had a fix on the time she was connecting from now - sometime around 1922. I shook my head slightly at Martin, confused. This house was not built until 1935.

"What happened next, Elizabeth?"

"He put a spit on my leg." I smiled at her misunderstanding of the word. "It hurts and it itches, and I can't scratch it. Mama gave me some medicine so my leg wouldn't hurt. It tastes bad and it makes me sleepy."

"I am so very sleepy," she yawned like she was about to nod off.

"What else happened, Elizabeth?" Martin asked, trying to keep her engaged.

"Mama!" came the frantic voice, suddenly. "Help! Mama, help me!"

"What is it, Elizabeth?" Martin asked.

"Mama, I can't..." she dissolved into choking coughs.

"Elizabeth, tell me right now what is wrong," Martin commanded.

"I can't breathe . . . It's hot," she was choking. She had a coughing spasm. "Where is my Mama? Mama!" she screamed. "Mama, help me.

"Fire!" she shrieked between frantic gasps and strangled choking.

"Fire!"

"Hot!"

"Help me! Hellllllp!"

The screams were awful. Deanne let go of my hand in horror.

"Don't break the circle," Martin shouted at Deanne. She grabbed my hand again.

"Elizabeth," he called out loudly but calmly.

"Elizabeth, come back to us. Elizabeth, come back to me, the fire can't hurt you again. Come back to me. I will help you."

He repeated this over and over, until finally a small voice came from within Clara again. Two tiny tears ran down Clara's face from her closed eyes. Deanne was weeping openly.

"There was a fire," Elizabeth said, quietly. "Our house burned down, but Mama didn't come for me."

I tried not to imagine her, abandoned, burning to death. A six-year-old child, terrified, alone, and screaming for help.

"Elizabeth," Martin said. "Can you be a big girl for me for a little while?"

"NO! I told you I don't want to look out the window!" she was adamant. "I am too afraid. I don't like this party."

"No, I won't ask you to right now, Elizabeth," he assured her.

"Are we still having our party?" She was calmed.

"Yes we are, Elizabeth. Do you remember what happened

next, after the fire?"

"No," she said quietly.

"Elizabeth, try to remember. I think you went through some doorways after the fire. You lost your way."

"The spit on my leg kept me back. I got lost from them, and I couldn't find my way, so I came back to my room to wait."

Had she really been waiting, alone, the past sixty years?

"Elizabeth, it's not really your room, your mama and papa are waiting for you in your new room, they have all your things ready for you there."

"Really?" she asked.

"Yes, Elizabeth. I must tell you something that will be hard for you to understand, but you must listen very carefully, and you must promise to be a big girl. Can you do that for me? Can you promise to be a big girl?"

"Yes," she said. "Are you my friend?" she added suddenly.

"Yes, Elizabeth, we are all your friends, that's why we are having a party."

"Do you have another game?" she asked with growing enthusiasm.

"Sort of, Elizabeth. But first I want to tell you a story, and while I tell you the story I want you to see if you can imagine it in your mind. Then you tell me what you have imagined looks like. Can you do that?"

"Sure, that's easy," she said.

"Elizabeth, first I want you to imagine your mother, how your mother looked when she gave you the medicine when your leg was hurt," he said. "Tell me what she looks like."

"Mama is beautiful," she said. "She has her nightgown on and her hair is long around her shoulders. She looks like an angel in the Bible."

"Now, watch your mother after she gives you the medicine, she turns and ..."

"She gave me a kiss and told me 'sweet dreams.' She always does that. She left the door open for me a little bit so I can see the light in the hall. She put the lamp on the table in the hall."

"What kind of lamp is it? Elizabeth" Martin broke in.

"Bright."

"Does it have to be lit with a match? Does it burn something?"

"Oil," she said. I was beginning to understand the source of the fire.

"Elizabeth, I want you to only think about after the fire, now. Don't picture the fire at all in your mind at all, but think past it, like you jump right over it. Now, what do you see?"

There was a long silence before she replied.

"We are walking, sort of, Mama, Papa, and me. We are walking through the cave toward the end. But I can't keep up with them."

"Can you see them now, Elizabeth? Can you see your mama and papa?"

"Yes, but they don't see me. They won't stop. They keep walking."

"Elizabeth, they were not able to see you just then. You have to understand that they could not see you. They did not mean to leave you behind. They just could not see you."

"Because it is so dark in the cave?"

Martin seized on that explanation, "Yes, that is right, Elizabeth. Because it is so dark in the cave. You are a big girl, you are doing a good job. I am so proud of you."

He paused for a moment. Elizabeth initiated the next communication.

"Are you still there?" she asked.

"Yes, Elizabeth, we won't leave you," he said. "I just needed to rest a little bit. Do you want to play some more?"

"Oh, yes!" she exclaimed.

"Elizabeth, look toward the end of the cave and tell me what you see."

"It is daytime outside the cave. We must be on a picnic because there is daylight and we are walking toward the daylight. Papa always likes to look at the cave on the picnics because it is cool inside."

"Can you go toward the light, Elizabeth?" Martin asked.

"No, I can't," she said impatiently. "I told you my leg won't let me. Besides, I am supposed to stay in my room." She seemed confused and upset. "Papa won't like it if I don't stay in my room."

"Elizabeth, listen to me. Your mama and papa are waiting for you. They have your room ready for you and are waiting for you, but you have to do something to see them."

"I am not going to look out the window!" she cried out, anticipating what was next.

"Can you see the light outside the window from where you are now, Elizabeth? Have you looked outside the window and seen the light?"

"Yes, but they are there too and I am afraid of them."

"Who are you afraid of Elizabeth?" Martin persisted.

"The ones outside my window. They are big and ugly and terrible and they scare me. They stand there all the time, waiting for me."

I knew what it was. I had forgotten the petition my elderly aunt included in her long blessing of the family's dinner at that first Easter in this house. She asked for the Lord to send his guardian angels to stand at all four corners of my house and protect it from all the evil that could befall it. It had seemed a little odd at the time, even coming from an old-fashioned woman who was a dyed-in-the-wool Baptist. Had her prayer brought down those angels and trapped Elizabeth inside in her fright? No wonder she was angry with me.

"They are angels, Martin!" I said in an urgent whisper. It was worth a try. "Tell her they are only angels!"

"Elizabeth. The ones standing there are angels, they are there to help you find your mama and papa."

"But they are ugly, they can't be angels. Angels are beautiful. These are ugly!"

"They are guardian angles, Martin. Tell her they are like that to keep the bad people away."

He told her as we listened.

"But I am bad," she said. "I made the man fall down the stairs and he hurt his foot."

"No! You are not bad, Elizabeth," I said out loud. "You did not mean to hurt my foot, you were just acting out your rhyme."

"Who is that?" she asked.

"You remember me," I said. "I fell on the stairs, but it was an accident. The chair I was standing on moved. An accident does not mean you are a bad person."

Martin shook his head at me. He wanted me to stop, to not confuse her.

"Go toward the window, Elizabeth," he continued, "but don't look at the angels. They won't bother you. Look only at the light outside. Your mama and papa are in the light and they will help you. The angels will help you. They will help you. They are good, but if they still frighten you just don't look at them."

"I am afraid," she said.

"I know you are, but I know you are also a brave girl," he said. "We will stay right here while you look, but you must go to the window and look for the light. Can you be a big girl and do that for me?"

"I can try," she said.

"That is a good girl. Now go to the window."

"Can I come back?" she asked.

"Yes, but you won't want to when you see your mama and papa," he said. "Go on and go to them, but we will still be here if you decide you don't want to."

There was no answer. We waited a while, then there seemed to be a reverse flow of energy through the chain. Clara came out of her trance.

"She is gone," Martin told us.

"Did she make it through?" I asked her.

"I can't know that," Martin said. "But I think she will contact us if she gets lost again. Let's wait around for a while, for a sign."

We released the chain of hands and stood from the chairs. It was nearly midnight. Almost two hours had passed and my back and legs ached from sitting so long. I suggested we move to the comfort of the living room.

I poured us all brandy and we stood in front of the fireplace, stretching our legs and telling Clara about the communication, who remembered none of it. I stirred up the fire and put on another log.

I was on edge and jumpy, half-expecting a rush of air down the chimney with a spooky apparition in the smoke. I didn't say anything about it because I did not want to look inexperienced. Clara came to stand beside me as I knelt at the fireplace and laid a hand on my shoulder.

She said, gently, "There won't be any smoke and mirrors, so don't be afraid. You are doing very well for your first time." She had read my thoughts, again.

She turned from me and looked around, changing the subject. "This is a very handsome room. Very comfortable and pretty, without being feminine. It has your personal ambience, your presence, imprinted on it."

"Thank you," I said.

Deanne and Martin were across the room, looking at the Christmas tree. The fresh scent filled the room, but I had not turned on the tree lights. In fact the house was quite dark.

Clara moved around the living room and then went into the dining room, looking around intently. She examined the framed print on the wall between the two front windows. She stopped in front of the buffet, reached out to the silver coffee pot, but jerked her hand back as if she had been burned.

"What is it?" Martin asked, we had followed her into the room. "What did you see?"

"Many images. Too many," she finally said.

I stepped forward. Martin and Clara knew all about the silver coffee service, but for Deanne's information I said, "This silver apparently belonged to the original owners of this house. They built this house in 1935.

"From what I have gathered, this silver was willed to one daughter who did not want it, but out of spite would not give or even sell it to the other daughter."

"How did you come to own it?" Deanne asked.

"The daughter who inherited it must have sold it eventually. I bought it just after I moved into this house, at the estate auction of a woman who had been in a nursing home for years. It was black with tarnish."

"Then, how do you know it is really the same set?" she asked.

"The other daughter came by the house one day out of the blue. I showed her the house and she recognized the set."

I picked up the coffee server and turned the base toward them. "Eva identified her parents' combined monogram on the base. This was a wedding present to them."

Clara placed her hand on the server again, lightly. She obviously received some type of mental image. She pulled her hand away and looked at me intently, searching my face.

"Look!" Martin interrupted. I turned to see him pointing at the chandelier over the table.

At first I did not see anything, but then it tilted slightly towards Martin and back. We quickly returned to our seats, joined hands, and Clara slipped back into her trance. Again there was the jolt through our hands that now told me our group had been contacted.

"Elizabeth, did you not make it through?" Martin asked.

There was a pause.

"Elizabeth?"

"No." A different voice came from Clara. "It's Madeline."

I was shocked. "The first owner of this house," I whispered, now frightened.

"We are here for you, Madeline," Martin said calmly. "Do you need to communicate with us?"

"I don't know," she said. "I am not sure what has happened."

"We want to hear you, tell us what you remember," Martin began.

"There is nothing to remember," she was becoming agitated. "I just left the house and now everything is changed."

"Why did you leave the house, Madeline?" Martin asked.

"Only to go to the party."

"What party, Madeline?" Martin asked. "Look around you and

tell us everything you can see and anything you can remember."

"The Christmas party! I am going to resign at the party. I'm finally quitting that lousy job, and I am going to do it in style in front of everyone instead of slinking off like a beaten dog. I will show every last one of them."

"Tell us about the party, Madeline," Martin said. "What happened at the party?"

"I don't know!" she said, more distressed. "I can't remember anything about it. I came back home and the house is different. Everything is changed. My patio is done, and the doors I ordered are installed, but everything is different. What is happening here?"

"Calm down, Madeline," Martin said soothingly. "We want to help you remember, but you must calm yourself. Don't worry about the house. Everything is alright."

"I'm sorry to be such a bother," she said. "I just can't remember. It is very upsetting."

"Let's go back a bit, Madeline, and see what you can remember," Martin continued. "Do you remember getting ready for the party?"

"Oh yes," she said. "See? I am really dressed up for once. It has been so long, but I am wearing my good pearls and my diamonds, and I had this dress specially made over for the party. It's my best black velvet and taffeta."

"That's very nice, Madeline. See, you do remember some things, so don't be worried," Martin reassured her.

"Thank you," she replied. "I also have my fox jacket, the one Jordan gave me." There was a note of tenderness in her voice at the name.

Jordan. Where had I heard that name?

"Alright, Madeline," Martin resumed. "Let's see if you can remember what happened next. Do you remember leaving the house?"

"Well yes, of course," she began. "I backed the car out of the garage and shut the doors. I wanted to take the car, even if it is getting old. It's so comfortable, and I didn't want to arrive on the bus or in a taxi tonight."

"Go on," he said. "What else do you remember?"

"Let me see. There was music on the radio - soft music Jordan would have loved. It was still early so I decided to take another route to the hotel so I would arrive after everyone else was there. I wanted everyone to be there when I arrived."

I could see her now, driving down Jefferson, turning left at the stop light. Light rain is hitting the windshield. She reaches out with a gloved hand and turns on the wipers.

"It was raining," she said, catching up with me. Then she continued in a pleased tone, "It was a cold, freezing rain that made me glad I had worn my fur, after all. I almost didn't make it to Levinson's before he closed. I had worked so long on the plans for my new business, I was running late."

I could see her rushing into the small downtown shop to retrieve the jacket.

"OK. So you stopped at the stop light," Martin prodded, keeping her on course. "What happened next, Madeline?" Martin prodded her.

"Well, I drove east through the colored section and then I turned south on the Boulevard."

The Boulevard. That was what they used to call National Avenue. It originally ran from Greenlawn Cemetery on the north end of town to the National Cemetery on the south. Until the street was widened in the 1960s it was a tree-lined boulevard. When St. John's hospital was built in 1953, the avenue was rerouted to continue straight south, rather than curving around toward the National Cemetery. After that, the National Cemetery was no longer the terminus and the 'boulevard' distinction was dropped. Now, it was simply called 'National.'

She continued in a cheerful tone, "I could never understand why the other wives thought they had to have a driver. I love driving, and our Cadillac is still quite beautiful. I don't drive it enough to wear it out. I always take the bus to work."

She paused a moment, reflecting on her beloved automobile. I could see that it was a beautiful and luxuriant machine.

"What happened next, Madeline?" Martin was struggling to keep her focused.

"I think I stopped for the traffic light at Chestnut Street. Yes. It held a long time, or at least it seemed so, and there was no other traffic. It was still raining and sleet was getting mixed in with the rain."

Beside me, Deanne gripped my hand tighter, squeezing my knuckles together almost painfully. I could hear the music from the radio, I could see the single traffic light hanging from cables crossed over the intersection, swinging in the sleet and wind. I could see the wipers swabbing the windshield.

Madeline paused and we waited.

"What then?" Martin asked.

She seemed embarrassed to continue, "I just kept thinking all of it would have been easier for a man. But can you blame me with what I had to go through with work and raising the girls and just trying to keep body and soul together after Jordan died?"

Jordan. There it was again. Where had I heard the name?

I felt the leather glove brushing against my lower lip.

"What happened next, Madeline?" Martin asked.

"The light changed and I put the car in gear. The streets were getting slick fast. I decided I had better go on to the hotel, before it got too slick. If it got any worse I would have to leave the car there and take a taxi home after the party."

I could feel the car slipping sideways until the tires caught on the slick pavement. With my right foot I eased the accelerator down lightly, edging the car forward. Deanne's grip was really hurting my hand now, crushing my knuckles.

"What then, Madeline?"

"I decided I had better go on to the hotel before it got any more slippery," she repeated, as if she was struggling to remember. "I was driving along, looking over at the buildings downtown. Then... then I... I don't remember."

Her last sentence faded away.

I feel the sudden jolt against my forehead. I squeeze Martin and Deanne's hands, making Deanne cry out. I can see the city lights reflected off the low clouds, the dark car coming up behind me fast. I feel my car lunge forward.

"What else happened, Madeline?" Martin asked, looking at me now, and knowing he was losing her.

I feel the low scream begin. I am falling. I try to turn the steering wheel away from the fall. Grasping Martin and Deanne's hands I scream, again and again.

"He's transferring!" Deanne screamed at Martin. "Stop this!"

My forehead is bleeding. I am falling, down and down, pressed backwards against the seat with the force of the fall. Through the rain-spotted glass of the windshield I see the rock floor rising up slowly toward me. I watch a single drop of blood fall from my forehead and splatter down against the glass. I marvel that it has fallen faster than the car. I scream. I look at the yellow radio dial - still playing the same song. I hear the wipers thumping against the window frame. I scream and scream again.

"Stop, Madeline!" Martin yells. "Stop now!"

I grip the steering wheel harder, pressing my foot on the brake so hard that my body arches backwards. I scream and push down on the brake pedal and scream again and then, mercifully, I lose my grip on the wheel.

My hands have broken from Martin and Deanne, the circle has broken, the fall has stopped.

Warm blood trickled from on my forehead. Martin slapped my face sharply, twice, calling out my name - Jack. I opened my eyes to see the dining room ceiling above me. I was lying on the floor. The circle was broken. Martin, Clara, and Deanne were leaning over me, frightened and concerned.

"You went into transference, or possession by the spirit," Clara said, holding my hands in hers and willing me to come back. "It can happen sometimes, especially with a novice who is receptive. You will be all right. You openly received what Madeline was telling us, but you could not control it."

Behind Clara, Martin and Deanne stared in silence.

"Like hell," I said quietly. "I didn't receive it. I was there."

"Come back to the table," Martin said gently. "You have had a bad fright. You could go into shock."

Gently he helped me up, set my chair upright and helped me sit.

I fell forward, shivering and smudging blood on the green cloth and my folded arms. The living room clock chimed three times. Could it really be that late? From somewhere a blanket was produced and placed on my shoulders.

"I was there," I insisted into my folded arms. "I really was there."

Martin's hands were on the back of my neck. I could feel his strength and calm flowing into me, but I was so exhausted I could not lift my head.

I heard them stir around me. Clara went to the kitchen for a wet cloth. Deanne came to kneel beside me, rubbing my shoulder and making small comforting sounds. For the first time I noticed how beautiful her eyes were. Martin's hands did not leave my neck. I could not stop trembling.

"I'm telling you I was there," I insisted again, knowing they did not believe me.

I am the first to hear it. A slight tapping overhead. What is it? Going back and forth. I hear the closet door of my bedroom softly close, the tapping resumes and then stops.

I sit upright, listening. Deanne tries to force me to drink water from a glass, I shove it away.

I think Martin and Clara must have heard it, too, just then. The snap of a radio being turned off. An old radio - like the one my grandfather kept in his bedroom to get the late news.

I leap from the chair and run from the dining room.

"Stop!" Martin shouts after me.

"Don't go," Clara begs.

She grabs at my wrist as I pass, whirling me around. "Let me go!" I shout and shake my arm free from her grip.

I run through the living room and up the stairs to the landing. They follow me, shouting after me to stop.

Deanne gives a low, authoritative command, undercutting the hysteria, "Stop, right there. Stop right now!"

I stop one step short of the landing, facing into the mirror where I can see up to the second floor. They stand behind me at the foot of the stairs, but they can also see what is in the mirror.

I can see my own reflection. I look frightened and I am trembling. Blood still seeps from the bruise on my forehead.

It has stained my shirt where I rested my head.

I see the walls of the staircase beyond the landing, but it is the old wallpaper, the last layer I removed, and the first that was put on these walls. It is the wallpaper that was on these walls thirty years ago. I turn and see only the newly painted walls behind me. I look at Martin, who nods slightly. He sees the old wallpaper too.

The tapping comes closer. It comes down the hall, hesitating a moment at the door to the guest bedroom. Then, I see her. She turns and starts down the stairs. First, her feet come into view - black shoes and silk stockings on good legs. Then, a black taffeta skirt, hemmed just below the knees, and rustling over a voluminous black crinoline.

Behind me, Deanne gasps and then whimpers. In the corner of my eye I see Martin's arm go to her shoulder to steady her. I know they are seeing her too. In my fascination, I take the final step up and I am standing on the landing.

She comes down the short flight to the landing. Now, I can see the luxuriant fur draped over her shoulders and the tailored black velvet bodice of the dress, then a strand of pearls with a diamond clasp come into view, and diamond and pearl earrings. I turn from the reflection to look directly at her beside me and see nothing but an empty staircase.

Clara gives a small cry of wonder.

I look for a moment at her face as it comes close to mine in the mirror. She has wonderfully high cheek bones, flawless skin, arched eyebrows and luxuriant dark hair. She wears little make up. She has no need for it. She looks content and confident. She stops for a moment at the mirror, presses her lips together, and dabs the corner of her mouth with a gloved finger. She turns her head slightly to one side and fluffs her hair, patting it upward from underneath. She adjusts the pearls at her throat and the fox jacket on her shoulders. I stare, not daring to breathe.

Then, in the mirror, she turns and walks directly into me, but she turns to look into the mirror one more time, and for one brief instant, her reflection is exactly overlaid on mine. Then she disappears into me.

I stood a moment longer staring at my own reflection in the mirror. A buzz started inside my head, growing louder and louder. The walls up the staircase were now reflected in the mirror as they really were. I could see Martin and Clara and Deanne standing at the base of the stairs, still staring up at me, almost frozen in time - motionless. I turned from the mirror and looked at them.

The message has been sent and received.

The meaning is clear, Madeline has come through.

Somehow, Madeline is me. I am Madeline.

I began walking down the stairs, but felt them tilt beneath me. As if in a dream, Martin and Clara rushed forward to catch me, but they are too late. I tumbled down the stairs, all the way to the floor, but not feeling the impact. Before I lost consciousness I felt Martin's arms around me for one brief instant. Then I continued to fall deeper and deeper into the whirling darkness.

The sun was high when I woke the next morning. I squinted in the bright light of my bedroom and saw Clara sitting on the bed beside me, both my hands in hers.

"Welcome back to Kansas, Dorothy," she said quietly.

I gave her a thin smile, remembering how she had read my thoughts the night before. In spite of the long rest I felt drained, exhausted by the events of the evening before. There was a sharp pain from my forehead. My banged and bruised knees and elbows ached. Curiously, my palms were marked a dark burgundy red where I had felt the steering wheel the night before.

Martin and Deanne were standing beside the bed. Deanne raised my head from the pillow and put a glass to my lips.

"Drink this," she said.

I drank deeply from the glass. It was more than orange juice. There were delicious nuances of other flavors.

"It's my special blend," she said. "Mainly orange juice and mashed bananas, but I spice it up a little with some of my own herbs and spices."

"You should bottle it and sell it," I said in a hoarse whisper. "We could make a million and retire."

They laughed softly at my remark, then without a word they

101

all got into bed with me. Martin and Deanne sat on either side of me. Clara knelt, facing me, and taking my hands again. Martin and Deanne both placed one hand on my head at the temple and the other on Clara's shoulders.

Deanne spoke first, "You are physically and emotionally exhausted," she said. "We will share our strength through this healing circle to you. Visualize a wick running through all of us that is drawing away your fatigue and diffusing it throughout the circle to us."

Although I wanted to bat them away, I relaxed and felt my strength returning, along with a sense of calm. I was amazed at the change that occurred in the next few minutes.

Later we sat around the table in the breakfast room. It was Saturday morning and I was ravenous, finishing my eggs and slathering jam on another slice of toast while the others ate.

My entire body was sore from tumbling down the stairs. My shins and forearms were striped with dark bruises where they had banged against the steps on the way down.

Curiously, my forehead was clear with no signs of bleeding. Martin told me that after they undressed me for bed, Clara decided to soak my shirt in cold water to keep it from staining and, only then, realized there was no sign of blood on it. The spot where I bled on the green cloth while I rested my head on the dining room table was also gone. Oddly, that part of the evening was wiped away - as though it had been a dream.

As I examined my bruises, I sipped a cup of strong coffee. Ultimately, I had to ask the question. "So, what is next?"

They exchanged brief glances and, by what seemed a prior agreement between them, Martin spoke.

"We all agree that you have gone too far, too soon, in this process," he began. "None of us expected you to be an active participant in the session last night."

I looked around the table at their contrite faces.

"Transference is a frightening experience, even to an experienced medium," Deanne said. "You have not developed the abilities to control it and to keep a claim on yourself."

"You were completely immersed in the transferred image," Martin continued. "We could have lost you."

I stared at him a moment. "What are you saying?" I asked.

"You were completely and physically linked with the memory that Madeline was communicating with us," he said. "Somehow you picked up on it and in addition to Madeline speaking to us through Clara, what she recalled was imposed on your physical body through your subconscious mind."

I remembered what I had seen. It was familiar. Bits and pieces of it had been familiar long before last night.

"What could have happened to me?" I asked. I had skimmed over these sections in the books Martin sent me.

There was a long pause, eventually Clara nodded at Deanne.

"There have been cases where the medium has received such a complete transference during a communication that they begin to experience the same physical phenomena that the subject is remembering. Some have developed the cough of advanced tuberculosis, some have experienced stroke-like symptoms, and sometimes there can even be spontaneous bleeding from an associated injury."

"Like a forehead bleeding after being banged on a steering wheel?" I asked, trying to keep the accusing tone from my voice.

They looked at me, silent.

"So I could have experienced everything that Madeline went through?" I asked them. "And just exactly where would it have stopped?"

Deanne broke in, "Martin was able to stop it. He made Madeline stop."

"No he didn't," I was angry. "I fell backward trying to stop the fall and broke the circle. That is when it stopped."

"We don't know that for sure," Deanne pleaded. "It seemed the circle broke at the same moment that Martin commanded Madeline to stop. We have reviewed the tape and it seems..."

"What?" I was really angry now. "What do you mean, 'the tape'? Did you tape the session without letting me know?"

"The sessions are always taped," Deanne said. "As a novice, we did not mention some things because we wanted you to be as relaxed as possible."

"So relaxed that I would become a transfer... a

transference...whatever, without knowing what was going on? I could have been badly hurt, or worse," I spat the words at them.

I glared angrily at Martin, "How could you let me get into this without at least warning me first?"

I turned away from them.

"I am so sorry," Martin began. "We did not realize that you were such a fertile medium."

As was my nature, my anger flashed and quickly subsided. I knew Martin would never willingly lead me into danger. None of them would.

"A fertile medium sounds like a prized vegetable garden," I observed, taking a sip of coffee. They smiled at the metaphor and relaxed.

"What do we do next?" I asked.

Clara who had been silent until now spoke, "You aren't going to do anything for a while. You need to rest from last night's experience and to regain yourself. After a few weeks we want you to listen to the tapes from last night, under our supervision of course, and see what else you can remember."

"The images are crystal clear to me right now," I said. "What good will it do to wait for a few weeks? Do you honestly think it will be any clearer if we wait?"

They exchanged silent glances around the table.

"Can you keep yourself removed enough to tell us what you remember from last night?" Clara asked me.

I nodded. Yes, I was sure of it.

"Try to separate yourself from what you remember, sort of like the difference between looking at a video of yourself and actually remembering being in the video when it was being filmed. Try to visualize what you saw as a film you are watching, then describe what you see."

That part was easy. All my life, I had been remembering disconnected parts of it. Those images had invaded my dreams for as long as I could remember. But only in bits and pieces. Last night was the first time they came together in one cohesive sequence.

Martin put a new tape on the tape recorder and turned it on. I began describing what I had seen from the afternoon when Madeline was running errands to get ready for her party until that evening when her car went into the quarry. As Clara suggested, it was like narrating a movie I was watching. They were soon totally engrossed, amazed at the detail when I described the jewelry and clothing Madeline was wearing, the way the house was furnished and decorated, the interior of the 1941 Cadillac, the last model produced before the war, and the street scenes along the route she had taken - down to the detail of the traffic light at the intersection and individual buildings in the downtown area.

That clear image of the downtown skyline made me pause. I was seeing the detail of buildings that no longer existed, cleared away years ago. I might have seen those buildings in my childhood, as I remembered them now, but I doubted it. What child could have such a clear and complete image of that skyline on a raining and cold winter night?

Martin stopped me when I began describing the sensation of the front tires bumping over the curbing, trying to ignore the sick feeling in the pit of the stomach.

"You have to stop," he commanded before the Cadillac hit the retaining wall. "Don't go any further. Erase this image from your mind and come back to where we are right now. Fill your mind with what you see in front of you right now and push all other thoughts aside."

It amazed me that I could exercise that much control over my thoughts, but as I looked around the table at the three of them, the images of the rain-filled night and the dark quarry faded away.

Later that afternoon, on my insistence, we drove downtown, retracing the route Madeline had taken, and to have a look at the old quarry.

We soon realized the quarry looked almost nothing like it did the night Madeline died. The mining company ceased operations in 1968. Then it was used as a dump for industrial waste. The dump caught fire in 1973 and smoldered until it was finally put out in 1976. Water had been dumped on the fire for three years and the quarry was still filled with murky green water. A high, chain link fence had been erected around the perimeter. A new retaining wall, built when National was widened twenty years earlier, was too high now for a car to go over it.

Between us and the old downtown area, a new office tower

blocked our view of the hotel. In its heyday, The Colonial had been the finest hotel in the area. It was host to touring dignitaries, presidential entourages, and visiting performers. The corner lounge with its wide windows overlooking the two busiest downtown streets was the watering hole of the well-heeled. Those who could afford it used it as the place to see and be seen.

Now boarded up for years, it was stripped of its interior architectural features. I was inside the hotel during the final auction of the fixtures, when Pamela bought my kitchen range. Closed for years by then, it was a shadow of itself with falling plaster moldings, frayed carpet in the lobby, and the grand staircase littered with pigeon droppings. These days, it was completely shuttered with only the tall red letters of the sign on the roof giving any indication of the hotel's former splendor.

On the way back to my house I knew I needed to tell them the rest of what I thought I knew, but I did not know where to begin.

"You have something else to share with us, don't you?" Clara said quietly beside me.

From the driver's seat, I told them about the dreams I had most of my life, and the debilitating grief I experienced as a child when I realized that in this life I was separated from my best friend.

There were also the odd flashes of memory I had while I was working on the house; the recognition of wallpaper patterns and even the old linoleum under the kitchen tile. All were things I had never seen, but were so familiar.

And although I had talked about it earlier, I tried to more accurately describe the driving force that dictated the remodeling projects I had undertaken - how projects had become obsessions until they were completed. I listed the purchases of furnishings I could barely afford but seemed strangely at home once they were in the house. I tried to describe how this had been beyond my control - like I could only obey what was dictated to me.

"It's very possible you are a contiguous spirit with Madeline," Clara said.

"A contiguous spirit," I repeated. "What is that?"

"Some also call it reincarnation – that the soul that was within her continues now in you."

"But how can that possibly be?" I pondered. "Our lives
106

almost overlapped. In all the books Martin sent me, the soul rests at least a couple of centuries before choosing another lifetime. Good grief, in this process, Madeline would have died just about the time..."

My eyes flashed to meet Martin's in the rear view mirror, and a chill went down my spine.

We already knew that Martin, Clara, and I shared the same birth date, born at precisely the same moment in different parts of the world. It also meant we had been conceived about the same time nine months earlier, just before Christmas, 1953. We realized that was the same time Madeline's car plunged to the bottom of the quarry.

"There may have been a need for an immediate return," Deanne said. "There may be a stronger purpose that required the bypassing of the usual rest period for the spirit, something that could not wait."

"Like a false hypothesis of suicide?" I offered.

"I don't think that would matter after the fact," Martin said. "That would only matter to the survivors who were perplexed at the reasons for the suicide, or blamed themselves. That would be theirs to deal with, not the victim."

I looked at Martin's eyes in the mirror and another thought swept over me. Was he the extension of Jordan? Had Jordan decided to come back to help Madeline? Clara too? Was that why we had all been born and were together now? Could things have really been that predestined all along?

"No, it would have been a more urgent need to complete unfinished business," Clara said. "Something that the person was intent on doing at the time of death, an unfinished requirement of the person's life."

"So you are saying her life was cut short, it was not the time for her to die," I said.

"Possibly by an accident..." Deanne offered.

"Or an intentional death," I finished for her. "Murder."

Had Madeline really been murdered? Was that what was always at the fringes of my final memory of her? I just could not see anything other than those fringes. Did another car really back up to push her over the wall? It was something I had seen in dreams most of my life, but why would someone do such a thing to Madeline, a middle-aged bookkeeper? Who could it have been?

We continued the discussion after we arrived at my house, sitting in the car in the driveway before moving inside to the living room. We examined every angle of what had happened to Madeline. I recalled Mrs. Poindexter saying that Addie never got over her mother's death. Once she even hinted that people had even blamed Addie - that she had driven Madeline to do it.

But from the appearance we had seen in the mirror, Madeline was calm and collected that night, dressed to the nines, and had a purpose and destination. She did not look like she was about to take her own life.

What Madeline had told us also made the suicide theory seem unlikely. The face we saw in the landing mirror was assured and content with an underlying sense of purpose. It was not the face of resignation or desperation.

Then I remembered something else that proved even more that it could not be suicide. I saw the Christmas tree in the living room as she left, freshly delivered and ready to decorate. Who would order a Christmas tree if she planned to be dead before Christmas?

I tried to dredge up the image of the other car bearing down on Madeline and shoving her over the edge. I was sure the car had to hit her twice to push her on over. Until last night, I had never seen it from her point of view, but as an objective observer - almost like I saw it from above, looking down on the dark hulk on a rain-slick street. Now, I had a better image of that second car and it fit perfectly in sequence with the rest of the scene.

I told them how, in the Cadillac's rear view mirror, I distinctly saw the car that slammed into Madeline's. If I relaxed my mind, I could almost make out the silhouette of the driver inside. After the first crash, I could see the car backing up, gunning its motor, and ramming Madeline again - shoving the Cadillac on over the wall. If these things were true, the two separate impacts meant it had been a deliberate act of murder, not a hit and run accident.

Clara looked at Martin and a silent communication passed between them.

"If there is any reason for all of this happening now," I

interrupted them, "it is that Madeline was murdered, and to put her to rest, the killer needs to be found and punished."

It had to be right.

"But the killer may not even be alive," Deanne said. "It was thirty years ago. He would be anywhere from fifty to ninety years old now."

"Or she," Clara added.

"But this has to be done," I insisted. "It has to be done to put Madeline to rest." In my mind I finished, 'and so that I can be free of the memory of her.'

Clara turned toward me, catching that thought.

"There is a lot of information still around," she said. "Newspaper accounts of the accident, old police files, and even people that she might have known. I think it would be best to examine them next."

As we continued in this vein for a while, I mentally ticked off a list of sources. It was getting late - past midnight - and Martin said they needed to get an early start in the morning.

I had a moment alone with Martin the next morning. I retrieved the gift I had for him under the Christmas tree.

"We won't see each other again before Christmas," I said as I gave the small wrapped box to him.

"You didn't need to do this," he said.

"You probably should see what it is before you say that," I teased. "It's just a small remembrance for you."

"Then I'll save it and open it Christmas morning," he said with a warm smile.

I almost asked him if he wanted to come back for Christmas, but did not. He would be alone, but his shop would be open on both Christmas Eve and the day after Christmas, so it would be a short visit with a lot of driving on busy travel days. Maybe he would get together with Clara on Christmas Day.

It seemed like he wanted to say something else but he only gave me a brief and powerful hug. He would not look directly at me after that. We walked to the car where Clara and Deanne were arguing about who got to sit in the front seat. I went to them, giving Deanne a hug first and thanking her for coming.

"I hope I didn't break your hand Friday night," I said.

"Don't worry about it," she said, lifting it and curling the fingers back grotesquely. "It's fine."

I turned to Clara. She held me at arm's length, searching my face.

"Be careful," she warned me, with concern. "Don't try too much on your own."

"Don't worry," I said. "After this I am sticking to old newspaper clippings and interviewing the little old ladies in the neighborhood."

I gave her a hug and she kissed me softly on the cheek. "You are a special and gifted person," she said when she released me. "Don't overlook your gifts or take them lightly."

I walked to Martin and hugged him again. He was impatient to get on the road.

"Hey," I said. "At least you guys sent Elizabeth on her way. Maybe I can sleep through a whole night now."

They climbed into the Jeep and Martin started the engine. As they backed down the drive, Clara waved triumphantly from the front seat. She must have won the argument.

I worried that something was not right with Martin, but he gave me a stiff, military-style salute that made me laugh. He stopped in the street to shift gears and Clara gave me the thumbs-up signal.

I waved as they drove away and deep inside I knew that I would not see Martin again.

Chapter Thirteen

After the holidays, my life went back to normal. January was always busy at work with end-of-the-year reports and I stayed late most evenings. Pamela and I had dinner a few times, but most nights I had had a quiet hour or two at home before going to bed. Elizabeth was gone and I slept soundly - the first time since I bought the house.

I did not forget my promise to investigate Madeline. I went to the library the first Saturday afternoon I was free and looked through old copies of the City Directory. There were missing volumes and my search was haphazard, but those musty old volumes showed that Madeline and Jordan were the first owners of the house. After a gap of missing directories, Addie and her husband were listed at my address in 1960 and after.

Back at work on Monday, my boss called me to his office. He reminded me that the next level required a Master's of Business Administration degree, which I lacked. I had put it off for years and he told me to get started. The first step was taking the Graduate Management Admissions Test - or "GMAT" - that summer. If I passed, I could enroll in classes in the fall. To satisfy him, I went to the college bookstore on my lunch hour, bought the review manual, and started studying.

My phone calls with Martin became more sporadic. For some reason, he was frustrated with my plans to go back to school and countered by saying he was going to sell his business and move to India. I think he was only teasing at first, but as time went on he grew more insistent. He said India was where he needed to be to advance his skills - a veiled implication that I was ignoring mine. Privately, I did not think his plans were rational and began drawing away - focusing more than ever on preparing for the GMAT.

I spent the entire Saturday before Valentine's Day re-reading the economics section of my review manual and working the problems. The telephone rang but I ignored it, letting it transfer to the answering machine. Daylight was fading when I finally put the book away, stuck a frozen dinner in the oven, and ran downstairs to transfer a load of laundry from the washing machine to the dryer. As I came back up the basement steps, the telephone rang again. I picked up the kitchen extension on the third ring.

"Hello!" It was sharper than I meant, so I said, "Sorry - Hello?"

It took a while for the caller to identify herself. It was Deanne and she was sobbing, almost without control. She told me that Martin and Clara had been in an accident on Friday evening. She finally found my number in Clara's apartment and was using her telephone to call me. She had been trying to reach me all day.

Eventually she calmed down enough to give me the details. On Friday evening, the three of them were driving to Lenexa, Kansas, on Interstate 35. They were meeting with a friend there to do a "reading." Martin and Clara were staying after for dinner, but Deanne had other plans, so she drove separately in her own car. She was following Martin's car, when a mile past the Overland Park exit, a car in the right lane blew a tire and started fish-tailing, out of control. It made it to the shoulder, but not before the tractor-trailer behind it swerved into the left lane to avoid running over it.

Martin, in the left lane, was braking hard and trying to stop, but the truck shoved him into the concrete barriers that were there to divide the traffic lanes where the road was narrowed down for construction. The truck dragged Martin and Clara along the retaining wall. Deanne locked up her brakes to keep from ramming them from behind.

She said that for a moment it looked like they would make it - that Martin would be able to stop. But they came to an unexpected break in the wall where some sections of the concrete barriers were missing. The truck pushed Martin's car into the opening far enough that the driver's side hit the next section head-on, stopping his car dead. Martin was killed instantly. Clara was thrown out the side door as the car spun around and to the right. She was alive, but her neck and back were broken. She had been in surgery all night. Her neck would heal, but her lower spine was severed. Deanne cried even harder as she told me Clara would be paralyzed from the waist down for the rest of her life.

The police told her that the time from the initial blowout to Martin's car hitting the wall was less than ten seconds, but Deanne said it seemed more like fifteen to twenty minutes. I was reminded of Madeline's car falling into the quarry. It had seemed like that too, even though I knew it was only a few seconds. It was odd how the mind can distort time like that.

I told Deanne I would drive up that night, but she insisted I should not. It was too late for me to start and she was going back to the hospital to be with Clara. They were not going to tell Clara about the paralysis right away, but Deanne wanted to be there when she woke up. She needed to be the one to tell Clara about Martin. She said Clara still loved Martin and it should not come from anyone else.

Deanne also confirmed what I suspected - that Martin had no family. She said she would go through his papers, but she doubted he had any funeral plans or other arrangements. He probably did not even have a will. We were only thirty years old and death was the farthest thing from our minds. Somehow, with no direction from him, Martin's shop would have to be closed and his apartment vacated.

I promised I would drive up first thing Sunday morning and take the next week off work to help her with what had to be done. It was the least I could do. It was too much for Deanne to do alone.

Chapter Fourteen

Martin was buried on Tuesday. The Westport Merchants Association sent a casket spray and a few of its members attended the service, but otherwise it was only Deanne and me, along with the neighbors from Martin's and Clara's building. There were not enough pallbearers so the funeral home's male staff had to fill in. Deanne's mother, who had met Clara, also attended, but Martin had no family left. From the lack of visitors at the hospital, it was becoming obvious Clara had no one else either.

They kept Clara in a drug-induced coma to let her stabilize and heal before facing her new reality. Deanne, crying almost nonstop, sat for hours at her bedside, but I could not bear it. Clara lay flat, connected to a web of wires and tubes that kept her alive. Both eyes were swollen shut and her face was a mass of raw and oozing flesh. One side of her face seemed to be held together with only a crisscrossed web of stitches. A plastic surgeon was already involved. She assured Deanne that, although more surgery would be required later, Clara had been lucky. There was no damage to the facial muscles and she would fully recover with only minimal long-term scarring.

Clara's legs were not so lucky. With her spinal cord severed, there was no hope of her ever being able to stand or walk. She may not be able to sit upright in a wheelchair without being strapped in. I could not imagine adjusting to that myself, but Deanne insisted to everyone who would listen that Clara was strong-willed and if anyone could survive what had happened, it was Clara Carson.

Deanne and I went back to Clara's apartment the night after the funeral, but there was little to do. I had expected to help Deanne go through Martin's things, but he had borrowed heavily for his business and had pledged his personal assets on the loans. As soon as they found out about the accident the bank seized everything, changing the locks on his shop and his apartment. A notice was put on the front door of the shop offering the contents for sale as a going business. Another notice was pasted to the front and back doors of his apartment, stating the property was under the probate court's jurisdiction and trespassers would be prosecuted to the full extent of the law. The contents of his apartment - lock, stock, and barrel - would be auctioned in settlement of his debts.

Believing Martin's personal belongings should at least go to Clara, Deanne dragged me to a meeting with a lawyer who offered no hope. If anything was left after the bank loan was paid, it would have been distributed to Martin's heirs according to his will. Since he died without one, the remainder would go to the State of Missouri.

Since Deanne only had a tiny one-room studio we were staying in Clara's apartment. It was laid out exactly the same as Martin's, but she had furnished it in a mishmash of post-war garage sale finds that somehow pulled together into a hip, Bohemian decor. She did not own a television and the walls were covered with rough shelves that were crammed full with books. More books were stacked on the floor, under her coffee table and end tables, and a stack of books weighed down her bedside table.

After seeing the attorney, when we were starting a second bottle of wine and Deanne was railing against the system that robbed Clara of Martin's assets, I said it was too bad that we couldn't get into his apartment. The bank had only just changed the locks and it had not been inventoried yet. If we could just get in, we could save a few of his things for Clara to have.

"Maybe we can," Deanne said and led me to the kitchen.

In the days when milk was still home-delivered, the milkman used the building's service staircase for his deliveries. The maids also set the waste bins in the service hall for the trash collectors. The staircase was no longer used, and could only be accessed from a locked door in the basement, but the half-door in Clara's kitchen was still there. Deanne was sure the door in Martin's apartment had not been sealed over either, and if she was right, the lock on his had been broken for years. The latch could be pushed back with a pen knife or any small blade - like a nail file, she added, producing hers from her purse.

We rummaged through the kitchen drawers, found Clara's flashlight, and opened the little door. Old, stale air flowed out to greet us, smelling of dust and long-dead mice. The flashlight's beam showed a network of cobwebs. No one had been on those stairs in years.

Silently, we crept down the gritty stairs to Martin's apartment.

Deanne stuck her nail file into the space between the door and the frame and wiggled it back and forth, trying to slide the lock open. The television in the apartment across the landing was on - hopefully loud enough to cover any noise we were making.

After whispering that we needed to go back upstairs and find something stronger than the file, the lock snapped open with a loud pop. We froze as the man in the apartment across the landing muted the television and came back to his kitchen to investigate. I shut off the flashlight. The overhead light in his kitchen was snapped on, sending slats of light around the little door and falling across Deanne's wide-open eyes. That was followed by tentative footsteps in the kitchen before the occupant stood in silence, listening. There were more footsteps and we heard the lock on his back door being unlocked and relocked, the porch light turned on, a shade being raised and lowered, and finally the porch light being turned off again.

We held our breath as his footsteps came back to the service door. The refrigerator beside it was opened. We heard bottles inside it ping against each other, the "pa-whoosh" of a beer bottle being opened, some gulps, and then a loud and explosive passing of gas. Deanne clamped both hands over her mouth to keep from laughing out loud. Eventually the footsteps retreated, the kitchen light was snapped off, plunging us back into darkness, and the television's sound came back on at full volume.

We waited a full five minutes until we tried the door. Luck was on our side and it swung open as silently as if the hinges had just been oiled. We crawled through the half-door into Martin's kitchen and closed the door behind us. Only then did I turn the flashlight on, keeping the beam low and away from the windows.

"Oh, man," Deanne whispered loudly, wiping away the cobwebs. "I thought we were done for when he farted." Able to laugh at last, we doubled over in silent laughter.

"I knew that guy was a fraud," she added and hiccupped. He did psychic readings for a living. "If he was really psychic, then he would have known we were hiding on the other side of the door. I think I wet myself a little bit."

After the past few days, laughter was a welcome relief. It also cleared the mental cobwebs from our brains. We agreed we needed to grab anything small and of value - sentimental or monetary - that we thought Martin would want Clara to have. We needed to go about it systematically, and in complete silence.

I know that what we did was illegal, it was burglary in fact, but it seemed to even up what the bank was doing to Clara in taking everything that belonged to Martin. Throughout the night we went through the apartment. Thumbing through his bookshelf, Deanne almost squealed when an envelope marked "India" fell to the floor with more than $3,000 inside. It must have been money he was setting aside for his move, likely unreported cash receipts from his shop. It was a great find, but it also meant we had to go through every other book in the apartment. That search only produced another $20 in smaller bills and some random photographs.

It was a little unsettling that everything was exactly as Martin left it. His bed was unmade and a bath towel was on the floor where he dropped it after his last shower. I picked it up and held it to my face, closing my eyes at his scent. I half-expected him to come walking in and ask what I was doing.

The ring he always wore was on the edge of the bathroom sink, obviously forgotten that night. Deanne said they were in a rush when they left Friday. I slipped it on the fourth finger of my right hand, the same finger Martin wore the ring, and had a rush of memory of him. Deanne insisted I should keep it - that he would have wanted me to have it. We went through every drawer of his desk, finding a stash of old Series E bonds that must have been bought for him as a child. Clara could cash those easily.

Silent as mice, over the rest of that night and the next two, we went through everything in the apartment. We took nothing that would be obviously missed when the bank inventoried his apartment. We rearranged what was left behind to look more natural with no obvious gaps between. In the mornings, as soon as the neighbors left the building, we carried the loot up the service staircase to Clara's apartment and stashed it in her guest bedroom. We wiped our footprints off the kitchen floor and made sure the latch was back in place.

Sadly, even counting the savings bonds, there was less than $10,000 to mark Martin's life. There were some nice things Clara would likely want to keep, and others she could eventually sell. Deanne helped herself to some of his books and I kept the sweater he was wearing the last time I saw him. Our theft was never caught, and no one, including the Country Club Bank of Kansas City and its agents, ever knew it had happened.

Chapter Fifteen

When I came home, there was nothing left for me to do but get to work on my MBA. Martin was dead. Clara had a long recovery ahead of her. I finished the GMAT, enrolled in the course, and spent all my free time studying. The next two years rolled by.

I was too busy to make many new friends, but Doug and I were both in the program and on the same two-year class schedule. Except for his coppery red hair and moustache, he reminded me a lot of Martin. Doug lived and worked an hour out of town. Our classes were Monday through Thursday evenings and we both worked Monday through Friday in the daytime. I knew how busy I was myself, and could not imagine how Doug managed to squeeze in that much driving time.

On weekends, we studied together when there was a project or exam coming up the next week, which was almost every weekend. Doug always arrived by noon on Saturday. We went straight to the college library and studied and quizzed each other until it closed at eight o'clock, then went out for a simple dinner. He usually stayed over in my guest room and on Sunday, as soon as we were up, we hit the books again until he had to drive back home and get ready for work Monday morning.

The arrangement worked well, although after two years we were getting worn out with our schedules. We both took a week of vacation from work during the last week of the last semester and burned the midnight oil getting things wrapped up for our final oral presentations and exams. By five o'clock that Saturday, confident we were ready, we closed our books for the final time and decided to celebrate.

Over the two years, we had gotten very relaxed around each other and sometimes walked in and out of the bathroom while the other was showering or shaving. Doug always teased me about not dating anyone, said that I was going to dry up and blow away, but as much as he liked to brag about his conquests, I doubted he had much time for it either. That final Saturday evening, I was a little self-conscious and wrapped up in a towel as soon as I finished my shower. I stood shaving at the mirror when Doug came in, stripped off, and got in the shower, but not before grabbing and ripping off my towel, then popping me with it.

"You dork," I said around the toothbrush, wrapping the towel back around myself as he pulled the shower curtain closed. He laughed, dipped his head under the shower and started singing, badly off-key, at the top of his lungs. I wrote it off to male bravado and the elation of finally being finished with two years of classes and studying.

Since Doug's car was parked behind mine in the drive, we took it to the pizza parlor near the campus. We ordered a pitcher of beer to go with our pizza. While we ate, the crowd picked up and more classmates came in and joined us. Everyone was in a celebratory mood and more pitchers were ordered. Around midnight I said I had to go. Feeling buzzed, I told Doug I would walk home, but he was indignant and wanted me to stay. A half hour later, others were drifting away and I stood to leave. Doug agreed it was time and we paid the bill. Stumbling out the door and walking to the car, he threw an arm around my neck, pulling me into him as we walked.

"Well, old buddy, this is it, isn't it? Next week - what the hell are you going to do without me?"

"Sleep!" I said, putting a hand against his side, hoping it would steady him. He was weaving badly. I probably needed to take the keys from him.

"Yeah, me too. I'm gonna sleep like a baby for a week." He laughed at how funny that was, stopped and shouted up into the night sky, "Like a little old bay-bee!"

He drove us home. He was excruciatingly careful - which I said was going to get him pulled over for sure. We made it, although he fell onto the pavement getting out of the car. He needed my help across the patio and up the steps, then slumped against me inside. I helped him up the stairs, to the bed in the guestroom and laid him across it the best I could. I thought about taking off his shoes, but I only pulled the blanket off the foot of the bed and draped it over him. He was snoring already.

I went to bed as quietly as I could. I undressed to my shorts and got into bed without even brushing my teeth. I was soon asleep.

Somewhere in the night, Doug got up and went to the bathroom; coming down the hall noisily, flipping on the overhead light, and splashing on the floor. I wished I had closed my bedroom door, but it was too late. I lay still, with my back to the door, feigning sleep until he went back to bed. I had to go too. When he was snoring again, I would use the bathroom and wipe up the mess he left.

Lying there, I heard him turn off the bathroom light, then there was silence. He must have come barefoot across the floor because the next thing I knew he was on the bed beside me, sliding under the covers and snuggling up against me, naked, with his hand on my shoulder and his bristling moustache at my ear, "I miss you," he whispered, pressing himself closer against me.

This was not what I wanted. I liked Doug, but not like that. I turned to tell him and when I did, there was no one there. I sat up in bed and turned on the light. My bedroom was empty and the sheets on that side were still in place. I went to the bathroom and the floor around the toilet was spotless and dry. I tiptoed down the hall to the guest bedroom and he was still lying on his back, snoring and covered just as I had left him.

I simply could not have dreamed it. The body pressed against me had been too real and the whispered words were still fresh on my ear. But it wasn't Doug.

The nightmare had started again.

Chapter Sixteen

The first thing I did on Monday morning was call Clara at work. She answered gruffly on the second ring, with "Detective Carson." I used the pretext of asking if she had received the graduation announcement I sent her.

"Yes, I did," she said. "Congratulations."

Feeling like I had been caught fishing for compliments I retreated. "Well, I just wanted to check. I don't expect you to actually come to the ceremony or anything."

"Why not?" she was defensive.

"Well. . . It's a long trip and I know it would be difficult for you."

"I am perfectly capable, you jerk," she said in such a tone that I wasn't sure if she meant it.

I paused, aghast at my gaff, and not sure what to say until she burst out in laughter.

"The department had a van adapted for me," she said. "I drive myself to cases and even to court and as long as there aren't too many curbs or steps involved I can go anywhere on my own. I can get my butt to your graduation if I want to. If you had bothered to come to see me even once in the last two years you would know all this already."

"Sorry about that, but it's been really busy, Clara," I said defensively. "I had classes every evening, each of them was three and a half hours long, and I had to study all weekend, every weekend. And on top of that I still worked full time - and even overtime, sometimes. . ."

"Oh, waa, waa, waah!" she almost sounded like a crying baby on the phone. "And I had to learn to do everything without legs, find a new apartment without stairs, and learn to drive a god damned conversion van without killing anyone. See if you can drive without using your feet. I really don't think you can ever top me for whining material, Jack."

I was laughing now, too. "And I suppose the next thing you're going to say is that you have to do it all better than a man would, too."

"Oh, I don't even have to say that, everyone already knows it."

She was suddenly serious. "You know what, Jack? It's actually made me better. People don't see me - or at least don't see me as a threat. They answer my questions more readily, are less guarded, and are more helpful. I am solving more cases than I did before the accident. It took a while for my boss to let me go out on my own again, but I'm doing better than ever."

We chatted a while longer until Clara asked me point blank, "So what's up? Why did you really call me?"

In a rush, I told her what had happened over the weekend.

"Have you found out anything else about the woman we saw in the mirror? Oh, what was her name?" Clara had suffered some memory loss of things that happened before her accident.

"No, and her name was Madeline," I prompted. "I'm not even sure where to start."

"Well, from what we saw, I'd guess she used to live in the house, and if she's a wandering spirit she probably did not die peacefully in her bed. Talk to your neighbors, especially the older ones, ask them about who lived there before you. If that doesn't work, see if your library keeps copies of your city directory, or something with a cross reference by street address. It's a pain going through the books, but they should show who was living in the house each year. Go back as far as you can. If someone named Madeline ever lived in your house, then you have a link."

I said I had done that already - before I started the MBA, but I did not remember the details and dates. It would be in my notebook, somewhere. I would have to find it.

"When you find that the name of the occupant has changed you can take the name to your local cemetery and cross reference their files for the date of death. If you have that, you can look up the obituary in the newspaper."

I admitted I had not thought of that.

"Your newspaper office or library will probably have those old editions on microfilm by now. If the obituary doesn't give any clues about her, then read the papers following the date of death for any articles. If she didn't die of natural causes, there was probably a newspaper story buried somewhere, especially back then. Those old newspapers used to list the police calls too. Once you have all that, I can see if your police department has a case file. I will have to have a complete name, date of death, and some reason to prove why we are suspicious or they will just blow me off."

I was making notes and a list of action items while she talked, and writing as fast as I could.

When Clara paused I said, "I talked to my neighbor a few years back. If Madeline was who she was talking about, she was the mother of the woman I bought the house from and there were rumors that she committed suicide back in the fifties. Does that help?"

"I'm due in a meeting in ten minutes, Jack. You have to do the legwork there, buddy, no pun intended." Clara was assertive and professional. "Once we have a verified name and date of death, I can ask to see the case file from your police department. Until then. . ."

"After the last two years, I don't know if I can stomach even ten more minutes in any kind of library," I said, risking a scolding for whining again. "I hoped I was finished with research for a while."

"Welcome to my world," she chuckled. "I really gotta go now. Call me the minute you have the information."

Chapter Seventeen

It turned out that while I was in graduate school, Mrs. Poindexter, the only remaining neighbor who might have known Madeline, went into a nursing home and had since died.

If Miss Addie was still living I suspected that seeing her would be out of the question. A call to the nursing home readily confirmed that she was not able to have visitors.

My next step was to contact Eva in San Francisco. I had received a brief note after her visit five years earlier, but I had not kept the return address, I called San Francisco directory assistance and got a list of possible numbers after I asked them to search under her last name and first initial. Because it was a shorter list, I started with the numbers for E. Montrose.

The first three were obviously not her. On the fourth try, I recognized her voice.

"Hello," she answered.

My throat constricted. I had not really decided what I would say. How could I ask about her mother who had been dead for so long? What would she think?

"Hello?" she said again into the empty silence at my end of the line.

"I'm sorry," I finally managed. "I have the wrong number."

As Clara suggested, I went to the public library on my lunch hour and looked through old editions of the city directory. This time the volumes were correctly shelved.

Within each directory, there was a section that listed every resident and business in town by street; first in alphabetical order by street name, then numerically by house number. For each address, the occupants of the house were listed, along with abbreviated information about them. I found the 1935 directory which showed nothing for my address. There was a rush of adrenaline when I found their names at my address in the 1936 edition.

The directories for 1936 through 1941 showed both Jordan(h) -

H for husband - and Madeline(w) - W for wife - Montrose as the occupants. The letters "dctr" followed, which I assumed was the abbreviation for doctor, and "hsw" I decoded as housewife. The directories listed the names of the two daughters, Evangeline and Adeline, along with their ages. The telephone number was only five digits.

There was a logical gap in the directories during the war years. The directories after the war only showed Madeline with a "w" likely for widow, without any occupation listed. Starting with the 1956 directory, the house was occupied by Adeline and her husband. In all the editions I checked after that, no children were listed. I made complete notes, but after my search there was nothing else in the directories that would help.

On another lunch hour, I had the idea of visiting the county recorder's office to review the property records. The recorder's clerk laid out the huge portfolio-type ledger of plat drawings that almost covered the entire table. On my lot, a small piece of paper was glued over the original structure with a pencil notation to the side showing the date of the revision, and an abbreviation the clerk interpreted to say the original structure, built in the 1890s, had burned. The outline of my house was drawn on the patch. Oddly, over time the outline of the first structure underneath had bled through, so that it was visible through the outline of my house. The first house was much smaller. Other than verifying that Elizabeth's story of the fire was probably true, there was no other useable information from this search.

On another lunch hour, I drove to Greenlawn cemetery and stopped at the office to ask for help in locating the Montrose graves. It was a long shot as there were other cemeteries in town but, after giving me an odd look, the manager soon located the names on her records and marked the location on a printed map they apparently kept ready for that purpose. I thanked her and drove to the plot, in the older section and not far from where my grandparents were buried.

It was odd to stand at their graves, reading their names on the headstone. It was a respectable marker, but not showy. With the minutes of my lunch break ticking away, I made quick notes of their full names, birth dates, and dates of death. The headstone said Madeline died December 18, 1953.

The next Saturday afternoon I made another trip to the public library and was admitted to the archives section tucked away in an airless room under the red tile roof. I told the reference librarian I was researching the family who had once lived in my home. He seemed mildly intrigued as I gave him the dates for newspapers I would like to see. He somewhat proudly told me that the library now routinely transferred newspapers to microfilm within weeks of receipt but, prior to microfilm, old newspapers had been stored in 'cribs' or long boxes, by month and year. It was a big project, but all of those were eventually transferred to microfilm, too. He added that the paper stock on many of those, especially the older ones, had been so deteriorated that many pages were partially gone or missing entirely on the microfilm.

I gave him the date of Madeline's death, saying I would like to start by reading her obituary to find a list of survivors. From a tall metal cabinet with shallow drawers he brought out a box of film with the typewritten label "Springfield Newspapers, 1953" and set it up on a microfilm reader for me.

He showed me how the lever below the screen ran the film spool forward and back. Satisfied, he left me alone with the instructions to wind the film entirely to the spool on the left when I was finished, to turn off the reader at the red power button, and to bring the film and its box back to him at the reference desk for filing.

By trial and error, I eventually advanced the film to the week of her death. The paper was filled with the holiday advertisements of merchants that I remembered but had long been out of business. I read some of these, remembering those stores from my childhood when the public square had been the main retail area.

At a time when the town's population was not quite a third of its present size, there were full morning and evening editions of the paper, signifying that television was still in its infancy and had not yet replaced newspapers as the primary source of local and national news. The local stories were almost quaint in comparison to current day reporting standards, and I found myself reading article after article as I scanned the pages.

Eventually I came to the obituaries for the day after Madeline's death. The section did not include her name so I rolled forward to the next day, the Sunday edition, and found her death notice in small print.

"Mrs. Jordan Montrose," it was headed. I was disappointed there was no photograph. I had hoped to confirm, once and for all, that the apparition we had seen in the mirror on the landing had indeed been Madeline. I read the brief obituary. Other than confirming her name, the name of her late husband, and the names of their children, the article provided no additional information. It was only mentioned in passing that after her husband's death during the war, Madeline was employed outside the home as a bookkeeper, with no mention of where she worked.

Slowly, I went through the rest of the paper, hoping to glean some news of her death. The pages were out of order. Apparently, whoever transferred this newspaper to microfilm put all the partial pages at the end, rather than keeping these torn or partial sheets in their original sequence. These tattered pages showed the effects of years of handling and storage. Some were taped together while others, in fragments, must have been glued to a base sheet before they were photographed for the film. Eventually I found the local page - or what was called the second front page - for that Sunday. The sensational headline was emblazoned across the full width of the page:

DOCTOR'S WIDOW DIES

Smaller type under the headline read:

Her Car Plunged Into
Boulevard Quarry
Coroner To Investigate

There was a photograph of a charred automobile being hoisted on a cable, with a grim crowd of onlookers and emergency personnel standing in the rain. Small, barely-visible type below the photograph said "AP Photo" and "3:05 Saturday morning" - the same time she always walked across my bedroom. From the first paragraph, the details of the story were sketchy:

'The widow of the late Dr. Jordan Montrose, noted Springfield physician, died late Friday evening when her 1941 Cadillac apparently skidded out of control on the icy streets and plunged over the retaining wall at the quarry on the National Boulevard. Dr. Montrose, whose offices were located in the Harris Building on Commercial Street, passed away in 1942.'

The article went on to say that Dr. and Mrs. Montrose had been members of the Springfield Club, the Springfield Country Club, and were active in many local organizations. They had been members of the Episcopal Church. Following her husband's death, Mrs.

Montrose withdrew from Springfield society and devoted herself to rearing her two daughters. She was employed outside the home as a bookkeeper after her husband's death.

A final paragraph reported, *'Mrs. Montrose is survived by her daughters, Mrs. Adeline Applegate, of Springfield, and Mrs. Evangeline Montrose-Song of San Francisco, Calif., and four grandchildren. Funeral arrangements will be announced, pending the arrival of Mrs. Montrose-Song on Wednesday morning.'*

I thought it was odd that Addie would be listed first, but it was likely switched by the reporter who wrote the article. If Eva was traveling, Addie would have given the information to the paper. I added a few more notes to my notebook.

There was nothing else in that day's paper. I scanned through the following weeks, finding nothing. Then, just before Christmas, there was a sidebar article buried in one of the back pages.

MONTROSE DEATH
RULED SUICIDE

The article stated that the coroner and police had jointly determined that the cause of death of Mrs. Madeline Montrose, widow of the late Dr. Jordan Montrose, was suicide. Their decision was based on the lack of tire skid marks on the street and the mental condition of the woman. Testimony from her coworkers indicated Mrs. Montrose had likely discovered earlier that day that she was passed over for a promotion she wanted and left work early, visibly upset and, according to one employee, bordering on hysteria. The article was continued on another page. I rolled the film forward and continued reading the text that filled the space between holiday advertisements:

At the inquest, a daughter, Mrs. Eva Montrose-Song, of San Francisco, insisted that at the time of the accident, Mrs. Montrose was traveling to a party at the Colonial Hotel, but police noted that the most direct route from the Montrose home to the hotel would not have passed the quarry. The coroner also stated that a rational woman driving alone would not go near the dangerous quarry on slick streets.

In additional testimony, the second daughter, Mrs. Adeline Applegate of Springfield, said her mother led a solitary life after being widowed during the war, was deeply devoted to her career, and was counting one-hundred-percent on getting the promotion left open by her retiring supervisor.

Mrs. Applegate said that her mother was the consummate career woman and would have been very disappointed, indeed, when she found out she did not get the promotion. She also added that her mother never left work early and it was rare for her to drive herself anywhere, especially at night. She always took the bus or a taxi.

While Mrs. Applegate admitted that, although they spoke by telephone, she had not seen her mother for several days before her death, she insisted she was close to her mother. Police added that the elder daughter, who was in California at the time of death, could not have reliably assessed the mental condition of her mother before the accident from such a distance.

Further, an autopsy was performed immediately after the remains of the body were recovered from the wreckage. The medical examiner concluded the injuries to the body were consistent with the accident, and did not indicate foul play. Dr. Joseph Song, a Chinese businessman, and the common-law husband of Eva Montrose-Song, asked to address the panel with his analysis of the autopsy report, but was denied. The body was interred prior to the hearing and will not be exhumed for further examination. No further inquiry will be conducted.

As I finished my notes, I was saddened for Madeline's daughters, who seemed to be divided at the inquest. Had Addie gone along with the suicide ruling just to have it over and done with? Had Eva attempted to find another explanation for her mother's death? What conflicting evidence did Eva's husband have that he was not allowed to present? Was the "common law" reference an intentional insult against the interracial couple by the reporter? Between the lines, the article carried an undercurrent of the shame and embarrassment for the family.

Thirty years later, suicide still put a blemish on a family name. At the time of Madeline's death it would have carried an even darker stigma, with implications of family insanity and inherited mental deficiencies. Was Addie's life ruined by it? Had the struggle to cope with the aftermath slowly driven her insane? Eva could escape back to San Francisco, but Addie had to stay behind, living in her mother's house. Addie would have been the one to feel the rejection and suspicion as the community shied away from her. Did she come to regret her words at the inquest that helped support the coroner's conclusion?

An unexpected wave of rage swept over me. From what I knew and what I had seen that night in the landing mirror, I could never believe Madeline had taken her own life. She had been confident and poised, with a purpose in mind. I recalled again the night of the séance, and seeing the darkened car backing up and charging forward to slam into Madeline's car again, finishing the job. She had not killed herself. Madeline had been murdered. The coroner's decision set her killer free. He did not have to pay for what he did to her.

Still staring at the screen, I slowly realized that the driver of the second car could also have been Addie. I remembered Mrs. Poindexter whispering that people thought that Addie was somehow responsible for the accident - if nothing else, she had driven her mother to do it. Mrs. Poindexter said that people thought Addie and her husband were having money problems and they took up residence in Madeline's house a little too quickly, before the funeral even. It just hadn't looked right, Mrs. Poindexter would say, shaking her head.

If what the article said about the inquest was correct, Addie certainly had done little to persuade the panel that it had been anything other than suicide. Had she helped steer it that direction to deflect attention from herself? And what possible motive could there be for her to kill her mother.

This line of thought made me even angrier for two reasons: first, that Addie might have killed her mother, and second, if Addie was innocent, that she was condemned and cast out by the neighbors, living her life under suspicion while the killer went free.

My indignation and anger meant my connection with Madeline was still there. I was beginning to accept my purpose: to explain her death and identify her murderer. Somehow, I had to find out who was driving the second car and, even though thirty years had passed, bring him - or her - to justice.

The overhead lights flashed off and on, signifying it was time for the library to close. I rewound the film, put it in the box, turned off the reader and returned the film to the librarian's desk.

"Did you find what you were looking for?" he asked with a smile.

"Yes," I replied. "Thanks for your help."

Other than the librarian and me, the rest of the library was empty. He followed me to the doors by the parking lot and locked them behind me.

Sitting in my car, I looked at the list of information in my notebook. I still did not know much:

Madeline Montrose
Wife of Dr. Jordan Montrose
Members of (possible leads to investigate?):
    Springfield Club
    Springfield Country Club
    Episcopal Church
Widowed: 1942
Died: December, 1953
    Ruled suicide.
    Limestone Quarry
    Murdered?
Autopsy performed.
    (Still available - Clara?)
Bookkeeper
    Who was her employer?
Two daughters:
    Adeline (Addie) Applegate
        Husband: David Applegate
        No children?
    Evangeline (Eva) Montrose-Song
        San Francisco
        Dr. Joseph Song.
        Chinese businessman, SF
        Four children?

I had very little information. It certainly was not enough to prove that Madeline did not kill herself, and it did nothing to identify her killer. Clara would say that the short list meant I was just getting started. The next steps would require more creative effort. After all, the trail was cold. It had been cooling since 1953.

As soon as I was home, I started another page and listed everything I could remember from the night we made contact with Madeline: her apparent confusion at first, seeing her image in the mirror on the landing, and retracing her drive from the house to the quarry. I listed what she was wearing, the dress, the fur jacket, her jewelry. I even listed her features and her approximate height and weight.

I did not know where to look next. The neighborhood was changing as younger people moved in and began renovating the old houses. I welcomed the renaissance, but it also meant that the traces of what had been were being stripped away like the old carpet and other rubbish I saw piled at the curbs for the trash truck. The trails to the old clues I needed were scrubbed away a little more every day.

I decided to call Clara and ask if she kept the tape from the séance in my house. She scolded me for using the term "séance" but said she would mail it to me. She sent it special delivery and it was in my mailbox when I came home from work the next day.

Playing the tape brought back vivid memories of that December evening when we gathered around my dining room table. In my mind, Clara was as she had been then. I had almost forgotten Deanne. I was overwhelmed with sadness at hearing Martin's voice and had to turn off the tape for a while. I would always struggle with the guilt that if he had gone to India when he first suggested it he might still be alive. I would always wonder if I had held him back from going when he should.

I listened to the entire tape again without stopping it, letting the memories flow back.

I rewound it and played it again, making notes on a new page in the notebook as the tape played - small things that might have some significance.

After the session ended the third time, I rewound back to the place where we had first heard Madeline. Something was troubling me, but I could not quite put my finger on it. I listened several times to the start of her narration and Martin calmly reassuring her when she grew agitated about the changes to the house while she had been away. I listened to her description of what she was wearing on that last night. I could visualize what we had seen in the mirror: the black dress, her pearl necklace with the diamond clasp, her diamond and pearl earrings, and the fur jacket. I could see her stopping to check her appearance in the mirror.

But something was not quite right. Something disturbed me. There was something I was missing or could not quite remember.

I rewound the tape again and listened to the beginning of her interview. I put the pen and paper down and was staring at the tape and leaning close to the recorder when the description of the clothing came around again:

'...and a dress I had made over for the party. My black velvet and taffeta.'

'That's very good, Madeline.' Martin's voice prompted her. 'See you do remember some things, so don't be worried.'

'Thank you.' (pause) 'I also wore my fox jacket, the one Jordie - my husband, Jordan, gave me.'

I stopped the tape. Jordie!

How had I missed it during the séance and all the times I had listened to the tape until now? It almost sounded like she had cleared her throat - unremarkable. That was what my mind was filling in every time I heard it until now. But this time I realized that she said the nickname and then quickly corrected herself. I rewound the tape to listen to it again.

'. . . fox jacket, the one Jordie - my husband, Jordan," I rewound slightly and pushed the play button again.

'. . .the one Jordie – my,"

"Jordie,"

I stopped the tape. It was something she probably never said outside their home. I knew there was something very significant about it, even if I could not put my finger on it. I jotted down the name in capital letters, underlined it twice, and followed that with three question marks then paused, staring at the page. What was it about the name that stirred something so deeply in me? What did it signify? Why was I so troubled by it?

For the next week I mulled it over in my mind. Sometimes at work I would think I almost remembered, but the telephone would ring or someone would stop by my office and the gathering mist of the remembrance would evaporate.

One evening I sat on the patio looking up at the stars and trying to remember. It was a cool night and the sky was perfectly clear and still, giving the sensation that you could reach out and touch a star.

"Help me, Martin," I spoke softly into the night. "Help me remember."

A few days later, it came to me in the shower - a clear memory from early in my childhood, one that was almost entirely forgotten. If I was right then I had an explanation, but I needed the corroboration of someone else to validate it.

That Friday, I parked my car downtown and sprinted through raindrops to the restaurant. It was in the first block of College Street, just west from the public square. The street had just reopened after being closed as a failed pedestrian mall for years and it was rapidly filling with new, owner-operated businesses. Café 303 simply took its name from its address. The narrow space still had its interior plaster walls. Some of the plaster was now deliberately chipped away to expose the old brick underneath. Support beams were painted in a faux marble finish and the wide tin molding at the ceiling was painted in bright contrasting colors. Round bistro tables and bentwood chairs provided intimate seating. The place was always packed for lunch. It was cheerful, light, quirky, and crowded, and my mother loved it. My three older brothers were married and had families of their own, but still single, I was the one who called Mom for lunch the most. Regardless what she was doing, she would always bend her schedule to meet me at Café 303 for lunch.

We passed over our favorite tarragon chicken salad sandwiches in favor of the special of the day: a salmon croissant with dill sauce and fresh peas on a bed of lettuce leaves. The croissant melted away to butter in my mouth, with the fresh dill bringing memories of my grandmother's garden on a hot summer afternoon.

Mom and I had not seen each other for weeks, and there was a lot of family news I had to let her report. The waiter cleared the entrée and served our dessert before I could ask the question that had been my purpose for meeting.

"Do you remember me having nightmares when I was a child?"

She paused, dipping the spoon into her sherbet while thinking back over the years.

"Yes," she said quietly. "The doctor called them night terrors. I think they terrorized your father and me even more than you."

"What were they like?" I asked.

Her face clouded at the memory.

"You were such a happy baby, overall," she said, remembering. "We couldn't believe you could have such bad dreams at night."

I waited a moment for her to go on.

"It was like you left us," she said her face visibly tightening. I thought she might cry.

"What do you mean, Mom?"

"There was nothing we could do. You were totally in terror of something. When it happened, it was like you were removed from us, like it completely consumed you."

"You couldn't wake me?"

"No, you withdrew into yourself, like were still sound asleep, even if your eyes were open. You arched your back and your entire body would go completely stiff, even when you were a tiny baby. All I could do was hold you," she said with a catch in her voice.

After a long pause, I asked, "How long did these go on?"

Misunderstanding my question, she replied, "Eventually, you would seem to wake from the nightmare, and begin crying, sobbing actually, although I have never seen another baby cry like that. Finally, we calmed you down and you went back to sleep, but you always had a death grip on me, my robe, my collar, whatever your little hands could grip. I'd have to hold you all night. You would wake up if I tried to put you back to bed."

"How young was I when it began, Mom?"

"The first time was the night after we brought you home from the hospital," she said. "I had never seen anything like it. I felt like a terrible mother. All I could do was cry along with you. Later on, the doctor wondered if you had been dropped in the nursery at the hospital and you were having some kind of seizures from that. He took some X-rays that didn't show anything wrong, and there wasn't so much as a bruise on you when we brought you home. I always wondered if someone in the hospital accidentally tipped over your bassinet and didn't tell us and you were afraid of that. Of course by the time we were figuring out what you were so terrified of, it was too late to find out anything from the hospital."

"What do you mean?"

"When you started talking, a few words would come through," she continued. "You would scream out 'fall' and 'no' and other words we could never understand."

It was amazing that my falling nightmare went back that far - even before I could put it into words. The dream had plagued me all of my life. They only stopped after Madeline revealed herself in the séance.

But this did not explain what I now needed to understand. Was there a name I called out during those nightmares? In my first memory of it, before my third birthday, I only recalled being held by my mother and weeping for something I was not able to put into words.

"Did I ever ask for anyone?" I asked, seeing that my sherbet had melted to soup in my dish.

"Not that I can remember . . . No, wait - once when you were a little older, three or four, there was a name you kept calling out one night, and then you cried even harder. I couldn't do anything for you. Georgie, I think it was, but I kept telling you we didn't know anyone by that name."

A tear slid down her cheek. I hated putting her through this. It must have been bad enough at the time it had happened without dredging it up again all these years later. I wondered what the people seated near us must be thinking of our discussion.

"I remember you kept telling me that," I said placing my hand over hers. But even more I remembered the grief that night, knowing I would not ever see him again. The memory had been suppressed all these years, surfacing again only now.

I waited while she dabbed her eyes with her napkin.

"When did they stop, these nightmares?"

"They were not as regular as you got older. Maybe they stopped by the time you were five. They may have stopped altogether after your tonsils were taken out."

I snickered at that. In the late fifties a tonsillectomy was considered the cure-all for almost every childhood ailment, but I'd never heard of the operation curing nightmares. My tonsillectomy had been the recommended cure for chronic ear infections.

I vaguely remembered the operation. I was really too young, not quite five yet, but the increasing frequency of ear and throat problems pushed my doctor into performing the operation earlier than he should. I fought the anesthesiologist when he placed the mask over my face. A nurse hand to hold my hands down. Under the anesthesia, I had frenzied dreams: of being chased by black-robed figures, the feeling of having my face inside our new television set with the deafening static buzzing around my head, then dark figures in the shadows taunting me. I could not run, I could not escape, until finally I awoke in my room, crying for water.

"You know, they nearly lost you during the operation," my

mother leaned forward to whisper. "They gave you too much ether, and it was touch and go for a while before you came back,"

"Came back?" I was intrigued at her choice of words.

"Before you recovered and came out from under the anesthesia," she clarified.

We sat a few moments, calming and collecting our thoughts.

"Could the name I called out have been Jordan?"

She did not understand my question at first, but thinking back over what she had told me, she shook her head and said, "I don't think so. I remember it ended in an 'ee' sound. You kept dragging out the last part, pleading in a sort of screeching scream. Anyway, we had never known anyone named Jordan or Jordie, so where would you have heard it?"

"I guess not," I said wanting to put her at ease. It had not been easy for her recalling this chapter of our past.

As we rose to go, she hugged me. Then she took my hand, looking deeply into my eyes as if searching for something.

"Don't look too far back, Jack. All we have is the present, and our future to look forward to. Whatever happened then is in the past, don't be troubled by it now."

Her advice came too late. All the same I was puzzled, wondering if she realized what I was up to. How much, in her mother's instinct, did she know? How much had she always known?

"Before I can have a future, I have to know what was in my past," I said. "I have to understand it before I will be able to let it go."

She did not argue her point further. She had confirmed what I had remembered: that as a child I had called out for Jordie. Beyond that, the real information I still needed was going to be more difficult to find.

At home that evening I made a few more notes:

"Jordie" was the name I called out as I sat on my mother's lap on that night, just weeks after my second birthday.

The grief that came with the realization that Jordie and I were separated ended only when I met Martin.

Martin and I had reconnected again for a reason, but if he was dead then the reason had passed. Was Martin the extension of Jordan, like I was the extension of Madeline? Where did Clara fit in all this?

I was beginning to exhaust all the sources of information I had available to me, and I had so little in my notebook that was of any significance in explaining why Madeline had been killed and who had killed her. Because I did not know where to turn next I called Clara.

"Give it some time," she said after listening to me detail my limited progress and my increasing frustration. "Let Madeline lead you. She will give you the signs. You can't approach this like it is a work assignment. It will take some time. Ask Madeline to guide you."

I wanted to shout at Clara. I had had enough of her hocus-pocus, smoke and mirrors, metaphysical ramblings. She was supposed to be the professional detective and I wanted concrete, action-oriented advice. I wanted a work plan and action items to check off. But I held my tongue. I had no other choice, I had to wait for Madeline to take the lead.

After my nightly yoga stretch I would always lie on my back with my open palms facing upward, breathing slowly, and calming my thoughts. That night, I visualized Madeline in my mind and sent her the simple petition, "Lead me."

Clara was right. Within the month, the sign I asked for fell into my lap in the form of an airline ticket to San Francisco.

Chapter Eighteen

With the seminar in San Francisco's Spear Tower it would have made sense to stay in the Hyatt Regency in the Embarcadero Center, but it was fully booked when my travel agent called so she reserved a room nearby in the Palace Hotel. She said I could take MUNI, the subway that runs under Market Street, and it was only one stop from the Embarcadero Center to Montgomery Street. The Montgomery Street subway exit on the south side of Market was just steps from the hotel's side entrance.

The lobby of the Palace was elegant, with lots of marble and gilding. When I arrived on Saturday, I couldn't help sneaking a peek at the adjacent Garden Court dining room. The domed glass ceiling was spectacular and I made a reservation for brunch on Sunday.

The rest of the day, I put off calling Eva. I strolled to Union Square and browsed through the department stores. Then I drove my rental car along The Embarcadero to Fisherman's Wharf and up Telegraph Hill to Coit Tower. The view from there was amazing, with the Golden Gate Bridge on the left, the Bay Bridge on the right, and the waterfront and downtown spread out between.

It was a sunny day with a cool breeze coming off the ocean. Street vendors set up shop on the concrete steps that encircled the parking area at the base of the tower. I chatted with a street artist and bought a set of street scenes. After that I drove aimlessly - past Van Ness and on to the upper end of Market. I parked near the shops that had sprung up in the old business district between Church and Castro. Art, antiques, and truly unique merchandise filled one trendy store after another. After an evening drive through Golden Gate Park and supper at Mel's Diner, I finally returned to the hotel. By then, I told myself it was too late to call Eva.

With the time difference, I woke early the next morning. I went for a run along the entire length of Market, going up the hill past Castro to where it becomes Portola and then on up to Twin Peaks before turning back to the hotel to shower and change in time for my brunch reservation.

Brunch was elegant, with bountiful, themed tables of artfully displayed food set up around the room. Champagne was included and was poured freely. I stayed as long as I could. After paying the bill, I went back to my room and lounged on the deep sofa, avoiding what I had to do.

I considered a walk along Union Street, but I was too lazy for that. Finally, I could avoid it no longer. I had to contact Eva and see if she would talk to me about Madeline.

I found her number in my address book. The phone only rang twice before she answered. I almost hung up, but I made myself speak.

"Hello, this is Jack Jackson," I began in a voice that was almost timid. "I don't know if you remember me. We met a few years ago. I live in your mother's old house."

"Of course I remember you," she said warmly. "It has been a while since we spoke, though, hasn't it?"

I remembered my last call and how I panicked and hung up at the last moment. Did she know it was me? This time I pressed onward.

"I am in San Francisco for a seminar and I was wondering if I could meet with you. I brought some photographs I found when I was redoing the master bedroom, and I thought you might like to have them."

I put the photographs in the suitcase just as I was leaving for the airport, thinking they might be my passport in getting her to see me.

"That would be nice," she said.

"I am staying at the Palace Hotel - on Market." As soon as I said it I realized how insulting adding the street name would be to someone who had lived in the city for years.

"Yes, I know where it is," she said pleasantly. "Have you seen the dining room there? It is magnificent."

"Actually, I just finished brunch," I relaxed a little. "Would you like to meet me here later this afternoon?"

"I'm so sorry," she said. "I fly to Asia later this evening, so I need to stay around home. Why don't you come here? You were kind enough to show me your home and I would like to return your hospitality."

She gave me the address and half an hour later I was parking in front of her house in Pacific Heights.

Just as Eva had done, I stood a moment and looked up at the house. It was an impressive example of Beaux Arts architecture. I usually thought the style was overdone, but this house was almost classic in its design, proportions, and decoration.

Although it was four stories tall, it was not overpowering. At first glance it only looked like a two story house - the top floor was tucked under a tall mansard roof with dormer windows and the ground floor was slightly below street level. A set of stone steps led to the front entrance that was actually on the second floor.

The recessed entry was two stories tall - crowned with a simple half-round pediment and flanked with false ionic columns. Tall windows on the main level suggested high ceilings and spacious rooms. All of the exterior ornamentation was painted a crisp white that tastefully accented the pale yellow facade.

I went up the steps, realizing they were white marble that was worn smooth in the middle, and rang the bell. Eva opened the front door almost immediately and welcomed me into the entry hall.

She had visibly softened; her hair style was less severe, her clothing was more casual, and she seemed more comfortable and relaxed. Her hair was a lighter shade of blond with hints of natural gray. There were faint lines around her mouth and eyes.

She gave me a tour of the house, and because she knew it interested me, described in detail the restoration after buying it in 1962.

"This has always been a good, stable area, but it was out of fashion when we moved here. The house had been neglected for years, just barely maintained, but I loved the space and the view and we could see the possibilities. We did things only as we could afford to and it took years for us to bring it around."

The first floor rooms were large and inviting. The central entry hall, with its curved white staircase and ornate black metal balustrade, was three stories tall. It was open and airy - with a dormer window set into the mansard roof high overhead. A long living room that had originally been two rooms was on the left, with a formal dining room and study on the right. The walls and ceilings in those rooms were heavily ornamented in plasterwork that would have been overpowering if not painted in varying soft shades of cream and white.

Although there were some beautiful antique cabinet pieces, a spectacular dining table with twelve chairs, and deep Persian rugs, the rooms were almost under-furnished. The matched living room sofas flanking the fireplace were sleekly contemporary and covered in a nubby raw silk that was repeated on the dining room chairs. The monochromatic severity of the rooms was relieved by wildly colorful artwork on the walls.

Eva was almost shy as she explained that she had long been an amateur collector of watercolors and oils by local artists. Oversized works hung on the living room and dining room walls and were illuminated by recessed pinpoint lights set into the ceilings. The rest of her collection was framed very simply and arranged, gallery style, around the entry hall and up the staircase. Some of the paintings were clearly defined, but others were so abstract they only represented energy and color. All of them had an Asian flair. The only traditional painting in the lot was a large portrait of Eva surrounded by four dark-haired children that was hanging over the living room fireplace.

In contrast, the bedrooms on the second floor were comfortable and homey. In the master bedroom there was a worn, hand-stitched quilt folded on the foot of the bed and needlework pillows on comfortably lumpy armchairs by the window that overlooked the rear garden and the bay. We had a quick peek at the fourth floor, still set up as a playroom under the eaves. Eva said her grandchildren used it when they visited.

She left me on the back patio and went down a few steps to the ground level kitchen. The patio was framed with a low bayberry hedge planted inside the stone balustrade and the air was fragrant with the blooming plants in large pots. Jasmine was heavy, blended with other fragrances I did not know.

Wandering to the balustrade, I realized the terrace was actually the flat roof of the garage that faced the side street. The street sloped off so sharply that the garage entrance was almost two stories below the front of the house. The kitchen to which Eva had exited had a delivery door on the side of the house that still needed a flight of stairs to the street.

Turning, I was surprised to see that the back of the house was as ornately detailed as the front. San Francisco row houses are usually finished plainly on the back, saving the showy embellishments for the street side. This detached house was delightfully detailed all around.

When Eva returned with tea and a plate of shortbread cookies on a tray, a small black and brown dog accompanied her. He eyed me with curiosity, but stayed close by her side while she served and settled in the chair facing me.

"I love your choice of colors," I said, after sipping my tea. "This yellow is so fresh and cheerful and it sets off the ornamentation perfectly."

She gave a slight laugh of surprise and looked up at it. "Actually, I always thought it looked like an overdone cupcake, but my husband liked the colors, so I kept them."

She became quiet, looking up at the house. "It must have looked like a band of gypsies had moved in when we changed it from the solid white it had always been. We were the first on the block to take the leap, but eventually the other houses began using brighter colors, too."

The dog came around behind me and sniffed at my pant cuffs. I am a magnet for dogs. They can single me out in a crowd as a soft touch. I gave him a crumble of shortbread and scratched him behind the ears.

"Shadow likes you," she said. "He is always protective of me with strangers, but you seem to have his approval."

"What breed is he?" I asked.

Eva laughed. "He's what my father used to call a Heinz 57 Varieties. Shadow's mother was our Sheltie, but we didn't know who his father was - some kind of terrier, maybe. Our youngest was ten years old and from the start, Shadow was always following him - like a shadow, my husband said. That's where his name came from. They got so attached that we had to keep Shadow."

Almost involuntarily, I made soft, comforting sounds for the dog and scratched him behind the ears. He closed his eyes and his tongue lolled.

Eva leaned forward, elbows on knees, and smiled. "He may want to go home with you, if you are not careful."

"Who keeps him when you're gone?" I asked, without thinking. It was really too personal to ask.

"My housekeeper will be here," Eva said. "She has the apartment downstairs. She is off today. When I'm away she takes Shadow with her when she goes to see her sister in Oakland on Sunday."

We chatted comfortably over the tea and shortbread. I did not really know how to approach the real purpose of my visit. I just handed her the packet of old photographs. She thumbed through them and seemed delighted.

"These were taken on my eighth birthday," she said with wonder. "I have not seen them since then."

I could see the memories flooding back.

"Some of my friends came home with me after school for the party. Mother had balloons all around the back yard, but she hadn't realized how hot the sun could be in April. My friends and I had a lot of fun screaming every time one popped." There were crinkles around her eyes at the memory. She slipped them back in the envelope and thanked me.

The visit was winding down without accomplishing my purpose. I could see the afternoon fog drifting across the bay and the air was noticeably chilly. Eva readjusted the sweater she had draped over her shoulders. She suggested that we move inside. As we settled in the living room I plunged in.

"Can I ask you a few questions about your mother? Would that be alright?"

She paused a moment looking directly at me, then bent down to bring Shadow up to her lap. She stroked the back of his neck a while before answering.

"She died so long ago. It has been a long time since I've thought about her. . . ," she said, looking out the window. The fog was starting to blot out some of the view.

"I'm sorry. You probably need to leave soon," I said, reaching in my pocket for my car keys. "I don't want to delay you."

She turned to me, "Are you having problems with the house?"

"No... what do you mean?"

"Addie always said it was haunted. At least I heard that from a friend. My sister and I did not talk much."

I could not find a tactful way to word the question I could not ask: Why, what happened?

She looked at me, considering, then said, "I guess there is no reason why I should not tell you."

I waited while she collected her thoughts. She took a breath to begin a couple of times but stopped as if she did not know where to begin.

"Addie and I were so very close as children," she blurted out, "but our lives after that went in entirely different directions."

That was obvious. I remembered the last time I saw Addie, deranged and disheveled, standing in her barricade of hoarded newspapers and ready to drop her flaming lighter and burn it all down. Eva could not be any more opposite.

"I used to think it was because she was so young when our father died. Addie was not quite ten and I don't think she could understand how it was for Mother. I was thirteen and could see the strain she was under.

"Mother made every effort to not change things, but I knew we were broke. I heard some girls talking at school. They said that we would lose our house soon. I think they were glad of it, too.

"Addie cried almost all the time. She complained that we couldn't go to the movies and that she had to wear my old hand-me-downs.

"Right after Dad died, Mother enrolled in the business college. She was married right after high school, so she wasn't qualified to do anything. I still don't know how she managed to do it. She sold one of her fur coats a month or so before she graduated from the business college, and that must have kept us going until she started working. There was no money coming in after my father died until she started work."

"Did she discuss it with you?" I asked.

"No, I think she didn't wanted us to worry," she replied. "I remember, a year or two after Dad died, that Addie complained because we didn't have any meat for our Sunday dinner. Mother said she had used all our ration coupons. We went without meat all week and I saw that a roast was among the groceries delivered that Saturday. I think she must have sold it."

"She ran her own black market?" I asked.

Eva smiled slightly and nodded, "Mother was always creative, and people weren't too particular about the rules toward the end of the war. She probably let on that she had accumulated some extra ration stamps and offered the roast to a neighbor for an extra dollar or two. If Addie had known what had happened, she would have thrown a fit."

"But was it really such a big deal? I thought that everyone was deprived during the war."

"The war was hardest on people who had comfortable lives before. I remember some classmates who actually thought they were better off because their fathers had regular jobs and regular paychecks every week - even if they were working in a war plant out of town.

"My father was a doctor, and even though he did not make the kind of money they do now, he still had a steady income all during the Depression. Because he was older, I think he was a little more prone to spoiling my mother, too. Her life was fairly typical for a doctor's wife in those times: she had a day maid, had only to ask when she needed money for the household accounts, and he always gave her an allowance above that to spend as she liked. We had a new car every year. My parents were members at the country club. They entertained at home and were invited to parties. Dad even sent my mother to St. Louis to shop every season."

"You're kidding," I said. "Why?"

"He thought the local stores were not good enough. The local department stores were nothing like the big stores in St. Louis. I especially loved going at Christmas time and seeing all the decorations. If we had enough time after shopping, Mother would hire a cab to drive us out to Forest Park before we had to go to Union Station for our train. We loved looking at all the big houses decorated for Christmas."

"You went on the train?" I asked.

"Oh, yes. Before the interstate was built, Route 66 had a lot of hills and sharp curves and it was very dangerous. It was faster and safer to take the train for a day trip. We would get up early Saturday morning and Dad would take us to the depot before he went to the hospital and made his house calls. We would have breakfast on the train and arrive by noon. We shopped all afternoon and the stores would send our packages on to the station for us. We had dinner at a restaurant and boarded the late train for the ride home."

"That must have been exhausting," I said.

"No, not at all," she replied. "We had a roomette for the ride home and when the train arrived in Springfield after midnight, the sleeper car would be set off on a side rail for the rest of the night. They would connect water, electricity, and heat so you could stay in the sleeper all night and leave in the morning. Business people used the service during the week so they wouldn't have to check into a hotel in the middle of the night, but sometimes, on the weekend, we would be the only ones in the car."

Her face brightened with the memory, "Mother would make a great adventure of it. We would have a late snack in the dining car and then the three of us would lie down to sleep in the tiny roomette with our shopping bags and packages piled all around us. In the winter she would cover the three of us with her fur coat. Sometimes, though, Dad couldn't stand for us to be away all night, so he would meet the train and have the conductor let us off so we could go on home. Mostly though, Addie and I wanted to stay on the train as long as we could, so he would let us spend the night, even though we were so close to home."

In my mind I had a clear picture of the car sidetracked at the old Mission-style depot in Springfield and Jordan arriving in the middle of the night and bundling his girls off the train to take them home.

"It must have been difficult for your mother to adjust when he died."

She thought for a moment. "I never once heard her complain. I will never forget when the man came to the house to tell us that Dad had died of a heart attack. I was supposed to be finishing my homework, but when the doorbell rang, I sneaked to the top of the stairs to listen. Mother let us go through dinner before she told us. She was so poised and collected, even at a time like that, that I thought I must have misunderstood. She only cried when she told us, and then she never cried about it in front of us again.

"A lot of times, when she was in the business college, I would sit at the top of the stairs and watch in the mirror as she studied. She took classes during the day while we were at school, but she never started studying until we were in bed. It must have been difficult for her studying at night like that, but she often sat on the sofa with the light burning beside her past midnight. I fell asleep sometimes, but I always woke up and was back in bed before she came up the stairs.

"Addie never knew how much it took for Mother to keep us together and how hard it was to stretch out the money so that we had some semblance of security until she could provide for us. A lot of women would have jumped at the first man who came along, but I think Mother always loved Dad too much to marry again."

"It must have been hard for you, too," I said.

She shook her head, "Not really, but I think after I heard those girls saying that we were out of money, I made more of an attempt to not ask Mother for things. I don't know if she realized it..."

'She did, Eva! She did,' came the voice from deep within me.

"...but I thought if we could just make it until she got a job, everything would be like it had been.

"Her classes ran late in the afternoon, so Addie and I came straight home after school to do our homework. That way, Mother said we could be together in the evening. She was afraid for us to cook without her there, so the three of us would usually make dinner together. Until she came home, I only had to see that Addie did her assignments and I took that responsibility to heart. I thought that if we did exactly what we were supposed to that everything would be alright. That was when Addie started hating me.

"Addie and I argued a lot. She wanted to play with her friends after school and sometimes she would not come home until just a few minutes before Mother came in. I would be frantic, but there was nothing I could do except scold her. Then she would start crying. I didn't want Mother to see Addie had been crying when she came home, or to ruin the evening with a bad report, so I always promised not to tell if Addie promised not to do it again. She quickly realized that she had the upper hand, and I think she made a sport of seeing how late she could come home and how much she could get away with."

"Did you ever lose patience with her?"

"Once. She discovered she could get almost anything she wanted by playing on Mother's guilt. Mother hated not being there when we came home from school and Addie used that. When

Addie begged Mother for money for an afternoon movie with friends after school and I realized Mother had to walk to and from her class that day instead of riding the bus, I yelled at Addie. She stuck her tongue out at me and said she wished that I would die, too, and I slapped her. It was too hard and she started crying. That made me feel like I was the wicked stepmother. She screamed that she didn't care if Mother had to walk - she could walk all the way to China and back. All she cared about was that she was going to the movies."

"It sounds like she was a handful," I said.

"It was a hard time for all of us. Mother lost a husband and had to make a lot of sudden changes. Overnight, she was left alone with the responsibility of supporting herself and two children. Even with the wartime shortages I had to forego many of the things my schoolmates had, but I was old enough to understand why. I was angry at Dad for leaving us the way he had, but at least I knew what I was angry about and could focus my feelings on it. Addie was too young to understand what was happening and what she was feeling. I think she focused all her anger on Mother."

"But it must have passed eventually," I said.

"That must have been what Mother hoped for, if she had a chance to even think about it. She started work right out of business school, and it had to be hard for her. She was so much older than the other women in her department."

"Where did she work?" I asked. It was one of the things I needed to know to continue my research.

"At Springfield Milling Company. It was downtown, where the tracks cross Boonville Avenue."

I knew the building, vacant now, and for some reason the name was familiar.

"I think it closed years ago," Eva continued. "But it was one of the major employers then and she started as a typist. It was a good job, but it was hard work and long hours - even for those days. She was promoted, several times, in fact. She seemed to have a knack for organizing and managing people."

"What about your sister?"

"By the time she started high school, she was even more out of control. The term 'teenager' had not yet been defined. Most people just said it was a transition period from childhood to being

149

an adult. I think Addie felt abandoned and was jealous of the time Mother had to spend away from her. But instead of taking advantage of the time they could have together, she started staying away from home as much as possible. She even cut school, until the truancy officer visited Mother at work. I guess these days it would be called a 'cry for help.' Mother felt too guilty to come down on Addie the way she needed. I think she kept hoping things would just smooth themselves out, or Addie would grow out of it.

"I was already in college when Addie started high school. I had classes in the morning and worked a part-time job in the afternoons, so Addie was left on her own a lot of the time. Mother paid her a weekly allowance to do some of the housekeeping and to prepare our evening meal, but more likely than not, Addie was nowhere around when we got home. I did quite a lot of shouting when Mother wasn't around, especially when I caught Addie smoking. Beside the fact that it was trashy for a woman to smoke, she left lit cigarettes everywhere and I was afraid she was going to burn down the house. If Mother ever knew about the smoking she never let on, or assumed I was the one doing it.

"Addie resented me more than ever. I think my life looked pretty glamorous and grown-up compared to hers. I was going to college, working at the book store in the afternoons, and meeting new people. She was stuck in high school.

"She never had the ability to look beyond the immediate present, to see that others had gone through the same thing, or that she would be coming into her own in her own future. By the time she was old enough to go to college, her grades were so bad that they wouldn't let her in. She really hated me then. I had finished college and moved to Los Angeles. I met my husband soon after that. I shared a three-room apartment with two other girls, but Addie was convinced I lived in Beverly Hills. I found out later that's what she was telling her friends.

"When Joe and I announced our engagement, I wanted to get married in Los Angeles. Neither Mother nor I could afford a big church wedding, so we planned to have a small civil ceremony with the families. Mother and Addie drove out for the wedding and Addie was a problem from the moment she arrived."

"Why?" I asked. "What happened?"

"Actually, my husband's father was Italian, but his name was changed to Song when he came through Ellis Island. With that last name, people in California assumed Joseph was Chinese and were always surprised when they met his father. Not that it mattered. Joe's mother was one-hundred-percent Japanese, so Joe was Asian to most people, anyway.

"From the moment they met, Addie was openly rude to my mother-in-law. Although she spoke perfect English, Addie only spoke to her in pidgin and imitated how she would bow her head slightly during conversation. Mother was furious with her."

"How embarrassing it must have been for you, too."

"Well, yes," she said. "Mama Niko was too refined to even acknowledge the insult, but I think my new father-in-law wanted to take a strap to Addie."

"It sounds like it might have done her some good."

Eva laughed at the thought, "I don't think anyone could control Addie by then. She was wild. She dyed her hair a bright reddish-orange before the trip and she openly smoked cigarettes at the wedding reception. She looked like a prostitute. Mother ignored her, but I could tell she was humiliated.

"After the wedding, Addie announced she was going to stay on in Los Angeles and get into the movies. For once Mother put her foot down and refused to let her. They had a big fight and Addie ran away in the middle of the night. We waited three days for her to come back. Mother finally had to drive back home by herself and Addie showed up later that same day, thinking she would stay with my husband and me. Joe was too polite, but I refused, and put her on a bus for home."

"Did she stay on it?"

"Oh, yes," she said. "In the days she disappeared I think she went to some of the studios and saw that she was one of hundreds of girls with the same ambition. She may have been high-strung and lazy, but my sister was never stupid. I think she realized how much work it would take - and that there were bigger fish to fry at home."

I laughed softly.

"All the same, she resented me more with every passing year. Joe and I both worked when we were first married. Then he went back to finish college and started medical school. We moved to San Francisco when Joseph did his residency. I worked and we had a tiny apartment south of Market, but in Addie's mind we were living on Nob Hill. By that time she had met David Applegate and was busy manipulating him. I never knew him very well, but Mother wrote that he was a good man and she hoped that he would be good for Addie. Addie pressured David into having a business, although I don't think he had any real passion for it."

"Did they have any children?" I asked.

Eva's face darkened for a moment, then she responded.

"Addie started their marriage saying she did not want children. In fact, she scandalized David, my mother, and practically everyone else for that matter, by saying that if she got pregnant, she would go to Mexico to get rid of it, even if she had to walk every step of the way. She wasn't going to wreck her body having babies."

"Did that ever happen?" I asked.

"No, but when I started having my children and she saw how much attention they were getting, she changed her mind. She was obsessed with it. She went to one doctor after another trying to find one who would tell her that she could have a child. I suppose it was for the best that she never did. I hate to think what the child's life would have been like."

"Your children were fortunate to have you as a mother," I said unexpectedly, surprising myself.

She looked at me for moment.

"Thank you," she said. "We have three daughters and a son. Todd was the youngest. They all have their father's eyes. We were quite a sight around the city when they were children. Some people couldn't understand what I was doing with all those Japanese children," she shook her head slightly and smiled at the memory, "even though they were only one-quarter Japanese."

She crossed the room to pick up a framed photograph from the piano.

"This is Todd," she said proudly. "He lives in Tokyo now. He runs the office there and researches his grandmother's family in his spare time. After being treated as Japanese here all his life, it amazes him that the Japanese see him as a Caucasian American. He has difficulty convincing some of them of his Asian heritage."

I took the photograph from her and looked at the handsome young man. There was, indeed, a slight Asian appearance around his eyes, but otherwise he had the same high cheek bones, brown eyes, finely arched eyebrows, and chestnut hair as Madeline.

"He looks like your mother," I said and wanted to bite my tongue. How could I possibly know what Madeline looked like?

She looked at me strangely for a moment, then went to the bookcase and pulled out a photograph album. She sat beside me and leafed through page after page of photographs. It had been her mother's album and, after the first pages of studio portraits, there were black pages filled with snapshots and captions written on the black paper in white ink. Her flowing script was beautiful with perfect loops. I ran my fingers across the writing, fighting against the distant familiarity.

Tucked between the pages of photographs was a formal, hand-colored photographic portrait of her parents from 1925. Her father was an amiable-looking man with a friendly smile, a thin moustache that stirred something deep inside me, and glasses. He was already thirty, but looked younger. Jordan Montrose looked like it would be nice to have him as a doctor. Beside him, Madeline was beautiful even in the odd-looking fashions of the era. Her bobbed hair was fashionably set in finger waves and her blouse hung loosely from the shoulders. Looking into the camera, she leaned slightly toward Jordan, lengthening her supple neck. Deep brown eyes smiled at the camera. Eva said that Madeline was only nineteen in the photograph.

We leafed through snapshots of their first child, Jordan Jr. "I barely remember him," Eva said. "He was hit by an automobile in front of our house when he was eight. I was barely five years old and Addie was a toddler. That was just before we moved to the new house. Our father never quite got over it."

But Madeline had. In her quiet strength she moved them all past the grief and made a happy home for the daughters.

There were more pages in the album: the family at Christmas, the girls having Easter egg hunts, car trips around the Ozarks, and all of the pictures carefully labeled by Madeline. There were photographs of the sisters in matching dresses for church, the family seated for Thanksgiving dinner with Jordan's chair empty as he took the snapshot, and always, the happy and radiant Madeline.

I knew Eva was watching me as we looked through the album. There were occasional flashes of memory. I fought them away, but I know I lingered too long over some photos. I was not sure how she would react if I revealed too much. There was more I needed to ask. I needed more time.

"You can see your home in some of these," Eva said quietly. "You have furnished it almost the same. Look at these chairs here by the fireplace, and the pictures on the staircase, and the mirror on the landing."

I turned to look at her, wondering how much she knew. Suddenly I remembered her flight. I looked at my watch, "Do you need to go to the airport?"

"Not for a while, yet. I hope this fog hasn't closed it down."

We decided she should call the airport to check the status. The airport was still clear and her flight was still on schedule. I could not waste any more time.

"How was it that your mother died?" I asked.

She paused a long moment, looking out the front windows to the street. The tree by the window was dripping. Beyond that, it was like the fog isolated the house in a shroud of secrecy. Finally she spoke.

"That was such a hard time. Joe couldn't get hired by the hospitals so he tried to have his own practice. Our oldest daughter was three and the second was still in diapers. With the babies, we had moved to a bigger apartment on Castro and were barely getting by.

"But Joe was never discouraged for long. He had an idea for a business. From his mother, he was fluent in Japanese and with the booming industrialization of Japan after the war he could see the opportunity for importing goods. Joe kept his medical practice open, and we borrowed everything we could to get it going.

"It paid off handsomely in the end," she added, glancing at the jeweled ring on her right hand, "but it was so hard in the beginning. I was his assistant and secretary. There were mountains of forms to fill out and we both worked day and night. We could have ended up bankrupt.

"We were so broke that year I didn't know how we were going to make it home for Christmas. We tried to go every year for Mother's sake, but the train trip was grueling. It took almost three days to go from Oakland to Kansas City and, even with a roomette, traveling that far with two babies was an ordeal. On one trip I got off the train in Denver and threw away an entire bag of used cloth diapers rather than trying to get them laundered on the train."

She paused before continuing. "The Christmas before, in 1952, we had a terrible falling out with Addie and her husband and I dreaded the thought of spending more time with them."

"What happened?" I asked.

"David's business was foundering and my husband offered some advice. Addie blew up, called him a stupid Jap and tried to order him out Mother's house. Mother stepped in and put Addie in her place, but it still made the rest of the visit uncomfortable when Addie and David were around. I dreaded going back all year. I was afraid something similar would happen again."

"But it didn't," I said.

"No. The Saturday before we were scheduled to leave, there was a telegram from Addie that only said Mother was dead. I tried to put a long distance call through to Addie, but she was already moving into Mother's house. I finally called Mother's telephone on Sunday morning and, when Addie answered, she lied and told me that the funeral arrangements were already made. She also said that Mother had killed herself, and it was all because of me."

Her voice was shaking at this point. Without thinking, I took her hand to comfort her. She did not draw away. Finally she regained her composure enough to continue.

"Because I could only get one ticket on such short notice, I took the Sunday afternoon train. Joe and the girls left, as we had planned, on Tuesday. When I arrived early Wednesday morning, there was no one to meet me at the depot. I had to take a taxi to the house. Addie met me on the steps and told me that she and David were living in the house now and I would have to go to a hotel. She said it was what Mother would have wanted. She said I had ignored and neglected Mother for years. It was my fault . . ."

Shadow's ears went up and he stood beside Eva on the sofa with his tail wagging.

Eva looked toward the stairs, "Carmen must be home early. She's my housekeeper."

Whatever Eva had been ready to say was lost in the flurry of activity that followed. Carmen came thumping up the stairs from the kitchen with Shadow's leash in her hand. As soon as he saw her, Shadow jumped from the sofa and ran to her excitedly.

Carmen knelt to pet him vigorously around the neck and ears and attach the leash to his collar. Shadow immediately pulled the leash to its full length, even standing on his hind legs to extend himself a fraction of an inch closer to the kitchen stairs in case Carmen had forgotten it was time for his walk.

Wrestling Shadow back, Carmen scolded Eva, "Hasn't your car come, Miss Eva? You will miss your flight."

"It must be the fog," Eva replied. She went to the desk, put on reading glasses, opened her address book, and punched the numbers into the touch-tone telephone. After speaking briefly, and with growing agitation, she returned to the sofa.

"They are running two hours behind. I told them I would take a taxi, but I'm not sure it will be any faster, now. Can you take me, Carmen? You can drive my car."

Carmen hesitated just long enough that I volunteered, "I can drive you. My car is parked outside. It's SFO, right?"

Carmen looked relieved to not have to go back out in the fog, but Eva resisted. "I couldn't ask you to do that."

I had to insist twice more before she agreed. She called the airport and confirmed that her flight was still leaving at the scheduled time, in exactly one hour and forty three minutes. While Carmen walked Shadow, I brought Eva's suitcases downstairs and loaded them in the car. Eva put on a light raincoat, covered her hair with a wispy chiffon scarf, and stood in the entry hall looking a lot like Grace Kelley. By the time Carmen returned, she only needed to say goodbye to Shadow, and grab an umbrella from the entry hall umbrella stand.

The fog was heavier than I expected, with visibility less than a block. We carefully made our way to Van Ness, then to Highway 101 which would take us to the airport. Before we reached the Candlestick Park turnoff, the fog had lifted and it was a beautiful evening. Although traffic going into the city on Sunday evening was at a standstill, the southbound lanes were moving along at about 25 miles per hour. Eva checked her watch again, and after determining we would make it, relaxed.

"You were saying that your sister was not very nice when you went back after Madeline's death."

I could sense her jaw tightening before she replied.

"She said I was to blame for Mother killing herself."

156

"Even if she resented you, that's pretty harsh," I said.

"I have never accepted that Mother killed herself. I couldn't believe she would do it. It was not in her."

"I read some of the newspaper articles before I left home," I admitted. "Addie supported the suicide theory right away, didn't she?"

"Some people were already suspecting Mother had been killed. I don't think Addie had an alibi for that evening. She insisted that she and David stayed home all that night because of the weather. But the police noticed when they came to tell her about Mother that their garage door was open and the car was wet. It had spray on the sides and icicles underneath like it had been driven the night before. It was the first storm of the season. Addie made the mistake of insisting they hadn't been anywhere that morning, either. Although David never wavered, there were suspicions about that from the start.

"On top of that, a neighbor said she overheard Addie arguing with Mother the week before. I never could understand why none of that came out at the coroner's hearing, but Addie could be persuasive and bullied people into agreeing with her. David certainly would have said anything she told him to say. I thought it was suspicious that she was so certain from the start that Mother had killed herself. She insisted that Mother wasn't well. She worked every tidbit of new information after that into her story, building evidence as she went.

"As terrible as it is to say it, I have always wondered if Addie had something to do with Mother's death."

"I think your mother was planning to quit her job that night," I offered, "and that she was planning to open her own bookkeeping and transcription service. Her plans for that would have been among her things. I doubt that she took them with her to the party."

I knew it was too much to say, and I really could not support it. That information certainly was not in the newspaper articles I read.

Eva looked at me, both relieved and troubled, but accepted what I said at face value. "If there was anything in the house to refute her argument of suicide, Addie had plenty of time to get rid of it."

"So you don't think it was suicide?" I prompted.

"No, and Joe didn't either."

I turned my view from the highway to her and raised an eyebrow of question. If she recognized the similarity to Madeline in that, she did not show it.

"After the funeral, Joe asked to see the autopsy records. Those included X-rays of Mother - of the body. He spent hours poring over them and in the end, he insisted the skull fractures were inconsistent with a suicide. He wanted the inquest reopened, even if the body was not exhumed, but it went nowhere."

"What did he think?" I asked. A green and white sign passing overhead showed the airport exit was in one mile. I put on my right blinker to merge to that lane.

Eva hesitated. "You have read the articles about the accident, haven't you?"

"Yes."

"There was a fire, but the coroner said the car hit the quarry floor first, nose down - if you will. It went into the quarry front-end first."

I struggled to stay focused on the busy highway and loosen my death grip on the steering wheel.

"When it hit the bottom, the steering wheel and the engine were shoved up into her, pinning her in the driver's seat. The body was still there when the crane pulled the car out of the quarry. The body was badly burned, unidentifiable really, except for her wedding ring. . . Is this too much for you?"

Eva was looking at my hands on the steering wheel. My knuckles were white. I pulled my right hand away from the wheel and shook it to relax it. "No, sorry," I said, "involuntary reaction, I guess."

"No, I should apologize. Having a surgeon for a husband all those years, I forget sometimes that other people aren't used to hearing these things."

"It's just so hard to imagine," I said, edging onto the exit ramp for the airport.

"Joe agreed with the coroner that the steering wheel was shoved into her chest and pelvis when the car hit the quarry floor.

It pinned her in the seat, so she stayed there when the car flipped on its roof and burned. The breastbone and ribs were crushed in a semi-circle from the steering wheel. It was the same across the pelvis. Since the autopsy showed her lungs were still clear and that she did not inhale any smoke or flames, Joe agreed that she died on impact. Mercifully."

"Yes," I remembered Elizabeth's screams at the séance. Thankfully, Madeline had been spared that. "So why did Joe disagree with the medical examiner?"

Eva did not hesitate, "Joe insisted that if she had driven the car into the quarry intentionally, the facial bones would have been broken differently. She would have braced herself, fallen with the car and slammed against the steering wheel when the car hit the floor of the quarry. It still would have broken her arms and legs and crushed her chest, but if her face was hit at all, the blow would have been straight on.

"Instead the bones of the skull were crushed from the top down, like the steering wheel hit her forehead first and dragged over her face down to the chin. In the X-rays, the nose was flattened downward and the lower jaw was completely broken away on both sides with the upper front teeth embedded in the lower jaw and the lower teeth pushed down and out. Those injuries can only match up with slamming into the curb unexpectedly and dragging her face across the steering wheel. The coroner finally agreed that could have happened."

"So what was the problem with that?"

"It gets complicated from there. Even if she was driving at a normal rate of speed, which was not likely in the rain and sleet, the car would have stopped when it hit the retaining wall. She had to hit the wall harder than that to cause those kinds of injuries. She might have had a bump on the head, or a broken nose, but not the type of crushing impact those X-rays showed. For that kind of impact, the car had to be going a lot faster when it hit the wall."

"Like it was being pushed?"

"Yes. Think about it. If her car was rammed from behind and veered into the wall, she would have been thrown back in her seat first. Joe said she would have stiffened herself reflexively - held the wheel and braced her legs against the pedals. If, a split second later, the car hit the wall and stopped dead, she could have been thrown forward, bending only at the waist if her knees were locked, and dragged her face across the steering wheel."

It was exactly as I had seen it happen. I couldn't help flinching.

"Joe got the coroner to agree to that much - that she banged her face on the steering wheel before she went over - but he wasn't going to reopen the case only for that.

"The thing is that Joe insisted the car would have stopped when it hit the wall. It might have bounced up onto the wall, but there would not have been enough force left for it to go on over. Remember, it was a Cadillac; heavy and a mile long, and pointing uphill at that point. With those kind of injuries to her face, Mother would have been stunned, dazed and bleeding. Even if she had started out wanting to kill herself, after having her face bashed in, would she still have had enough sense left to put the car in gear, press hard on the accelerator, and drive on over? Would the rear wheels have enough traction on the icy street and sidewalk to do that?"

"It would take something else to push her over the wall," I agreed. "A major push from behind and from something equally big."

"Another car, right?" Eva nodded. "I can understand someone accidentally rear-ending her if it was dark and it was raining. They could have been drinking, driving too fast - or both - and swerved at the last minute, pushing her sideways and up onto the sidewalk. But a second hit, to push her on over, would have required them to stop, back up far enough to build up speed and hit her again, and straight-on this time, too."

The airport's departures lane was like a parking lot. I was creeping forward slowly, keeping an eye open for a place to pull over.

"Joe argued that had to be what happened. He even took the coroner to the police yard, where Mother's car was impounded, to have a look at the rear bumper. There was damage and paint that could have been from another car on the rear bumper, but the coroner said it could have happened any time. This was a woman driver, they were talking about, and surely, no one was going to run a middle-aged woman off the road in the middle of an ice storm, were they? They were talking about Springfield, not a B-movie. He tried to make Joe feel like a fool - like he was imagining things and making trouble. As far as the coroner was concerned, it was over and done with."

I finally pulled over to the curb. A skycap came forward with luggage tags.

"I still can't believe Addie would have done something like that," Eva said, fighting tears.

"I can't either," I said, motioning to the skycap to give us a minute. He probably thought that we were mother and son, or rich lady and young boyfriend, and needed more time to say goodbye.

I remembered Clara. "I have a friend who is a detective with the Kansas City police. I could ask her to have a look at the autopsy records."

"I don't want to," she said, then stopped and almost laughed at herself. "Automatically, I was going to say, 'I wouldn't want to upset Addie,' but I guess that doesn't matter so much anymore."

"She would be very discreet. I would check with you before we did anything else."

"Yes - go ahead. I think I have the right to know. If Mother killed herself, then I will have to accept it, once and for all."

"She didn't."

She turned and looked at me. A tear escaped. The skycap was at her door again, but seeing Eva dab at her eyes, he waved an apology to me and went away.

"You know, don't you?" she asked, unsure of how I would react.

I could only nod.

"You know that you have a connection to her - to Mother. I saw it the first time I visited you in her house - in your house. There is something of her in you, some connection."

"My friend, Clara, calls it a 'contiguous spirit,'" I offered. "She's the detective I mentioned, sort of a psychic profiler. I don't understand it very well, but I do understand that I have to do this. I know that your mother did not kill herself. My gut tells me that your sister didn't do it either. And as crazy as it may sound, I have to find out who did for Madeline to be able to rest."

Eva put a gloved hand over mine, "I don't think it's a bit crazy. In a way, it makes me happy, just hearing you say it."

She checked her watch, then flipped the sun visor down to check her face in the mirror. I was surprised there was a mirror there. She pressed the tissue below her eyes, then took a compact from her purse and dusted fresh powder on her cheeks.

I got out of the car and went to the trunk while the skycap opened her door. I set the suitcases on the curb. Eva showed him her tickets and pressed a five-dollar bill in his hand, an extra-generous tip for his trouble. He checked his watch as he pocketed the tip, thanked her, touched his cap and assured her he would check in the baggage for her.

"But you better hurry, ma'am. They are boarding now."

Eva came back and kissed me on the cheek. "Promise you will stay in touch. I will be back in a month. Call me any time after that, collect."

"You'd better run," I said.

She took a few quick steps to the door and, as they slid open, she turned back and called out, "Thank you!" Then she disappeared inside.

The skycap looked up from tagging her bags. I winked at him slyly and he winked back. The prolonged goodbye, the tears, the kiss on the cheek, and the final farewell - it was the rich lady and her young boyfriend now, for sure.

Chapter Nineteen

I called Clara as soon as I got back to the hotel. Instead of calling from my room, I went to the bank of pay telephones off the lobby, and placed the call with my new Southwestern Bell Calling Card. The card allowed me to access my home telephone account from anywhere in the United States. I bought a block of evening and weekend minutes each month. After those were gone, I was charged a nominal rate. Doug talked me into it while we were in graduate school so we could call each other as much as we needed. I meant to cancel the account after that, but I was using long distance more than ever.

After hitting the "0" key, followed by my area code and home telephone number, I waited for the tone to enter my four digit access code. When I got the special dial tone, I entered Clara's number. It was late, especially with the time difference, but she answered on the second ring.

"Hello?"

"Hey, Clara, it's Jack."

"What? Where are you?"

"Still in San Francisco."

"Come on, Jack! Everyone has a calling card these days. No one is impressed with it except you."

I laughed, "Guess who I just saw."

"Michael Jackson?" she said. She loved to tease me about my real name. "It had better be him or somebody famous if you're gonna call me this late."

We paused a moment, listening to the hum on the line. "I just got back to the hotel. It was an interesting talk."

"What's she like?"

"Rich, sophisticated, beautiful. Pacific Heights, the house could be in *Architectural Digest*. We talked most of the afternoon, then I drove her to the airport."

163

"The airport?" Clara was impressed.

"Flying to Tokyo as we speak. Son lives there, runs the office for the family business."

"Family business? Sheesh. What is it?"

"Imports. Eva and her husband started it in the fifties, about the time Madeline died."

"Do you think she could have killed her mother?"

"No, they were in San Francisco that weekend. Had train tickets later that week to go home for Christmas."

"They could have hired someone to do it."

"No," I said, "I don't think so. If she was telling me the truth they were flat broke, barely could afford the tickets that year. Her husband was half-Japanese and couldn't get work as a doctor. Still too soon after the war. That's why they started the import business. Apparently they kept it going after he was hired as a surgeon."

"If they were that strapped for cash, all the more reason to bump off Mom for the inheritance."

"She let a few things slip, intentionally maybe, but Addie and her husband took everything after Madeline died - the house and everything in it, lock, stock, and barrel. Addie claimed that Madeline wanted it that way. I bet if you look at the probate records, she got the house with some sort of promissory note to Eva for her half. Sounds like Addie was quite a stinker, even then. She manipulated everyone, including Eva. I don't think Eva would want to do anything, even now, to upset her."

"A real female dog, huh?"

I laughed. Clara always said that when she meant a woman was a bitch. "I'm sure Addie was insanely jealous of Eva," I said. "Especially by the time Madeline died."

"Insane?" Clara repeated. Clara was coaching me on acceptable terminology. She would remind me that Miss A could tell Miss B that she was "insanely jealous" of Miss B's new shoes and no one would think that Miss A was the slightest bit unbalanced, but let the police or detectives use the term and lawyers would be expecting us to have the doctor's certification in hand, signed and notarized.

"OK, she was 'extremely' jealous of her sister."

"So you are pretty sure this Eva is on the straight?"

"Yes. If anyone is telling the truth, it's her."

"It is she," Clara corrected. "Did she give any indication she suspected her sister."

"Well, yes, by insisting she could not believe that Addie would do it I think she has always thought it was the case. From the start Addie, and I quote, "built her case" that it was suicide. Eva said her husband had a look at the autopsy and inquest records when he arrived in Springfield. From the post-mortem X-rays, he was convinced it was not suicide - the way the skull was broken from the forehead down and the body being pinned by the steering wheel. Anyway, Eva said that Addie and her husband swore they had been home all night that night, and even the next morning, but their car had salt spray on the sides and icicles hanging on the bottom like it had been out in the sleet and rain. Something wasn't right there. Eva also said that Joe had a look at Madeline's car and there were marks and paint on the back bumper like it had been hit."

"Did she say it matched up with her sister's car?"

I had not thought of that angle, but I thought back over the conversation, "No," I answered. "No, I'm sure she didn't. I would have remembered that. She only said the coroner said it could have happened any time with a woman driving a car."

Clara exhaled in disgust. Before she could comment I continued, "Eva is still indignant about that. Don't you think Eva and Joe would have had a look at Addie's car while they were there for the funeral? I don't think Eva would leave something like that out. She was pretty straightforward during our talk."

"Or maybe she wanted you to think she was being straightforward."

"Don't we have to believe *someone* is telling the truth?" I asked, my voice rising with impatience. "Unless Eva is a pathological liar, I think the truth is that in December, 1953, she and Joe were broke, starting a business, stretching to buy train tickets home, and the tickets they had were for the week after Madeline died. I think she was genuinely surprised when Addie's telegram came that Saturday. If she is concealing anything, it's the suspicion she's had since then that Addie was somehow responsible for their mother's death."

"OK, OK, Jack," Clara said. "Do I have to remind you that we have to talk about every possible angle to eliminate the false ones? I agree it would have been nearly impossible for Eva to do it. I am not one-hundred-percent convinced she's telling you the complete truth, especially where Addie is concerned, but for now we have to go with what she says at face value."

"Alright."

"So, where does this leave us?"

"I would like to see the autopsy report, and the transcription of the inquest, if there was one. Is that something you can get your hands on?"

"Not easily," Clara said. "But I have a detective in Springfield who owes me a favor. I'll call him in the morning and see if I can get him to send me a copy by facsimile. . ."

"Clara," I interrupted.

"What?"

"I know what you mean, but almost everyone under fifty just calls it a "fax" these days."

"You jerk," Clara said.

"Maybe you could make a note of that on your stenographer's pad and total it up on your automatic tabulating machine."

"I'm gonna kill you," Clara laughed.

"Let me know as soon as you get something." I said.

"Shall I send a telegram in confirmation, sir, or should I place a person-to-person long-distance telephone call?" Clara said in her Ernestine the Operator's voice, complete with the double snort, and hung up leaving me with a dial tone on my end.

On Monday morning, wearing my best suit and a new tie, I entered the lobby of the Spear Street Tower, showed my registration confirmation for the seminar to the guard at the desk and was directed to the elevator that would take me to the thirty-third floor. There were four others standing in complete silence on the elevator with me. With only the button for the thirty-third floor depressed, I guessed that we were all headed for the seminar. Like me, they all probably carried the seminar materials, notebook and name badge in their briefcases. Clara's observation techniques were rubbing off on me. If pressed, by the time the elevator doors opened, I could have given a pretty good description of the others who rode with me.

The seminar was surprisingly interesting, mostly because of the instructor, Janelle Johnson. It was no surprise that she was a junior partner for the accounting firm that provided the meeting room for the seminar. It was probably a feeder for their auditing practice - that is, they hoped the participants would recommend contracting with their firm for audit services in the future. However, it was information I needed for work, so I made careful notes and references for things to look up at the library when I was home. I could also give a good trip report to my supervisor, who was not enthusiastic about me missing work.

We were on our own for lunch, but I joined Janelle - she had insisted we all be on a first name basis - and several others from the seminar who walked to the Embarcadero Center. We ate together at one of the small restaurants on the ground level, facing toward the modernistic concrete cubes of the fountain in the Justin Herman Plaza, with the ugly, elevated Embarcadero Freeway between us and the old Ferry Building. It was a beautiful day and Janelle joked about continuing the seminar outside as we walked back across Market and up Spear to the building.

We had a break at three o'clock and Janelle had just placed the first transparency for the final afternoon session on the overhead projector when the receptionist for the thirty-third floor knocked on the door and entered the room. She crossed to the instructor, holding a pink "While You Were Out" message in her hand. Janelle glanced at it briefly and called out "Jack Jackson?" I raised my hand and the receptionist motioned for me to follow her.

I recognized the number on the note as Clara's work number. The receptionist had not only checked the boxes "please call," "ASAP," and "Urgent" but had filled in the message area with almost the same words, with "Urgent" underlined.

"I promised I would deliver it to you right away," she said in a low voice as soon as she closed the conference room door behind her. Everything about this woman, from her sleek hair, tailor-fitted suit, and perfectly polished nails, shouted big-city, no-nonsense efficiency. I followed her, almost at a run, back to the reception area. She went behind the desk, set a telephone on the counter, and said she would give me an outside line. "Just push 9 when you are ready."

I said I could charge it to my office, but she just waved it off, "We have a WATS line. Don't worry about it." She sat down behind the desk and put on the headset for the telephone system.

Clara's line rang four times and was transferred to another telephone.

"Jack Jackson, returning Detective Carson's call," I told the man who answered, noticing a flicker of interest in the eyebrows of the thirty-third floor receptionist. I made sure to say "Clara!" in a friendly voice and loudly enough for her to hear when Clara came on the line.

"Jack! I have the transcript."

"That was quick." It was only a few minutes after one o'clock in Kansas City.

"Yes, amazing this technology these days, isn't it?"

"What's so urgent?"

"You are not going to believe this," she said. "I read through everything. Nothing much we didn't already know. The coroner railroaded right over Eva and her husband at the inquest. It was a done deal by then, I'm sure."

"You called to tell me that?"

"No - listen. Detective Woods in Springfield sent me more than just the copies of the inquest transcript and the autopsy report. There was a later affidavit in the file."

"Yes?"

"Yes! Dated July, 1978, from one Mister David Applegate. He completely recanted his testimony at the inquest, Jack. Said he lied about Addie being home that night. Looks like they had a big fight early in the evening and she took off in their car. He didn't know where she went and she came home completely plastered after the bars closed. Said she was so drunk he had to carry her in the house. He was going to let her sleep it off in the car outside, but she kept blowing the horn. He carried her in, put her to bed, then went out and pulled the car in the garage, where it was when the police came the next morning. Addie made him lie about her being home. He said he was sure it was only because she didn't want to be embarrassed with people knowing she had been out all that night when her mother died. He said he couldn't ever believe

Addie had done it."

"Is that it?"

"Yes, I summarized, but that's the gist of it. It's signed, witnessed and notarized. It was enough to reopen the case, Jack, but there's a note clipped to it that David died of lung cancer four months later. It's like a death bed confession.

"So, it looks like Addie did it, after all?"

"Not so fast," Clara cautioned. "It only means they were lying about her being home that night. I admit it's possible she could have planned it all out; knew her mother was going out to the party that night, picked a fight with hubby, took off in the family car, followed her mother to the quarry, pushed her over the wall, and then spent the rest of the night getting roaring drunk. But I don't think so. Most criminals don't go on a drinking binge right after the fact. They focus on covering their tracks."

"Unless she was celebrating," I suggested. "If they needed money, mama's would be coming in now. She could have decided to throw back a few, to celebrate, to calm herself down, or both."

"Jack, my gut tells me she would have hightailed it home. She was the first one the police would come to see when her mother was identified. Turns out the quarry wasn't completely abandoned. There was a skeleton day crew and a night watchman. He was inside the shack because of the freezing rain, but called the police right after the explosion. If her alibi was going to be that she had been home all night, she would have gone home, cleaned up the car, and been in bed with hubby when they came. She did none of that. It's just way too sloppy this way. I am leaning toward David's story being true - or at least his 1978 version of it.

"I just wish we could talk to her," Clara continued. "I'd like to hear her explain all this. Between us, we could tell if she's lying."

"A senile old woman?" I said. "Even if she remembers it, do you think anything she says would be reliable? And even if she's completely lucid, she was pretty devious before - when I nearly had to evict her from the house. Do you really think she's going to confess to anything now? She'd probably spit in my eye and stick to her story just for the fun of it."

Clara said she would make a photocopy and send it to me special delivery. It should be in my mailbox when I got home. I said I would call her after I read it. There wasn't much more to say, so we ended the call. I thanked the receptionist, ignored her inquisitive look, and went back for the final half-hour of that day's session.

The package Clara sent never arrived. It was not in the bundle of mail my neighbor brought over as soon as I returned home. I waited a couple of days, thinking it could still come, before I called her. Clara was annoyed, saying it was the last time she would send anything "Special Delivery." She put a tracer on the package, resulting only in the Post Office declaring it "lost" mail. We could go to the lost mail offices in Kansas City and Springfield to see if we could identify it. I had a look in Springfield, a lost hour that produced nothing, then told Clara not to bother with it at her end. If I needed to read the file I surely could make the trip downtown and have Detective Woods show me the file.

We had reached yet another dead end.

Chapter Twenty

Clara will never accept that there is such a thing as a dead end. If it seemed like there was, it just meant something had been missed along the way. It was time to go back over everything, talk to everyone again, turn every stone a second time, cross every "t" and dot every "i." Hopefully, we would see something we missed or that something else would be revealed that was not on the first pass.

Weary with her metaphors, I agreed I would go over everything again at my end. I went back through my notebook, read everything I had in the file, and came up with nothing. I called Eva's house and, when Carmen answered, asked her to have Eva to call me when she returned to San Francisco. The month passed slowly and when Eva called, I told her about David's 1978 confession.

She said it confirmed what she had suspected all along, that they were lying about Addie being home all that night, but she also agreed with Clara that it really proved nothing else.

She surprised me by adding, "I think it's time to talk to Addie about this."

"Can she have visitors? I would have to get past Nurse Jones somehow."

Eva laughed at that. "She was intimidating, wasn't she? No, Addie is not there any longer. When she could not go back home, I moved her to the Montclair. Do you know it?"

Yes, I knew the Montclair - the new retirement residence for the country club set. It was quite a leap from the old motor court Addie had been living in.

"Yes," I managed. I didn't want to ask too much, so I only added, "I didn't realize they provided nursing home level care."

"They don't. Addie has private nurses around the clock." Then to clarify, "I wanted to help Addie for such a long time, but she wouldn't have it - at least she wouldn't take it from Joe and me. When it was clear she couldn't go back home, I arranged to get her in at the Montclair. They take her social security check, give her a spending allowance for the month, and I pay the rest. She doesn't know that, though, so I will appreciate you not saying anything about that when we see her."

"Yes, of course," I replied. I felt like I wasn't keeping up. Did Eva just say "we" would be seeing her?

"If you come to Springfield, you are welcome to stay here with me. The guest room is always ready."

"Thank you, Jack," she said. "That is very kind of you, but I always stay at the University Plaza Hotel when I see Addie. Do you know it? The restaurant is actually quite good."

Yes, I knew the hotel, the newest and nicest in town. It was atrium-style with glass elevators. The hotel was built by a local self-made millionaire as part of a new downtown complex that included an office tower and a second tower of swank residential condominiums. While the surrounding area was in decay, the new project was drawing interest and investment back downtown. I was not surprised Eva would stay there, but I was surprised that she had been coming to town to see Addie.

"Maybe we could have dinner there one evening after seeing Addie," she offered. "I am being selfish, but that is the loneliest time of the day for me when I'm there."

"Of course," I said. There were at least half a dozen things I wanted to ask. I settled for, "How is Addie?"

"No better. Some visits are better than others. The last time she knew me, but the time before that she did not recognize me at all. I try to see her every other month, but it's always a toss-up what her condition will be."

I was surprised Eva had been coming back that often. I thought she had not been back since the day she came to my house, years ago, but in reality she had been here every eight to ten weeks. I wondered momentarily why she had not contacted me, but immediately understood. Until I called her in San Francisco last month, the ball had been in my court. It was up to me to make the next move.

"Let me say again, that you are always welcome to stay here, Eva."

"Thank you," she said, then hesitated. "Jack, please don't take this the wrong way, but I really cannot come to your house again. Most of my memories there are not happy ones, and seeing it that one time brought them all back. It's hard enough sometimes just being back there. I wouldn't do it at all except that I am the only family Addie has left. I can't . . ."

"Of course. No explanation needed," I said.

"But I do want to see you when I'm there - and for us to go see Addie together. I have a trip booked next month, but I will call my travel agent and get something booked this weekend, if that will work for you."

I had nothing to do outside work except Clara's assignment of going back over everything again. I agreed and Eva said she would let me know as soon as her plans were made.

The next Sunday afternoon Eva and I entered the lobby of the Montclair just as the residents were finishing lunch in the dining room. I left all the arrangements up to Eva and she wanted us to arrive together. Sundays were the busiest time for the residents, when families and friends were most likely to drop by. No one would notice me walking in with Eva.

The Montclair was like a luxury apartment building and not at all like a nursing home, except most of the residents were at least eighty-years-old. I had dinner with Eva at the hotel the night before and she said the residents could come and go at will. There was a morning check by the staff, presumably to find any who had died during the night, a restaurant-like dining room, group activities, and field trips. There were intimate conversational areas around the property for people to stop, sit, and visit.

She also said her sister took advantage of none of these. Addie stayed in her one-bedroom apartment, only leaving when her nurse accompanied her for a doctor visit or to have her hair done. The live-in nurse, who wore a uniform and whom Addie believed to be her personal maid when she was coherent, brought Addie's meals on a tray. She interacted with none of the residents, knew no one, and complained bitterly to Eva about her "reduced circumstances." She said the Montclair stole her monthly social security check and only gave her $25 a month to live on.

Addie was sitting in a chair in the living room when we arrived, looking better than I remembered. Her clothing was clean and neat, and the sweater matched the dress. Her hair, although completely gray now, looked freshly shampooed and was in a stylish blow cut. If she wore any makeup it looked natural.

Her nurse, after greeting us, asked Miss Addie if she needed anything else and left us. She carried a pager that Eva could call if she was needed before her scheduled return time.

Addie looked at me and demanded, "Who the hell are you?"

"Addie," Eva was calm. "You remember I said yesterday I was bringing a friend today. This is Mr. Jackson."

Addie ducked her head, patted her hair, and straightened her sweater, "Well, if you'da told me we was having company, I'da fixed up."

Addie soon forgot me and launched into a litany of complaints that I suspected were regular. They were stealing her checks and leaving her penniless. The maid was stealing from her. She couldn't keep anything in the house, things disappeared all the time. The maid had stolen all the jewelry and the police wouldn't do anything. Remembering me, she turned and asked, "Are you the police?"

Eva, seeing the opening, nodded slightly and I said, "No, I'm only a private detective, ma'am."

"Well, finally we are getting somewhere. This place is a den of thieves, I tell you. Every bit of my jewelry is gone, all my money too. Do you have a cigarette?"

Eva slightly shook her head and I remembered the facility was non-smoking. "No, ma'am, I quit," I said truthfully. With Martin's insistence, I had stopped for good on my thirtieth birthday.

Addie slapped the arm of her chair, "Well, crap. No one smokes anymore."

"Do you want to tell me more about your jewelry?" I asked, taking a pen and small notepad from my jacket.

For the next fifteen minutes, I made notes. Addie seemed to have a complete and detailed memory of her jewelry, some of it likely imaginary. Eva nodded and agreed at times, realizing the process was building trust and putting Addie at ease.

"David gave me that brooch," she stopped and held a tissue to her nose.

"David was your husband?" I asked.

"Yes, thirty-eight wonderful years," she sniffed. "If my

174

David was here, none of this would be happening. He took care of me."

"When did he pass, ma'am?" I asked.

She looked over at my notebook and slowly dictated, "November twenty-second, nineteen-hundred and seventy-eight."

"Can I ask you a few questions about him?"

"You can - and you may," she said, smiling coquettishly.

"May I…" I said with a slight, agreeing nod and let my eyes smile back at her. "Was your husband ill?"

"Lung cancer," she said readily, looking down at her hands. "Suffered terrible with it. It was a mercy in the end."

I looked at Eva and raised an eyebrow. We had talked about it and she knew I was asking if I should plunge ahead. We both knew it was going to be a leap that could shut Addie down. She nodded her permission.

"Do you know if David - your husband - filed any police reports before he died?"

For a long while, Addie only stared at her hands. She seemed to shrink into herself. I was about to ask the same question, slightly rephrased, when she spoke. "He said he had to do it."

"Had to do what?"

"He said he had lied long enough and wasn't going to go to hell because of it. I begged him not to, but he had to make it right."

"Make what right?"

"That's what I said! He said he lied about me being home all night, and I said he didn't really know that I wasn't so it was not a lie. He was out all night, looking for me, and I couldn't remember where I had been, so I could have been home while he was looking for me, couldn't I?"

She looked at the opposite wall, "I still don't remember where I was, David. You can't tell them now or they will lock us both up."

She was slipping away. Eva moved to sit beside her on the edge of the chair and took her sister's hand. "Addie. Addie, it's alright. No one is going to lock you up."

Addie looked around, "I guess I'm in jail already, ain't I?"

"Can you tell me what happened, Addie?" I asked. "What happened that night?"

"Nothing. We had a big fight and I took off in the car. We was so broke I only had a dollar in my purse. I think someone started buying me drinks at the tavern. Next thing I know I'm wakin' up in the back seat of the car down by the tracks and I drove home. It was almost light and David was sleeping, but someone called to tell me Mother was dead - drove her car off into the old quarry."

She paused, remembering, "It was creepy, like they was accusing me. They said they heard us fighting that week over money. I told David we had to say we had been home all night or the police would think we did it. David's business was about bankrupt by then. I told him we was alright as long as we stuck together and kept our story straight. We had to act like it had to be suicide and keep everything together."

She turned to Eva her face screwed up in tears, "I didn't kill Mother, Eva. You gotta believe me. I can't remember, but you know I could not of killed her. When things settled down, before you was there, I went out and looked at our car. If I'da pushed her car into the quarry, there would'a been some kind of dents or something on the bumper wouldn't there? That old car was pretty banged up, but I knew all the dents - I put most of them there. I'm telling you, there wasn't nothing new when I looked. Unless I was driving someone else's car, or was riding around with someone and made them do it, I tell you I didn't do it!"

Crying now, Addie's spine rounded forward even more, as though she were collapsing into herself.

"I believe you, Addie," Eva said gently. "I believe you."

After a while, when Addie was in control of herself again, she sniffed and straightened herself, looked at me and asked, "Who the hell are you?"

I called Clara from Eva's hotel room. Eva was on the extension, and after the three of us talked, Clara agreed it was unlikely Addie had killed her mother. It was too bad her life had been haunted with it since then.

Chapter Twenty One

Within the week, Addie had a stroke. Eva, in San Francisco by then, flew back to be with her sister. Eva called me a few evenings later. With the stroke, Addie's dementia had worsened. When she was in a lucid state, she thought David was still living and did not recognize Eva. She needed nursing home care now and would not be returning to her apartment at the Montclair.

I was afraid our talk might have brought on the stroke, but Eva, as if reading my thoughts, said she was glad we talked to Addie when we did. That conversation would be impossible now and it had helped her decide, once and for all, that Addie was innocent.

Further supporting her sister's innocence was Eva's recollection that Addie and David's car had been a smaller, two-tone gray coupe. In reality it was only a few years old at the time of Madeline's accident, but it was indeed banged up by then. A gray coupe did not match up with the memory I had of a hulking black automobile bearing down on Madeline. I reviewed this additional tidbit of fact with Clara, and we agreed to presume Addie's innocence and take our investigation in another direction. We just did not know what direction to take.

For the next couple of months, our investigation stayed on the back burner. I was busy with work and Clara was immersed in a gruesome murder investigation. I was sure that having fresh evidence to work with was more rewarding to her than our dead-end case. We talked almost every weekend, avoiding discussing Madeline. It was fall when it came up again. I said I would go back to the library and read the newspapers again. Clara said she would have another look at the police file and do some cross-analysis. Neither of us had much hope of uncovering anything we had not already found.

On a rainy Saturday, I went to the library and asked the same librarian to see the same microfilmed newspapers from December, 1953. With the rainy day, the library was busy. This time, the librarian simply handed me the boxes containing the film for December as well as January, 1954, confident I could load the film

177

on the reader and operate it myself.

One thing my accounting work had taught me was that when you go over and over an analysis or reconciliation that should work but doesn't the best thing to do is to start at the beginning and fill everything in again. Starting over with a blank slate sometimes showed what you had overlooked, or what you were seeing but not really seeing. Before I loaded the film on the reader, I turned to a blank sheet in my notebook. I would read everything again and force myself to make new notes, instead of reviewing the ones already written. I loaded the film in the machine and advanced it to December 18, 1953, the date of Madeline's death.

I did notice a paragraph I had missed, buried in the morning edition's society column "About Town." It only said that the Springfield Milling Company would be hosting its annual Employee Christmas Gala that evening in the ballroom of the Colonial Hotel, and listed the names of the executives and their wives who would be in attendance. I entered the names on the blank sheet.

In the following papers, I found nothing more than the articles I had seen before: *Doctor's Widow Dies* and *Montrose Death Ruled Suicide.* I read the articles again and made careful notes that I was sure I had listed previously: no tire tracks, icy street, mental condition, coworkers' testimony, passed over for promotion, hysteria.

I scanned the papers through the end of December and the first weeks of January, finding nothing else. Leaving the microfilm spool on the reader, I flipped back to the first set of notes to see if anything was different. Other than changing the placement of the apostrophe on coworkers' where I previously showed it in singular form, the two sets were almost identical. Was there really any significance that more than one coworker testified that Madeline was visibly upset when she left work early that afternoon? It only seemed to give more support to the suicide theory.

Disappointed at the wasted afternoon, I closed the notebook and started rewinding the microfilm. I held down the rewind lever, but instead of rewinding the film went into high speed, advancing forward by several weeks-worth of newspapers before I realized what I was doing. It almost ran off the wrong end of the spool before I managed to stop the machine.

The reverse rewind began slowly at first, with the pages passing one at a time rather than whizzing by in a blur. With the film passing at a slowly increasing speed, I caught a glimpse of a familiar face in a photograph as it crossed the screen. Again I stopped the tape and backed it up page by page until I found the picture again.

My breath caught at the sight of Mr. Knight. Even now, I could barely look at his photo. His slick lips were stretched over a wide smile not yet stained by incessant smoking and the full head of wavy hair was almost laughable, except that after all these years my stomach still constricted with dread at the sight of him.

It was my first job after college. I was hired by a junior partner while Knight was out of the office on an extended vacation. When he returned, I was introduced and he took an instant dislike to me. He bullied me daily, to the point of mental torture. Apparently terrified of Knight himself, the junior partner I worked for did nothing to defend me.

Knight's final words when he fired me still rang in my ears. Now, years later, I could still see the satisfied smirk as he handed me my final paycheck, with the hours I would not work that afternoon meticulously deducted.

"You will be lucky to get a job as a bank teller after this," he declared. "You wasted your time in college, I could take a bum off the street and make him into a better bookkeeper than you will ever be. Now get the hell out of my office."

Seeing his face on the screen, I could still feel myself trying to hold it together and walk out of the office carrying the box of personal items from my desk he had someone else pack while I was being fired. As a young graduate with less than a year of experience it was devastating. For weeks I wanted to hide in my apartment instead of trying to get another job without any references. He had destroyed my confidence, both in myself and in my work. It was years before I was able to take a stand on anything, even when I had the documentation to back me up.

Barely breathing, I stared at his photograph at least five minutes before I was able to read the text below it. The first paragraph said he was scheduled to speak at a luncheon meeting of the Springfield Club in the Garden Room. Below that, the page was torn away at a diagonal. There were several partial paragraphs that seemed to sing his praises and list the local organizations he belonged to. Almost nothing remained of the last paragraph. Against the right margin I could only make out

ief Account-
ling Co. of

The rest of the page was missing.

I looked at the date at the top of the page: January 25, 1954. Knight had been at it long before I was born, schmoozing and boozing his way to the top. I had never had a chance against him.

It was a while before I could hit the rewind button and correctly rewind the film. After the film was completely wound on its spool I put it back in the box and took the boxes back to the reference librarian.

As I walked to my car, I felt sick and wished I had never looked at the January microfilm. Not only had the afternoon been a complete waste of time, but I had dredged up all the anxiety of that first job and the humiliation of being fired by Knight. Even though I told myself I had gotten past it - that I made a success of it all in spite of Knight; I wanted to go home, get in bed, and pull the covers over my head. I settled for going home, tossing the notebook on the coffee table and downing a beer while standing in front of the open refrigerator door. I took the second of many more that evening upstairs to the den to sit, unseeing, in front of the television until sleep would finally come.

Chapter Twenty Two

Like she was not going to let me give up, Madeline walked across my bedroom that night. She didn't wait until three o'clock. I had the dream many times, each seeming more insistent, until around four o'clock I sat up in bed, turned on the light and sat with my back against the headboard. I picked up a book, hoping that reading would clear my mind and allow me to go back to an undisturbed sleep. Madeline was going to have nothing of that though. While I sat, trying to read the book, the footsteps began at the desk, went through my bed to the door, and down the hall. I got out of bed and left my bedroom - Madeline's room - and went downstairs to the kitchen.

I made coffee and had two cups, wondering if I should just sell the house and be done with it. I had nothing more to give. If Clara had uncovered anything else, she would have called me. When I heard the Sunday paper hitting the sidewalk, I turned on the porch light, unlocked the front door, and went out to get it.

After I picked it up, I stood there a while, looking up at my house. I could not put Madeline to rest, probably never would. She needed me to identify her killer, to prove it had happened and bring him, or her, to justice. Until then, Madeline was stuck where she was, and I was stuck with her.

I talked to Clara that afternoon. She was as discouraged as I was. She had cross-examined and cross-referenced her notes, had been through the autopsy and hearing transcript, forward and backwards - as she put it - and had come up with nothing. I said I had no better luck looking at the old newspapers.

"You sound really down, Jack," Clara said.

"Just bummed about this," I said. She waited until I said, "And some old work stuff I kind of dredged up and need to get over."

I also told her about Madeline's multiple appearances the night before, and the footsteps across the bedroom after I was fully awake. "I can take a dream once in a while, but I can't take this anymore. I think I should just sell the house and be done with it."

"You can't quit now, Jack," she said gently. "And besides,

181

increased activity like that could be her sending a message that you're onto something."

"But what?" I shouted into the telephone because I wanted to cry. "What am I onto Clara? I'm going over the same exact stuff, over and over, and it's the same every time. What could she possibly think I've got now?"

Clara was silent.

"Sorry," I said. "I'm just worn out with this. I can't do anything else."

"What you have is something that you don't realize you have, something right in front of you that you're not seeing," she said quietly. "Or it's me. I have it. We can't quit now."

"And how are we supposed to find it? It's like asking me to see something that's invisible. How am I supposed to do that?"

"Madeline," Clara spoke aloud to her. "We need to take some time off from this. Let us have a day or two away from it. We promise we won't stop. Jack needs to rest, and so do I. Let us rest, now."

"Will that work?" I asked.

"I hope so."

Madeline was quiet all that day and night. I slept soundly and went to work Monday morning, feeling refreshed. It was a productive morning and I was rapidly checking items off my work list. Before lunch, my supervisor knocked on my door, "The director wants all of us in a meeting at two o'clock."

"Big announcement," she added and gave me a teasing "butter won't melt in my mouth" look to let me know she already knew what it was, and was bursting to tell someone.

"What?" I said, grinning at her.

"If I tell you then I have to tell everyone else and then everyone knows," she said, ducking back around the door.

Exactly. No one else knew. That was what we had been missing all along.

I picked up the phone and punched in Clara's number. Hopefully she was at her desk and had not left for lunch yet. It rang through to her backup. I asked for Clara and there was a shrill whistle and he called her name. Clara came back, talking to me on his telephone.

"Jack? What is it?"

"Do you have your notes with you?"

"Yes, the file is in my briefcase. Do I need to get it?"

"Madeline worked for the Springfield Milling Company, right?"

"Yes," Clara was puzzled. We had been over that a dozen times.

"The newspaper article about the inquest said a co-worker or co-workers, plural, testified."

"Yes, three or four, I think," Clara replied. "Their testimony unanimously supported the suicide theory. They were all questioned individually and separately by the coroner."

"Did they all say they knew Madeline didn't get the promotion that afternoon? That they already knew when she left early, upset?"

Clara was thoughtful, "I'm not sure, Jack. I think so, but I would have to look again. Harvey! Transfer this to my phone."

I waited while Harvey transferred the line. As soon as she picked up I could hear Clara rifling through her papers. "Let me see, no - not this one, she doesn't mention it specifically." There was a pause while she continued reading.

About to burst I asked, "Do you have their names there? Can you just read off the names to me?"

"Um, sure. First is Lou Johnson. She was the clerk in the payroll department. Then, oh let's see, there was a Frances something in personnel, and..."

"Any men?" I interrupted. I waited while Clara shuffled through more papers.

"Yes, there was, a Keith . . ."

"Knight," I finished with her.

"What?"

"Keith Knight, my old boss - the monster I told you about. He was Madeline's assistant. He was the one who got the promotion instead of her."

"He killed Madeline," I added. I was sure of it.

"No, Jack. It wasn't him. Why would he kill Madeline? He got the promotion. He said that was why she left early. Because she was upset about it.

"He didn't know yet when she left the office, none of them outside the personnel office did. I bet it was going to be announced that evening at the party. Knight didn't know he had it until he got to the Colonial. Something in the way Madeline left work that afternoon made him think she found out early that it was her, that she had it. She just came from the personnel office. He killed her on the way to the hotel. He didn't know that they picked him."

I could hear Clara shuffling the paper as she scanned back through the recorded testimony considering this new angle.

"Frances, a secretary in the personnel department, said her boss was talking about the promotion with his door partly open when Madeline walked into the office . . . with the pay envelopes. She said it was down to Madeline and Mr. Knight on the final decision. Frances wasn't sure if Madeline heard that it wasn't her, but she must have. She wanted to say something to her, but it would have meant Frances' job if she did. From there, she's crying and saying she wished she had chased Madeline down the hall or at least gone by her house on the way home that night. She was so sorry. She was excused after that. I don't think Frances would have told anyone else, Jack."

Clara then skimmed Lou's testimony. It looked like she didn't know until the party either. None of them did. We had completely missed that until now.

Clara read Keith's testimony aloud to me. My stomach churned. He was slick and smooth. He said that Madeline must have been upset about not getting the promotion - that was why she left so early. If he had been cross-examined it would have come out that he did not know the news when she left early. The personnel manager would have verified that. Knight filled in that small detail later. He too readily offered that he wished he had stopped her from leaving. He said it was sad that he had not, and her death, and the shame and grief it caused her family, might have been prevented if only he had.

"Every implication from him is that he already knew he had the job when Madeline left the office," Clara confirmed. "It's clever. Why would anyone suspect <u>him</u> of killing <u>her</u> that evening if he was the one who got the job? She was out of the way. What possible reason would he have? It puts the anger and suspicion off himself and onto Madeline. The only hole in his story, is that he didn't know they hadn't chosen Madeline over him until after he already killed her. It's clear to me now that it wasn't announced until the party."

"I am going to take him down," I said deliberately through clenched teeth.

"Jack! No!" Clara cried out. "You are not going to do anything. This doesn't prove a thing. It's only a theory."

"He did it," I said.

"You know that and I know that," Clara agreed, "and I'm sure Madeline knows it."

"She led me to him," I said. "I can see that now."

I told Clara about the malfunctioning microfilm reader that took me to Knight's photograph. I could fill in now that the missing parts of the article's last paragraph were "Chief Accountant" and "Springfield Milling Co." In January, 1954, Knight had the job that Madeline deserved. I could see the smirking and self-satisfied smile in the old photograph. Clearly, Madeline had led me to it.

All along, I knew Knight's name and would have recognized it, but since my copy of the transcript was lost in the mail, I never saw it there. Clara had the transcript, but the name meant nothing to her. It was what we had missed, the missing link. Madeline had to lead us to it.

"We have more work to do on this," Clara said. "Now that we know, we have to build our case and prove our evidence. We have to present it to your police and they will have to arrest him. You cannot do anything until then, Jack."

It took a while for Clara to talk me down, but I eventually saw that I could not just drive across town and confront Knight half-cocked. We needed to do our homework and plan how to present it to the police. We would let them be the ones to approach him.

"I have some vacation I need to use," Clara said. "How about if I drive down Wednesday morning and we spend the rest of the week on this?"

My supervisor would not be happy about me taking more vacation that week, and with so little notice, but she would just have to get over it. As soon as she was back from lunch, I told her I needed the rest of the week off, starting on Wednesday, for a personal matter. Like Clara, I had a bank of vacation hours built up that I was going to forfeit soon. Although she wasn't happy, she approved my request.

The meeting that afternoon turned out to be nothing. The company was buying new personal computers for everyone in the department. It meant we would have our own computer on our desk instead of having to go to the computer lab when we needed to use one. Prices were dropping so dramatically, especially compared to when they had been first introduced several years earlier, that the company could afford to buy one for everyone.

I was barely able to concentrate on my work after the meeting. My supervisor stopped by my desk shortly before four o'clock and quietly asked me if everything was alright.

"Just some old business I need to take care of," I said. I told her Clara was coming down Wednesday morning to help. It probably raised more questions than it answered, but my supervisor had met and liked Clara and did not ask anything else.

I puttered around the house that evening, reading through my notes once again, knowing now that Knight had killed Madeline. I couldn't find anything else I had missed.

I sat in the darkening room remembering the first time I met Knight. I was happy with the new job until then. When Knight returned from his vacation, my immediate supervisor, the junior partner, took me to Knight's office to introduce us. Looking back, I could see that Knight intimidated my supervisor, like everyone else.

When I was introduced, I stepped forward and put out my hand, but apparently that was too forward and presumptuous for Knight. It was what I had been taught when I went through the interview skills seminar before graduation, so I was surprised at his reaction. He merely stared down at my extended hand like I was infected with something, sniffed, and turned away to pick up a cigarette. He sat on the edge of his desk, lit the cigarette with a lighter he took out of his pocket, took a long drag while sizing me up, and blew the smoke out toward the ceiling. For the next fifteen minutes he grilled me about everything he should already know from my employment application and resume. Toward the end he made a slightly off-color comment I was not sure he meant as a joke. I was surprised and struggled to contain my reaction. Since the junior partner did not laugh, I was glad I hadn't either.

Keith put the cigarette in his mouth where it hung from his lips, glared at me, and said, "Since I am paying you so handsomely, don't you think you should actually be working?"

The junior partner said nothing, and feeling like I was hung out to dry, I could only nod in agreement. I turned to the junior partner who effectively dismissed me saying, "I will check with you later." When I left Knight's office, he closed the door behind me.

What had Knight seen in me in those first moments that made him hate me so much? In the dark, I kept going over it in my mind, until I remembered something Eva said about the first time we met. I turned on the lamp beside the sofa and looked at the clock. It was still early enough to call her.

"Hello?" Eva answered in a stiff and formal tone.

"Hi, Eva, It's Jack. Are you busy? Did I catch you at a bad time?"

"Hello, Jack," she was instantly friendly. "And no, not at all. I just finished dinner and was thinking about taking Shadow for a long walk. How are you?"

I said we were making some progress on the case, and without revealing what we suspected about Knight, asked Eva if the name meant anything to her. When she could not remember him, I said he had worked with Madeline, and that his name was in the inquest transcript.

"Oh yes, Keith," Eva said. "I think Mother was involved in training him those final months she worked. She only mentioned him a few times. I don't think she liked him very well."

"It looks like he got the promotion instead of Madeline," I said, "just before she died."

"Oh dear," Eva said. "But he wasn't the first, Jack. That's how it was for women in those days - more than today. I guess she had gone about as far up the ladder as she could."

I couldn't say anything more so I asked the question, "Eva,

187

something you said a while back puzzles me."

"Yes?"

"Well, you said once that you recognized something of Madeline in me the first time we met. Do you remember that?"

"Oh, Jack, don't worry about that. I shouldn't have said anything about it - really."

"No, I'm glad you did, and it could help with something we are working on right now. Do you remember what it was?"

"Clearly," she replied.

"There was something familiar about you as soon as you came around the side of the house, brushing paint chips out of your hair. The more we talked the stronger it was, until I was afraid you were going to think I was unbalanced or something, the way I was staring at you. Then, I said something and you raised your right eyebrow slightly, either in surprise or disbelief, and it was like looking at Mother. Later, when we were on the patio, you brushed your lower lip with your left forefinger. That was something she did when she was thinking. As my grandchildren would say, it creeped me out. I think that was why I made such a hasty departure. It wasn't until weeks later that I figured out the connection and even longer to accept it."

"That helps," I said. "Thanks."

"Jack, what is going on?"

"I can't say anything just yet. Only a lead we are working on. I will say though, that it's looking less and less like your mother's death was suicide."

"Is this Keith Knight involved?"

"Eva, please forget I said anything. And please, whatever you do, don't say anything about this to anyone else. I will let you know the moment we come up with something. Right now, I'm afraid anything that gets out from anywhere can ruin it."

"Mysterious," she said, "but you know you can count on me. Mum's the word."

"How is Addie?" I asked, wanting to wind the call down.

"About the same. No, that's what I tell the family, but I can tell you Jack that she's getting worse. They think it may be Alzheimer's disease now."

"I'm sorry. I don't really know much about it, but I am sorry."

"No one knows much, including the doctors. But they are doing everything they can for her."

"Alright. Well, I won't keep you any longer."

"Jack?" she said.

"Yes,"

"Thanks. I mean thanks for doing this, and thanks or caring. You will never know how much it means to me."

"OK. I'll call you as soon as I can."

After the call, I sat a while longer. I finally understood why Knight had hated me from the start. If I reminded him of Madeline, he might have thought I was a relative - a nephew possibly. His guilt drove what he had done to me. This realization took some of the sense of failure away from me. It also reinforced that he had killed Madeline.

Madeline only walked through my room only once that night. I woke moments before and was wide awake when she made her way from my desk to the doorway. I rolled over, facing away from the door and was almost asleep again when I sensed someone sliding up against me in the bed. Again, there was the bristling of the moustache against my ear, but this time I sat up quickly and turned on the light. Again, there was no one there.

Since the last time it happened, when Doug was sleeping in my guest room that final weekend of school, I would sometimes remember it. Although Martin did not have a moustache, I eventually convinced myself that it was him. I did not have the heart to mention it to Clara, who still grieved for him. She had mentioned no contact with Martin, even though I thought the connection they shared was even stronger.

Now I understood that it was Jordan, Madeline's husband, coming for her. It had to signify that we were getting closer to the truth, and in doing so, would release her to join him.

Clara arrived Wednesday morning. I should not have been surprised to see Deanne sitting in the front seat of the van. Both of them waved cheerfully as they pulled in my drive. I went to the driver's window and Clara, after leaning in for my kiss, said "Watch this!" and pressed a series of buttons to open the side door, rolled herself onto the lift and then used the lever to activate the lift and remove herself from the van to the drive. I clapped as Deanne came out of the rider's side door, laughing.

I helped Deanne unpack the van. They both would stay in the guest room. Clara assured me that she could get up the stairs with Deanne's help and she brought along a small folding wheelchair for use on the second floor. The rest of the van was packed with a variety of equipment, including a new whiteboard on a stand and a packet of colored dry-erase markers.

I just could not understand all the excitement about these whiteboards. They were installing them in the conference rooms at work. It was the latest thing in office equipment, but I couldn't see any advantage over a regular old-fashioned blackboard and chalk.

That is, until the board was set up against the dining room wall and, after the files and other equipment were spread out on the table, Clara explained the color coding we were going to use for the markers. Regular text would be in black, names would be in red, places in green, and everything else in blue. She started calling out things for Deanne to write on the board, pointing from her chair where to write it on the board, and fifteen minutes later we had a working diagram of the case. Deanne flipped the board over and started a timeline on the back side with four categories along the bottom;

Pre-Dec 18, Dec 18, Dec 19, after Dec 19.

Clara told her where to plot what we already knew on the timeline. Not only were the bright colors more visible against the whiteboard, the variety of colors helped sort the data and changes were easily made, rubbed out with a dry-eraser or cloth, and written elsewhere. Thirty minutes into our meeting, I was a whiteboard convert. It was like a giant erasable flip chart and I said whoever invented it deserved to be a millionaire.

We worked late into Wednesday night and were back at it over our coffee on Thursday. Most of the morning was devoted to playing the section of the séance tape after Madeline appeared. More notes were made on the board. The board became so full that we started taping typing paper sheets of details to the margins to keep track of them. We worked through lunch without stopping and at four o'clock ordered pizza. We stopped only when the delivery man came to the door and we worked late the second night. On Friday morning, feeling that everything was in place, we had the narrative of what had happened. We had started with the bones, now the flesh was on them.

Clara started the tape recorder and told the story.

Chapter Twenty Three

December 18, 1953

On the evening of the last day of her life, Madeline Montrose realized she had never been as enraged as she had been that afternoon. It was not like her and now, as the anger faded, she was drained. If she were not so determined, knowing exactly what had to be done, she would have cancelled her plans and put herself to bed.

She pressed her lips together as she leaned back from the mirror and set the lipstick on the dressing table. How she had changed! She had never been as sure of a decision as she was now. If nothing else, being alone the last eleven years had taught her to make decisions and to stand ready to enjoy the benefits or suffer the consequences. No one from her old life would recognize her now.

She took a small brush from the tray and leaned forward on her elbows, sharply evaluating her reflection. She rarely wore makeup these days, and tonight it had to be perfect. A few strokes of the brush shaped her eyebrows. She applied just a touch of shadow to accentuate her deep brown eyes and brushed a final dusting of powder across her high cheekbones and slightly upturned nose and was done.

"Well, Jordan," she said to the mirror. "It looks like the old girl can still pull it together when she has to."

Almost as an afterthought she took a small bottle of perfume from the tray, dabbed her wrists with the applicator, and traced a line from chin to neckline.

Satisfied, she slipped off the dressing gown as she stood. While she fastened the diamond clasp on her strand of pearls, she looked at the dress in the dressing table's long mirror, first for any problems that would have been hidden under her dressing gown, and then in the overwhelming realization that she once again looked the part she had lost so long ago.

The black velvet was perfectly tailored from the shoulders to her still-narrow waist. The black taffeta of the skirt swept in full billowing folds down to a fashionable mid-calf length, whispering over the stiff crinoline underneath. Turning slightly she could see the low back line in the mirror. She knew the women at the party would think the dress was not appropriate for a woman of forty-seven, but she really did not give a fig about what they thought tonight.

She took the fox jacket out of the furrier's bag and draped it over her shoulders. Gathering up her black gloves and purse, she paused. Before she turned off the radio she stood looking at the room.

Jordan and Madeline had shared this room from the time they built the house in 1935 until his sudden death during the early days of the war. They selected this wallpaper one cool June morning lying side-by-side on the tall poster bed with their packing boxes still stacked around the room. Dr. Jordan Montrose had been such a special man, strong and stern when it was needed, but warm and tenderhearted with Madeline and their two daughters. Back then, this house always seemed to wait in silent anticipation when he was away, only to come alive the moment he walked through the door. Even now, Madeline felt a piercing longing for him, an indulgence she seldom allowed herself.

He died without warning on a regular Tuesday evening in the spring of 1942. Walking to the car after his last office appointment, he had a heart attack. His doctor said he was dead before his body had completely fallen to the sidewalk, as though that would be a comfort to Madeline.

One of her husband's associates knocked on the front door that evening while she was putting the final touches on a meatless wartime dinner. He broke the news to her as gently as possible. When he was finished, Madeline calmly stood to thank him, shook his hand at the door, and called her daughters to dinner. After the meal, she gathered the girls to her, told them the news as gently as she could and held them close while the three of them wept.

Sleep did not come easily for a long time after that. First there was simply too much to do: arrangements for the funeral, wires to send, and long-distance telephone calls to make. Then there was the crush of people filling the house after the funeral. That was followed by a silent and empty house. For weeks, she caught herself speaking in hushed tones to the girls as they resumed their routines of daily living.

It was not only the shock of the loss and the loneliness that kept her awake at nights. In the weeks after the funeral, Madeline discovered that they had been spending almost everything he earned.

After writing the checks to pay the funeral home, the florist, and the minister, she called at the bank to ask for a transfer to cover the expenses for the next month. Jordan preferred that she handle their expenses in that manner - to write the checks once a month, and then go to the bank to transfer money into her household account to cover those checks. It saved him a trip to the bank, and gave him one less thing to worry about.

When she called at the bank that morning, dressed in the same black suit and hat she wore to Jordan's funeral, she thought the teller was behaving strangely. Moments later she was sitting in a private room with his supervisor. Questions were asked that she could not answer. As soon as the bank manager returned from lunch she found herself in his office. He was a kind and grandfatherly man in a rumpled suit with a smudged pince-nez perched on his nose. He carefully laid out a series of papers in front of Madeline for her to see. The news was grim.

Although eleven years her senior, Jordan apparently believed he still had plenty of years ahead of him. He had generously indulged their every whim. Now, other than the proceeds of a small insurance policy that would barely cover the burial expenses, she was left with the car bought just before the war started, a small savings account, and the house - along with the mortgage payment book.

Because there was a shortage of civilian doctors, and thus no one locally interested in buying Jordan's practice, the banker pressed her to shut down his office immediately. He said she could sign a power of attorney authorizing him to settle the accounts, pay the final bills, and get what he could for the furnishings and equipment. It was obvious that after the accounts were settled Madeline could expect to receive little or next to nothing.

She was at a loss all that weekend, confused about what had happened to their money, absorbed with her daughters, and distracted when friends called. She knew it would not be long until the meager savings account was depleted and there would be nothing left to live on. The banker had hinted it would be financially advisable for her to marry again - but with the war there were so few eligible men in town that was not possible, even if she wanted to.

She could not understand how this could have happened. She had grown up with nothing and she was frugal with what she spent in running the house and buying necessities for herself and the girls. But then, it always seemed that if she saved a dollar, Jordan would spend three to reward her. She would scout around for a sale on shoes for the girls, only to have Jordan bring her a gaily-wrapped gift from the very same store the next day. It was the closest they ever came to having a real argument, the gift was always something that she had admired or an acquaintance had flaunted at the club. If she scolded him, he would say that he just wanted his family to have the best of everything and be second to none. It was impossible to be angry with him. Because of that, her household budgeting had still been a challenge, but it was more like a parlor game with the calm assurance that Jordan would always cover whatever she spent.

Late into the night all that weekend, she went over every check she had written during the previous twelve months. In an attempt to make some kind of sense of it, she posted every check to one of three lists. The first list was items that were an absolute necessity and they could not live without, the second list was the things that were nice to have, and the third were the luxuries they would have to live without. Through those long nights, many items found their way from the first list to the second, and sometimes even to the third. The first light of morning would find her still at her desk, revising her lists, adding and re-adding the columns of numbers, and trying to find a way.

She also prepared a fourth list. It started with the house and the car, the antiques and the furniture, the silver, and even her jewelry and furs, although there was likely no market for those during wartime. A big liability, the monthly mortgage payment of fifty-eight dollars, was written at the bottom of this page, underlined many times with her dulled pencil.

Madeline was determined, at all costs, to keep the house. It was in one of the best neighborhoods, but with the war there was no market to sell it if she tried. There were entire neighborhoods of lesser homes standing vacant and boarded up - their owners in the war or out of town working in the war plants. Somehow, she had to come up with the payment each month. Anyway, if she sold the house there was nowhere else for them to go. She had no family and Jordan's one elderly aunt lived in a house too small for three more people.

If worse came to worst, she might be able to rent out the girls' bedrooms. The three of them would crowd into Madeline's room, but the thought of strangers sleeping just down the hall - how tongues would wag. A widow opening a home as a boarding house was only one step from the poor farm, and well on her way to being considered a woman without virtue. For the girls' sake, that had to be the absolute last resort. There had to be another way.

She would have to let the housekeeper go. From then on, Madeline and the girls would do all the housework, along with keeping the grass cut, and the gardening. It was getting late in the season, but they could still plant a victory garden. The girls might even think it was a fun and patriotic adventure. She would cancel the weekly laundry service and do all their washing and ironing. She would cancel the club memberships and save the dues - the appropriate thing for a woman in mourning, anyway. It would be equally excusable for her to withdraw from the garden club, her bridge club, and give up lunches with friends. Madeline and the girls would borrow books from the library instead of going to movies. They could even go to bed at dark and keep the radio off to save on the light bill. But after cutting everything to the bone, she knew that she would have to find work for them to live.

On Monday morning, she took her furs - a mink coat and a fox jacket - to her furrier for summer storage. She put the pearl necklace and the diamond earrings that had been a tenth anniversary gift in the safe-deposit box at the bank, then went to the tellers' window and withdrew fifteen one-hundred-dollar bills and some change, closing the savings account. Back at home she carefully parked the car, closed and locked the garage doors, and then hid the $1,500 and the mortgage payment book in a lingerie box in her top dresser drawer. With those tasks complete, she walked to the corner to catch the bus downtown and enrolled herself in classes at the business college.

The course of study took eighteen months, keeping her up most nights long after the girls were in bed. She read every chapter in her text books over and over until she had mastered the hieroglyphics of stenography, understood the intricacies of double-entry bookkeeping, could quote the essential internal controls of a basic customer billing process, and could prepare profit and loss statements from a general ledger.

There were nights when she lay awake in bed, wondering how long she could keep it going. Even with the war, there were still social invitations from loyal friends that she routinely declined. With wartime shortages, everyone was beginning to look a little down at the heels, but she even lacked the funds to keep up with those lowered standards. Their shoes were wearing out and their clothes were becoming frayed.

With the passing months, social calls at home from past friends grew less frequent as she withdrew even more, but the lack of social contact mattered less than she had expected. Obsessed with how to pay the grocer, she lacked the cleverness to participate in a spirited game of bridge or even the casual chatter of an afternoon tea that she had once enjoyed.

Then, even with careful management of their expenses, her funds ran critically low when there were still two months until graduation. Expenses could be cut no further. The girls had been brave and understanding, but there was nothing left for any of them to give up. Madeline carefully took another inventory of her assets, decided what would be missed the least, and one afternoon after classes took her mink coat out of storage and offered to sell it back to the furrier.

Although Mrs. Montrose was meticulous about paying her storage bill on time, Mr. Levinson had known this day was coming. Like clockwork, she came into his shop the day before the payment was due and made pleasant conversation while his clerk processed the payment. There had never been any problem with her account, but he had overheard tidbits of gossip among other customers in his shop. Wealthy women, solidly assured of their own positions, had openly discussed the problems of Mrs. Montrose as though he could not hear and understand their conversation.

He thought back to the early days when he came to this city. The community was barely large enough to support a synagogue and he had struggled through the early years of establishing his business. At first he had thought his wife's sickness grew from her loneliness in this strange country. Ultimately her lingering symptoms had led them to Dr. Montrose.

The doctor treated Mrs. Levinson when others had refused them. The hatred here was more veiled than it had been in Europe, but it was still present. The kind doctor had even allowed him to make payments on their account, which, at times, could not have even covered the cost of her medicine, let alone the time the doctor spent with her. His attitude was always one of empathy and concern, with gracious appreciation when payments were made. Levinson only paid the account in full three years after his wife's funeral, at a time when his business was finally on solid footing. In the following years the doctor had become a friend, stopping to chat when he saw Levinson on the street and never once smirking at his attempts to translate his words into the difficult English.

Dr. Montrose bought the luscious stroller-length mink from him shortly before Mrs. Levinson passed away. It helped pay for her funeral. The pelts were rich and luxuriant and after all these years the coat was still soft as butter to the touch. Levinson had thought how beautiful his Marta would have looked in it, in the days before her illness when she was still a great beauty. The coat, worn by the also-beautiful Mrs. Montrose, had helped Levinson Furs establish a well-heeled clientele. The Montroses were the first crossover of their social group and had been a turning point for his business. In time, the furs he sold were purposefully draped at the best social occasions to reveal the Levinson label stitched to the lining.

Even without the gossip, he would have guessed at Mrs. Montrose's precarious financial condition. He saw her entering the business college each morning as he walked to his shop. One afternoon in the bank, while depositing his weekly receipts, he accidently overheard two men in an office behind the counter discussing her loan and that she had closed the savings account. One had said it was just a matter of time until she would be placed on the foreclosure list. Mr. Levinson thought it was to her credit that she had managed to avoid that for this long.

Now Mrs. Montrose stood before him. After having him retrieve the coat from the storage locker, she wanted to sell it to him. She calmly explained that with the war she had no opportunity to wear it, but he could see a veiled expression of anxiety behind the beautiful brown eyes. A slight embarrassment accompanied her offer.

He wondered about the two little girls he had seen in the photographs so proudly displayed on Dr. Montrose's desk. How old were those girls now? Possibly twelve and fifteen years? At long last, this was his chance to repay some of the kindness Dr. Montrose had shown to him and to his Marta.

"I don't have many asking for this type of coat these days," he began. He did not want to make the gift too obvious. Let her think she had struck a good bargain.

"Dr. Montrose always said it was the very best," she said firmly. "There is always a demand for quality, isn't there Mr. Levinson?

"Yes, yes, my dear Mrs. Montrose," he agreed, "but most of our customers are only having their coats restyled these days. I should not do this but I could, at best, offer you three for it."

He realized for one awful moment that she had misunderstood his offer. She had barely hidden her shock.

"Three hundred dollars, Mrs. Montrose," he added quickly, in clarification. "That is my best offer."

After the shock of thinking he had offered her three dollars for the coat, she realized he had made a generous offer. She knew that Jordan had paid not much more than that seven years ago and now with the war and most husbands away or otherwise preoccupied, she had not hoped for even half as much.

She drew herself up proudly, "Three-fifty, Mr. Levinson, or I will put it back into storage."

He paused for a moment, going through the charade of turning the coat inside out, examining its perfectly maintained lining. He fluffed the fur along the collar as if looking for wear, and pulled it close to his spectacled eyes for closer inspection.

"Three-twenty-five. No more."

"Done," she said, beaming at him and holding out her hand for him to shake on the deal.

He thoughtfully took the coat with him into the backroom while he retrieved the cash from the vault. There was no need to leave her alone with the coat to grieve over its loss.

While she waited, Madeline allowed herself to remember only briefly the morning Jordan had given her the coat. He had prepared her birthday breakfast himself and, after setting the tray on the rumpled bedcovers, he slipped the luxuriant mink around her shoulders. She had screamed with delight, bringing the girls running from their bedroom. His eyes had misted over at her happiness, as hers did now at the memory.

She heard Mr. Levinson approaching the curtain that hung over the door to the backroom and quickly blinked her tears away. She resolved it would be the last of Jordan's gifts that she would sell to keep them going. From then on she would provide for their needs as he had provided for them in all the years that had gone before.

Mr. Levinson counted out the bills on the counter, and then placed them in an envelope. He handed the envelope to her and thanked her, although she was not sure why. She thanked him in return, and bid him a good day.

After she made a generous payment on the grocer's bill and set aside enough for her daughters' Christmas, the funds from the sale tided them over for the next two months. On the same day she received her certificate of completion from the business college, she went directly from the ceremony to the personnel department of the local milling company and was hired as a typing clerk.

Madeline worked her way up, first with a promotion to the position of statistical proofreader and eventually to supervisor of the entire transcription department. She consciously patterned herself after Jordan, being firm and demanding when necessary, but also developing a reputation for understanding and compassion with the younger women she supervised. As a result she earned their admiration and affection, along with their respect.

After three years, a position was posted in the bookkeeping department, and Madeline created quite a stir in the company by bidding on the job. To Madeline, the choice was simple; the salary was considerably better and the department offered more opportunities for advancement than the typing pool. Until then, no woman had ever worked in the bookkeeping department, and she endured hours of interviews with the man who would be her immediate supervisor, as well as the chief accountant, before they were satisfied that she could handle the simple responsibilities of entering and adding endless columns of numbers in the company ledgers and keeping them in balance.

Building the trust and respect of her coworkers in the new department was a slower process than it had been in the typing pool. The war was over and most women quit the jobs they had taken while the men were away, but over the next five years she again earned a reputation of competency and reliability, along with honesty and sound judgment. She worked her way to the back desk, a symbol of competence and expertise, equipped with its own filing cabinets, telephone, typewriter, and electric tabulating machine. In this position she acted as the unofficial assistant to Mr. Morrison, the chief accountant. She even had her own secretary.

In June, 1953, Mr. Morrison announced his retirement, which had been moved forward several years earlier than expected. The company began looking for his replacement. Once again, Madeline endured long, anxious interviews in her bid to replace the retiring chief. Weeks dragged into months, and no decision was announced. Countless applicants from outside the company were paraded through the department, until one afternoon in late November the word came down from the mill president's office that an internal applicant should be preferred for the position. After that ultimatum, the list of qualified contenders was narrowed to two: Madeline and the young man whose desk was directly in front of hers.

Although she could work circles around Keith Knight, who was almost twenty years her junior, she worried that his degree from State Teachers College might be a determining factor in the selection process. To her credit, she had the advantage of working with the company longer and the strength of her own maturity, but the strongest card in her hand was that she had almost single-handedly trained Keith in his current position.

On the first of December, the interview board announced that a decision would be announced by the end of the month, and then the following week a memo was posted saying that their selection would be announced at the annual Christmas party.

The Friday morning of the annual party dawned crisp and clear. An undercurrent of excitement ran through all the departments in anticipation of the evening. For many it was their only night out in style for the year. Madeline found it difficult to concentrate on her work, not only in anticipation of this one party she attended each year, but in the sickening dread of the announcement that would be made there. She alternated between the calm assurance that she had to be the one selected - if only in recognition of her experience and seniority - and a sinking anxiety that Keith would be selected because of his degree from a "real" college.

From her desk, she could see directly into Mr. Morrison's office. His polished desk and leather chair seemed to beckon to her. She tried not to imagine her own name on the door, her coat hanging on the rack in the corner, and photographs of her daughters, their husbands, and her grandchildren in the frames on the credenza behind the desk.

After lunch, a little after one o'clock, she decided to help Lou, the payroll clerk, by distributing the weekly pay envelopes. Lou always had a heavy workload on Friday afternoons and gladly accepted her offer. It meant she could leave on-time and get ready for the party. Madeline thought the walking would help clear her head and calm her nerves while providing a diversion from waiting for the hour hand to reach the Roman numeral five on her desk clock.

Even with everyone in the company knowing what was going on, Madeline found herself enjoying the walk through the various departments. On the loading dock she received the crew's unanimous wish for good luck, and she scarcely passed a desk without being offered some type of warm words of encouragement. As she made the rounds, her confidence grew. Surely the interview board had recognized how popular she was with the workers in this company. Surely they would realize the boost to the workers' morale in knowing that a typing pool employee had eventually worked her way up to one of the company's executive positions.

At her last stop, in the personnel office, Madeline handed the pay envelopes to Frances, the departmental secretary. She was taking a telephone call, but smiled up at Madeline, put her hand over the receiver, and mouthed the words, "Good luck!" She was just turning to leave when she overhead the director's voice coming through his partly-open door.

"...wanted a man for the job," he was saying into his telephone.

Madeline froze, not wanting to believe what she was hearing.

"Well, Sam, the official reason is that the kid has a degree, but, frankly, the board just wasn't too keen on having the job go to a woman. It's really a shame they decided to..."

Madeline did not hear the rest. After colliding with the door on her way out, banging it back against its stop, she found herself going almost at a running pace down the stairs and back to her desk. She paused only to pick up her purse and coat and turned to Keith, struggling to maintain control of herself. On Monday he would be her new boss, the company's Chief Accountant. It was almost impossible to look him in the eye.

"Tell Mr. Morrison I am taking the rest of the afternoon off."

With his bulging blue eyes, Keith Knight stared at Madeline in stunned silence, almost dropping the cigarette that seemed to hang perpetually on his full lips. With those eyes and lips, and the curly dark-brown hair that he continually smoothed back, most women thought him handsome, but he disgusted Madeline. His ashtray would be overflowing by the end of the day, and the fingers of his left hand, the one he smoked with while he wrote with his right, were perpetually stained yellow with the nicotine.

Looking at him now, Madeline realized how much she really detested him: his thinly veiled disrespect of her authority, his willingness to point out to Mr. Morrison all the errors she and others made, the way he interjected himself into conversations with the people he thought were important, and the insincere and almost leering flattery he slathered on any female who came into the department.

Although she had been nothing but polite and professional to him from the day he was hired, her hand itched now to slap that perpetual and self-satisfied smirk off his face. She imagined slapping him so hard that his cigarette flew across the room. Instead, she raised a solitary eyebrow of disdain, an involuntary expression for her that he had started mimicking recently, pulled on her gloves, and walked briskly and purposely from the room.

For Keith, this was completely unprecedented. Unlike others, Mrs. Montrose had never left early for any reason in the two years he had worked here. From the cocky way the old bitch was acting, she must have found out something about the interview board's decision, and from the calm and assured glare she gave him just now, it looked like she was the one getting the promotion. Probably the first thing she would do when old man Morrison was gone was hand Keith his walking papers and kick him to the curb.

Madeline managed to keep her composure until she got off the bus, but walking to the house the tears began. She let herself in and collapsed on the living room sofa in choking sobs. How could she have made such a stupid fool of herself, bidding on a job she would never be allowed to have? Why had she kidded herself all these years, thinking that she could compete? Why had she given up all her evenings and lunch hours so willingly to train the boy who would now leap frog over her to become her boss? How would she be able to hold her head up at work again?

Madeline cried tears that she had not allowed herself for years; the frustrations she had felt since Jordan's death, the disappointments in not having him around, and the lack of support from fading friends who seemed to believe another husband would be the solution for everything. She also cried for all the time she had missed with her daughters and grandchildren because of the investment she thought she was making in an independent future for herself.

Finally, when her tears were spent, she stood and walked into the kitchen. Washing her face at the sink, she had the sudden clarity of what to do now. After making a strong pot of tea, she sat down at the kitchen table with a stenographer's pad and began a list of estimated expenses and the capital requirements for opening a bookkeeping and transcription service. She listed everything she could think of, including office rent, supplies, the purchase of two typewriters, desks, and a small nest egg to cushion the business during its startup phase. She made a second list of contacts who would need her service. They were professional men who had been associates of Jordan, business owners they had known through the club long ago, and other favors she could call in. By five o'clock, she had roughed out a good beginning of a business plan.

Even though she took the car, Madeline barely made it to her hairdresser's appointment and had some trouble persuading her regular operator to cut her hair in the new fashion - a modern style that was a shade too young for her. With her hair brushed out and ready for the party, she crossed the street to the bank to get her pearls and earrings out of the safe deposit box, and then stopped at Levinson's to take her fur jacket from storage.

Refreshed and revitalized by her plans, she set about getting ready for the party. This would be no dowdy and out-of-date Madeline in a pleated wool skirt and gray sweater with her hair up in a bun tonight. When she announced her resignation at the party, she would give them a glimpse of the woman she used to be: diamonds, furs, and all. The Cadillac would not be hidden away in the garage while she arrived by bus this evening. She would right drive up to the front door and let the valet park her car. She would sweep up the Colonial Hotel's wide staircase to the grand ballroom and stand in the doorway for a moment as if surveying the room, with the diamonds at her ears sparkling in the light from the chandeliers. Then she would let the maître-d remove her coat.

She finally snapped off the dressing table lamp and walked through the bedroom and down the hall. As she paused a moment at her daughters' rooms that were already made up in anticipation of their arrival for the holidays, Madeline realized that now she would have the entire week to prepare for and then enjoy their visits, rather than trying to squeeze everything into the evenings after work. Like old times, she would have everything perfect when they arrived this year; a fire crackling in the fireplace, frothy eggnog in the silver punch bowl, and even sheet music ready on the piano rack.

She hoped it would be a pleasant holiday. Her two daughters were so different from each other. Eva, short for Evangeline, the eldest, had been a great help to Madeline during the first years she was widowed. Mature beyond her years, she was always ready to offer help without having to be asked. Addie, short for Adeline, was difficult - spoiled, in fact. Madeline had found it almost impossible to enforce any rules and discipline for the younger child.

Eva never seemed to need anything. Even now, as a young mother who had worked to put her husband through medical school, and was working to help him start a business, she flatly refused any offer of help, financial or otherwise. Instead, Eva always managed to stretch her tight budget enough to bring her family from California every Christmas.

Addie was the complete opposite. Madeline could only blame herself for whatever her younger daughter lacked in character now. She was a daddy's girl and was too young when her father died. It had been a terrible shock for her when Madeline had to go to back to school and then started working. Addie naturally resented having to help out with the household chores, especially when they used to have the maid who did most of that. It seemed she had been angry and resentful of Madeline since Jordan died. Madeline had to constantly keep herself in check and not give in to every demand that her younger daughter made.

Against Madeline's wishes, Addie quit school and married entirely too early, to a young man she completely controlled, it seemed. Almost immediately, and with Madeline's help, David Applegate bought an established corner grocery store. It should have been enough, but Addie was ambitious and they immediately expanded the space and inventory to offer more variety. Then they started giving free delivery service to attract more customers. Business increased, but costs increased more and it was always a struggle. Recently, two new supermarkets had opened in town and business for all the small grocers was off. Madeline could see that it was the beginning of a slow and irreversible decline. She tried to tactfully advise her son-in-law to cut his losses, sell the store for what he could get out of it, and to then apply for a store manager position with one of those new supermarkets. With his experience they should hire him in a second, and at a good salary, she insisted.

When Addie heard about it she hit the roof. She drove herself to Madeline's house and stood on the front porch, yelling at her mother through the screen door like a fishwife, almost foaming at the mouth as she berated her mother for interfering and "belittling" her husband when he was doing the absolute best he could. They would never sell the store. Her husband was not going to go to work for others and be their lackey, constantly at their beck and call like a common servant. People were not going to look down on them for losing their business. He would not fail. She would not let him. Her mother would see and then she would be sorry when she had to come crawling back on her hands and knees to apologize to him.

David always did exactly what Addie told him to do, and the store continued to struggle. Even though Addie was still angry, and now blamed her mother for most of their troubles, she was not above asking her mother for money, saying it was only to "tide them over" until things picked up. She needed things, after all. She could not go around looking like a charity case and have their customers think the store was not a success, could she? Madeline owed her that much.

Lately, Addie had even started demanding that Madeline go ahead and give both daughters their share of the house their father had left them. She insisted she did not mean Madeline had to sell the house, but she surely had enough saved by now that she could pay both the sisters their one-third share of the value. Although Madeline knew she was going to have to refuse, and had to try to reassure her daughter that the house, along with the rest of the minimal estate, would be divided equally between the two sisters after she was gone, she was waiting until after Christmas to tell her. Until then, Addie was on a "campaign of niceness," it seemed, until the cash was handed over. Madeline hoped that putting off the decision until after the holidays would ensure they all had a more enjoyable Christmas. Addie would have to be on her best behavior.

On the stairs Madeline paused in front of the mirror on the landing before descending into the living room. Without a window there, the mirror had been a necessity. But while she would have been satisfied with a simple glass mirror, Jordan had insisted on buying the over-sized Duncan Phyfe reproduction that hung there instead. It was exactly like the one they saw in a movie while the house was being built and he would have nothing less. She had almost sold the mirror in those final days before she finished her studies, but she realized after placing the advertisement in the newspaper that she could not part with it. It was too much of a reminder of him, and she had to admit it was perfect for the space, even if it was ostentatious.

After checking her reflection in the glass and gently patting her newly-cropped hair into place one more time, she descended to the living room. The Christmas tree, just delivered and ready for decoration tomorrow, filled the room with its fresh wintery scent.

When she turned off the living room lights she realized that her plans for the new backyard patio, as well as the French doors she had selected to replace the two windows that flanked the fireplace, would have to be put off once more. Her carefully-hoarded savings were needed now to set up the bookkeeping service and provide some security until it could generate a steady income. Maybe by this time next year she would be able to start thinking about her remodeling plans again.

Carefully she backed the car out of the garage, parking it momentarily to close the double doors, and then proceeded down

Jefferson Avenue toward downtown.

The car radio was on, a sadly romantic song she remembered from the lonely war years. Her watch read exactly eight o'clock. She was already running a little late for the party, but it was better to not be right on time this evening. She would let everyone else arrive before she made her entrance.

Turning left onto Division Street to take a more indirect route, she relaxed and began to enjoy the drive. The elegant old car always made her feel pampered, gliding along the pavement and smoothly absorbing the bone-jarring bumps she would have felt on the bus. The fur on her shoulders was warm against the chill of the evening. As a light rain began to spatter down on the windshield, she switched on the wipers and their muted whir and thud seemed to be in perfect tempo with the old song on the radio.

When she reached National Boulevard, it was raining harder and she saw that sleet was mixed in with it. With a careful right turn she headed south on the wide avenue that would take her about a half mile east of the hotel. The street lamps glistened on the wet pavement and she found herself humming along with the radio as she approached the traffic light at Chestnut Street.

Waiting there for the light, she propped her elbow on the window ledge of the driver's door, absently brushing the back of her left forefinger against her lower lip. It was an old habit Jordan used to tease her about, but it helped soothe the dark and frightening thoughts that swirled around her. If she let them, dark thoughts of losing her life savings and having to beg to get her old job back would force their way in and steal away her confidence.

Surely everything would have been so much easier for a man, she thought. It would have been easier for a man to be left alone with young children during the war years. Easier for him to work his way up in a company. Easier to have been recognized for her accomplishments. Easier to deal with the pressures after the war to step aside and provide a job for a returning hero. Easier to have fought and clawed like she had for everything she was going to give up tonight.

She willfully pushed these thoughts from her mind and, as the light changed to green, proceeded cautiously on the rapidly slickening street into the next block that was bordered by darkened warehouses. Crossing over the tracks beside the quarry she had a sudden panoramic view of the entire downtown area. It was a view she loved and partly why she had taken this route. The lights of the tall Landers and Woodruff buildings hung as bright and clear as new stars in the cold night. The darkened twin minarets of the Shrine Mosque rose in silent silhouette, and the low and luminous night clouds softly reflected the lights of downtown. The big red letters that spelled out the hotel's name on the Colonial's roof dominated this city scape, reminding her with an almost sickening dread of her destination and her purpose, but from this vantage point, the view was peaceful and inviting.

As she admired the view, Madeline did not think about the old quarry on the west side of the street, lost in darkness. If she had looked down, the low retaining wall along the sidewalk and the wire fence would have seemed out of place against the spectacular view. She avoided looking because the yawning abyss always pulled at the balance of those who stared too long into its murky depths.

In the dark, she did not see the other car coming up behind her fast on the empty street. Even if she had been looking in her rear view mirror, with the rain and sleet she would not have seen it. Keith Knight had turned its headlights off and the hulk of the car was barely visible against the black night. And even if she had seen it coming she could not have reacted in time to avoid the collision.

Just before impact, Knight swerved left, clipping the Cadillac's back bumper. Madeline was thrust forward and to the right, with her front wheels jumping the curb and sidewalk, smacking hard into a dead stop against the retaining wall, and then bouncing up and rolling over it. The underside scraped along the top of the wall, grinding the car to an abrupt and precarious stop.

First, Madeline was shoved back against the seat with her head snapping back painfully. Then, when the front end hit the retaining wall and the car came to a sudden stop, she was thrown forward, dragging her face, from forehead to chin over the edge of the steering wheel, peeling a wide strip of skin and muscle away from bone, crushing the bridge of her nose, pulverizing her cheekbones and breaking off her front teeth before the wheel finally snapped the jawbone away from her skull.

Dazed, she stupidly held her grip on the steering wheel, struggling to comprehend what had happened. Blood from the loose flap of skin was streaming into her eyes. Blood was gushing from her broken nose and gaping mouth. With her headlights reflecting upwards and off the low-hanging clouds, she struggled to collect herself, trying to understand what had happened. Pressing and holding the loose flap of skin on her forehead away from her eyes and back in place with her left hand, she eventually realized she had to shut off the engine and get out of the car that was now partly extended out and over the low retaining wall - if only she could let go of the steering wheel.

Behind her, the dark and unseen car ground its gears loudly into reverse and backed away wildly, as if in escape. With the engine still roaring and the gears grinding, Knight hesitated a moment on the deserted street. Then the gears found their place and it lunged forward again, accelerating as it came.

The second impact finished what the first had not. As her rear wheels scraped heavily over the low wall and the front end passed through the wire fence as though it was the delicate strands of a spider's web, Madeline realized the true horror of the situation. Her hands, both now on the wheel, futilely tried to steer the airborne front tires away from the fall.

From a distance, she heard the gurgling scream rising from her throat, while a calm part of her brain watched in detached fascination as her headlights reflected a moment on the opposite rim of the quarry and then down and down into the quarry's depths. Helpless now, she saw her bloody, gloved hands still clamped on the steering wheel, the wipers still swabbing senselessly at the glass, the center post of the windshield, and the yellow glow of the radio that was still playing the same song. With her heart bursting in her ears she watched the rock floor of the quarry rising up in slow and silent motion to meet her.

Then, somewhere between the crushing impact that flattened the Cadillac's front end into the stone floor - pushing the steering wheel through her ribs and driving the scalding hot engine through the firewall to break her legs, with the momentum of the fall flipping the car forward to land upside down and the brilliant explosion that followed, Madeline mercifully slipped away.

Chapter Twenty Four

When Clara shut off the recorder I rose from the dining table, gathered up the cold coffee cups and went into the kitchen to make another pot.

"So, what now? Do we take this to the police?" Deanne asked.

"Not unless we want to be laughed at," Clara replied. "This is only a theory of what happened. We need physical evidence, witnesses, or a signed confession. Since the only witnesses were Madeline and Knight, we can't go there. The only physical evidence would be Knight's car and that is likely long gone."

She wouldn't say it, none of us would. We were finished.

"At least we can tell Eva what we think happened," I said. "It will take the guilt off her sister, and maybe it can give them both some peace, even if Knight got away with killing their mother."

Clara sat up straight in her chair and stretched her arms high overhead. "I'm starving," she announced.

We all were. After eating only pizza and snacks since Wednesday, it was time we had some real food. I opened the refrigerator. About the only thing I could offer them was a cheese omelet and toast. Deanne made a face and we all agreed to go out for lunch.

The next hour was busy with the three of us taking showers and getting dressed to go out. I went first, quickly shaving and showering then closing my bedroom door behind me while Deanne set up the portable chair in the shower and helped Clara into the bathroom. When I was dressed, I went downstairs, straightened up the dining room, living room, and kitchen. I had just started the dishwasher when Deanne came into the kitchen and asked if I could help her carry Clara downstairs. With Clara's arms around our shoulders and her sitting on the human chair we formed for her with our wrists and hands, we went down the stairs and settled Clara in her regular wheelchair. I realized I was getting used to this new normal for her. We all were. Nothing about it seemed the least bit out of the ordinary.

It was really best for Clara to go to the restaurant in her van. Deanne could ride with her, of course, but with the lift equipment taking up the space where the back seat would have been, there was no place for me to ride, except sitting on the floor. We decided I would drive my car and they would follow.

I thought they would like Café 303, so I drove there. The only hitch was that Clara had to go down the block to find a ramp where she could wheel onto the sidewalk. She was cheerful, saying it was the scenic route, "I get to see all the things that people with two good legs miss."

We had a table near the back with plenty of room for Clara's chair. I knew exactly what I wanted, but Deanne and Clara studied the menu carefully, asking me questions I could not answer about dishes I had never tried. Finally they decided the daily special sounded best.

We had a leisurely lunch, with none of us really in a hurry to get back to work. Clara said she thought she would go to the police station on her way back to my house and look through the case file. It was possible there was real physical evidence on file. She explained it would most likely be in a cardboard file box stuffed away in some storeroom in the basement.

"Are you not wanting us to go with you?" Deanne teased. "That certainly is not very effective marketing."

Clara smiled, "I doubt there is even that much. I can paw through it well enough on my own. They will likely assign a clerk to stay with me, anyway. If you like, you two can live it up this afternoon."

"A nap sounds pretty good to me," Deanne said.

It was Friday afternoon. I really needed to do some laundry and a few household chores before the weekend. A trip to the grocery store was in order, too, especially if Clara and Deanne were staying through the weekend.

We had dessert, more iced tea, and were waiting for the check when Deanne said, "It would be nice if Knight would confess, wouldn't it?"

"Ha!" Clara said. "That only happens in movies. Even if he did confess, he would say that it was under duress, or some such nonsense like that, when it actually came to court."

"What if he did it voluntarily?" I asked. "And in front of
211

witnesses?"

"If he denies it later, then the witness testimony would only be hearsay evidence in court. That's not a very strong case and almost any defense attorney can have it thrown out, or get the jury to ignore it. Knight could still deny everything."

"What if he was recorded, like on tape - his own voice?" I asked.

"Well, it is better, but do you really think Knight is going to confess if you say, 'wait a minute while I turn on this here tape recorder,' and 'please speak directly into the microphone, now'?"

Deanne laughed. I waited, then asked, "what if he doesn't know it's being recorded?"

Clara looked at me, opened her mouth to say something, stopped, then said, "Are you talking about wearing a wire? I'd have to get a court order, and that's not very likely."

"What if I carried a pocket recorder? I've seen them. They run on a battery and fit in your pocket. What if we went to see Knight, confronted him with what we know, and recorded the whole thing?"

"Jack, this man is dangerous, remember. He probably isn't going to say anything and what do you think he would do if he found out it was all being taped?"

"That's why we go together. If he gets belligerent, you can flash your police badge until the real police get there. The worst case scenario is he doesn't confess and we have to call the police for protection, then we have him for threatening us, don't we?"

"Or murdering us - then he would be convicted for sure. I'm just not willing to risk that."

"He's an old man," I said. "I don't think he can overpower the three of us,"

"Two," Deanne objected, holding up her hands to stop us. "I didn't sign up for this."

"Two," I revised. "It could be that he wants to confess anyway. There's always that possibility."

"Do you really think so?" Clara asked.

"Not really," I said. "It would be nice though."

"And just how do you propose that we get in to see him?" Clara said. We can't just invade his office.

Actually, I had thought about that. "I used to work in that office, remember? I know that Knight is greedy. He can never turn down meeting a potential new client, especially one that is referred by someone important. All I have to do is call and set up an appointment for us to see him, under fake names, of course, and say that Knight was recommended to us by a friend. The friend would be an actual person. He plays golf with my supervisor's father and he is in Europe until after Thanksgiving, so Knight can't verify the referral before he meets with us.

"So, we set up an appointment with Knight on the pretext of turning over our business accounts or doing our taxes," I continued. "Since he has never seen you, you could go in first, saying I was on my way. Just seeing me may be shock enough to get him to confess. With the tape recorder hidden - in your purse or in my jacket pocket - we could lay out what we know about him killing Madeline and see how he takes it. We could set up an evening appointment when most of the staff is gone so it's less likely anyone would recognize me. What do you say? Should I see if I can get us in?"

Clara looked at her watch, it was going on three o'clock. "Not today. I don't think it's a good idea, Jack. In fact, I think it's completely harebrained, but I can't come up with anything better, myself. I think it might work, but we need to give it a lot of thought first. In the meantime, I'm heading to the police station to see if there is anything else I can uncover as real evidence. With any luck, there will be a home movie in the file showing Knight smiling and waving at the camera before he pushes Madeline over the edge."

"Are you OK if I set up an appointment with Knight in the next couple of weeks? We can always cancel it."

"I guess so. Just allow enough time for me to drive down before the meeting."

Clara headed to the police station and Deanne rode home with me. I put off calling Knight's office until I unloaded the dishwasher and put a load of towels in the washing machine. Just before four o'clock, with Deanne snoring lightly in the guest room, I went to my bedroom, closed the door, and used the extension to call.

"Knight, Cunningham, Bristol, and Jones, how may I help you?"

Thankfully I did not recognize the voice. The regular receptionist, Dorothy Daniels, had a thing for remembering voices and might still recognize mine. On the principle that the best lie is one that is almost entirely the truth, I said I was Michael Andrews. On a sudden inspiration, I said that my wife, Clara, and I lived in Kansas City, but were moving to Springfield. We were in town for the weekend and a mutual friend had referred us to Keith Knight for our accounting and tax work.

She politely asked if she could have the name of the person who referred me and seemed suitably impressed when I gave the name of my supervisor's father's golfing partner. I asked when we could see Mr. Knight. Late afternoons or evenings were better for Clara. In fact, if Mr. Knight was available, we could meet him for drinks and dinner over the weekend.

It was a blunder. A person in the position I was pretending to be would have included Mrs. Knight in his invitation, but I already knew Mrs. Knight rarely attended anything beyond the annual Christmas party. She certainly did not accompany her husband to meet prospective clients. Fortunately, it went unnoticed - or she thought I was rude.

"I'm sorry, Mr. Knight will be out of the office until the first of November. Perhaps one of his associates could meet with you?"

"But Mr. Knight is the top man there isn't he?" I asked, more aggressively.

"Yes, he is the partner in charge, but any of his associates are capable of . . . "

"No, we want to meet with Knight. Is there any way I could just speak to him?"

"I'm sorry, Mr. Andrews. He is here, but he is finishing things up before his flight leaves this evening. He asked not to be disturbed, but I can see if I can put your call through to him."

"No," I said with a sigh. "Don't bother him. I guess it won't matter if we don't meet him until November will it? There aren't any taxes due before then, are there?"

"No sir," she said. "I can schedule you for a five o'clock appointment on the ninth of November, with dinner after that at his

214

country club. Will that work for you and Mrs. Andrews?"

When I agreed, she asked if she could have a telephone number. I hesitated, then gave her Clara's home telephone number in Kansas City. Then, in case she was wondering why I hesitated, I added that it was an unlisted number in Mission Hills. Whoever was on the other end of the line at Knight, Cunningham, Bristol, and Jones was probably thinking Michael Andrews was a nouveau riche social jerk, but she did not show it. I made a mental note to tell Clara so she would could play the stuffy, country club wife if they called.

After the call, I knew in my gut that this could not wait until November. Everything would all fall apart by then. If Knight was leaving town tomorrow, we had to see him tonight. Still wearing the slacks and dress shirt I had worn to lunch, I opened my closet and threw on a sport coat and put on my shoes. I stuck my wallet and keys in my pockets as I was walking down the hall to the guest room. Deanne was awake but still lying in bed. When I told her to call Clara at the police station and give her the message to meet me in the parking lot outside Knight's office, she tried to talk me out of it. Ignoring her protests, I told her to tell the police operator it was an emergency to get Clara to the telephone, and to tell Clara that she was to meet me there "ASAP." Deanne was shouting after me as I ran down the stairs and to the garage.

As I backed the car out of the garage it was starting to rain. I drove down Jefferson and made a left turn onto Division as soon as traffic cleared, but still against the red light. I drove above the speed limit and made a right turn on National, a route that would take me to the electronics store near the Southwest Missouri State University campus. I pulled into the lot, leapt out of the car, and told the clerk I needed a pocket tape recorder and I was in a hurry. He pulled three off the rack. I picked the most expensive one, thinking it was likely the best. He unpackaged it for me, put in the batteries, and showed me how to turn it off and on. Instead of using a credit card, I put four twenties on the counter, told him to keep the change, and ran out to my car.

Friday evening traffic was getting heavier when I pulled back out onto National. Looking down the road and seeing traffic backed up at the stoplights as far as I could see, I wheeled onto a side street, hoping to avoid traffic. It was raining more heavily now, making the streets slick and slowing traffic even more. Hoping Clara was not far behind me, I careened around the deeper puddles and even bounced over a curb to go around a car that was barely moving.

It was after five o'clock when I pulled into the parking lot at the accounting firm and parked at the back of the lot. It was far from the door but still close enough that I could see in through the plate glass windows. I shut off the engine to wait for Clara. It was only then I realized that I really did not know what I was going to do next. I just knew that I had to do something.

Chapter Twenty Five

Getting into Knight's office was easier than I expected. The same routines were followed as when I worked there, and I still had the spare key to the door. While I waited for Clara, I watched the staff leave. The senior partners were first, then the junior partners, and finally the underlings were free to go. Sitting in my car in the rows behind the employee spaces, I was invisible to them as they ran to their cars. All they wanted was to get out of the rain and home to their waiting dinners.

With the rain it was getting dark early. This side of the building had floor-to-ceiling windows and where the lights were still on I had a clear view of both the reception area and Knight's private office. The other partner offices, along the front of the building, were dark except for the rectangles of light where the doors opened to the main hall.

After setting up coffee for Monday morning, straightening up the waiting area, and watering the plants, Miss Daniels put on her raincoat, and, as she had done every evening for the last thirty-odd years, transferred the phones to the answering service.

Through the windows, I saw her walk the length of the hall to the one remaining lighted office that was Knight's, speak briefly to the chair that had its high back turned to the window, pick up some papers from his out basket, and walk back to her desk. While tying the strings on her plastic rain bonnet, she opened the telephone line to his desk again. Then she shut off the overhead florescent lights in the reception area, and left.

From my darkened car, I watched her drive away. I checked my watch, wondering where Clara was. Inside, I saw Knight stand and put on his jacket. He was getting ready to leave. He went back to his desk, and after sitting down heavily in his chair, gathered things to put in his open briefcase on the floor.

I couldn't wait for Clara any longer. I hopped out of my car and darted through the rain to the door. It was locked, but my key still worked. The door opened with a hoarse whisper. I caught it to soften the closing thud and left it unlocked for Clara.

In the dark I went behind the reception desk and transferred

Knight's line back to the night service. Creeping down the hall, I was amazed with how little things had changed since the summer afternoon I was ushered out. The carpet had been replaced since then, but it was the same dull brown and was beginning to show the same signs of wear. The paneling of the walls was the same, just a little more faded where the sunlight came through the open office doors. The same faded prints were on the walls and the same stale odor of ledgers and cigarette smoke hung in the air. As I approached Knight's office the pungent reek of his cigar was still present.

Likely thinking it was Miss Daniels coming back, he did not even look up as I stepped in.

"Still smoking that vile cigar, I see," I said from the door.

He was startled by my voice, but looked up calmly, pulled the cigar from his mouth with his left hand, clutching it between the thumb and first two fingers, the pinky finger with its diamond ring extended arrogantly, as always.

"Well, well, well, the prodigal failure returns," he said with a sneer.

Ignoring this I moved toward the desk. "Yeah, you said I would be lucky to get a job as a bank teller. Quite the benevolent mentor you were for a struggling young man fresh out of college. Maybe you should move on to being an advisor for high school dropouts and troubled teenagers."

He leaned back in his usual self-satisfied way in the chair, the leather creaking heavily under his bulk. He took a long draw on the cigar and casually puffed out three smoke rings toward the ceiling. I could remember him doing as many as five rings during a meeting, signifying his boredom and fascinating himself with the way they enlarged until they disappeared. I sat in the armchair across from him, uninvited. If I still worked for him, that action alone could have gotten me fired.

"You surely didn't come back to discuss why I fired you. Christ, that was twenty years ago!"

"Actually, more like ten," I corrected, "and maybe I did. We both know that the real reason you fired me wasn't what you said it was back then. But I doubt if you would ever admit it."

He shifted his gaze from the ceiling to me. Silent and cold, the bulging blue eyes that had overpowered me years ago had no effect now.

"Why were you so hard on someone just starting out?" I asked. "What was it you could not tolerate about me?"

"You were a schmuck," he said. "No balls. Castrated. A gelding."

"Yeah, right. As if any of your staff could have had an opinion of their own. You couldn't stand it that I did not automatically go along everything you said. You hated me because I did not spend all my time with my nose completely up your ass like everyone else."

I stopped myself, not wanting to fall back into the old anger, not wanting to lose the thin edge on my control. He had that effect, using anger and defensiveness to put his opponent off center and off-guard, then moving in for the kill. I held myself in check.

"You were a loose cannon then, Jackson, just like you are now," he said with disgust. "Clients didn't like you."

"Maybe they didn't, and maybe they did. At least they got the truth from me - and most of them asked to have me assigned to their jobs again."

"There were plenty of other of reasons I couldn't stomach you," he cut in.

"Yes, I know," I agreed, disarming him.

I continued. "So, what really happened that day you fired me, Knight? What did you see that scared you so much?"

He stared at me with contempt. "Bull," he spat out in sarcasm. How could someone as insignificant as me frighten him?

I paused, willing myself not to look away.

"There was something you saw in me, wasn't there?" I asked calmly.

I leaned back in the chair, letting my elbows rest confidently on the arms of the chair and placing my fingertips together, forming a temple of calm.

"It was something you finally put your finger on, wasn't it? I did something that totally scared the crap out of you, didn't I?"

I could see his confidence was slipping away, his stare was more uncertain now, wavering.

"There was something that you recognized, something that came back to you, but what was it?"

Deliberately, with my hands in my pockets, I stood, and as if trying to remember, and faced the window. Outside, the parking lot was nearly empty - no sign of Clara.

I took my hands out of my pockets and turned back to Knight. I slowly lifted my left hand and traced my lower lip with the back of the forefinger. My eyes remained on his.

"Was it a gesture? The turn of a phrase? What was it? Who did you recognize in me that completely scared the shit out of you?"

The tremble of his hand was almost imperceptible as he grabbed the cigar from his mouth and set it on the edge of the ashtray. He said nothing, but reached for the phone.

"Oh, the phones are all transferred to the service," I cooed. "I took care of that. You can't call out, so just answer my question. It's really quite simple. What did you see? What was it that you were so afraid of?"

I gave a little satisfied smile at him now, never breaking eye contact. I allowed my right eyebrow to elevate slightly, emphasizing my question, just so, just the way Madeline would do it.

His pills were never far away. He reached for the bottle he kept on his desk and shook out the last one. The skin around his mouth was taking on a bluish cast as he put it under his tongue.

"There's no need to be so upset! Just answer my question. What did you see?" I traced my slightly-parted lower lip with my left forefinger again. "What did you see . . . Keith?"

I let her speak through me. When I said his first name, it was Madeline he heard. His eyes bulged even more, as if they would burst from their sockets.

"Damn you!" he said, lowly at first, "Damn you straight to hell! It's where you belong!"

"Tell me Keith, I want to know, what did you see?"

"Damned bitch!"

"How can that be, Knight? It doesn't make any sense does it? How can Madeline possibly be here?"

No response.

"Didn't you know I would be back, Keith?" Madeline continued smoothly. "I've always been here, haven't I? I have been with you every day since then, haven't I? You just can't get away from me, can you?"

I sat again and crossed my right leg over my left at the knee, a calculated and feminine gesture that was not lost on him. I lowered my chin and looked up, mocking him. I allowed Madeline to shine through me.

He stared at me, not wanting to believe. He shifted his weight like he was going to stand, but did not. I could see how thin and weak his legs had become from so many years of sitting at this desk. It was difficult for him to stand now.

"After all I did for you, you turned on me," I said in a low voice that was not my own. "I showed you everything didn't I, Keith? I taught you everything you needed to know."

He had slouched forward slightly, with small beads of perspiration showing on his forehead, his breath irregular and heavy.

"DIDN'T I?" Madeline shouted at him. The shout echoed back down the hall outside his door.

His hand almost went to his chest before he realized I would see it. He picked up the medicine bottle again, but it was empty. He tossed it aside. There was a loose pill on the desk. He fumbled and dropped it. Without looking, I was aware of it rolling on its edge across the desk and dropping onto the carpet.

I showed a slow Madeline grin at the lost pill, raising a visible panic in him.

"What are you going to do?" he asked, almost a whisper.

"Nothing."

"What do you want from me?" almost pleading.

"Nothing, nothing at all, Keith. I never asked you for anything, did I? Not once!"

His confusion was pronounced. He straightened slightly but did not stand, his breath coming in gasps now. I looked away from his face, at the cigar on the ashtray, staring at it with my eyebrow raised in Madeline's way, watching until a length of ash fell. I remembered the tape recorder, put my hand in that pocket and pressed the button with my thumb. The whir was barely perceptible.

"When did you first see Madeline's car that evening, Knight?" I asked him.

No response.

"Did you follow her from the house? Were you waiting for her to leave? How far did you follow her?"

"She was in the way," he said hoarsely. "She was in the god-dammed way of everything! She was screwing up everything for me!"

"But I'm so curious how you did it," I purred. "How you managed it. Tell me, did you just happen to pass her on the way to the party and decide to do it when you saw her alone on deserted streets? Or were you too smart for that? Did you have it all planned out for a long time?"

"She was in my way," he repeated.

"OK - so you saw her on the street. No one else was around, and you took your chance."

He stared at me, fish-eyed now. A purple vein at his temple throbbed visibly.

"How long were you driving behind me with your lights off, Keith?" Madeline asked. "Did you pull up behind me at the stop light and decide to do it then?"

"You were in the fucking way!" he croaked, clutching his chest. He wanted to shout the words but could not.

"There were only the two of you on the street, Knight," I said. "She never even saw you. You could have left and she never would have known."

"You were screwing everything up, you bitch. You fucking bitch!"

"Did you really think you could push me all the way over with just one hit, Keith?" Madeline mocked. "Did it surprise you when I didn't go in the first time?"

A thin trickle of blood from his nose surprised me. He sniffed and wiped at it with the back of his hand, but I continued.

"Even then, you still had a chance to change your mind after the first crash, didn't you, Knight? How long did it take you to back up? How far back did you have to go to get enough speed to push her on over. How long did it take to grind those gears into first with the car still rolling? When was the very last moment that you could have swerved and saved her?"

I sank back into my chair, bringing my fingertips to the temple again.

"Did you watch her go over, Knight? Did you see the gas tank explode? Did you stick around to watch her burn to death?"

He was slumping forward now in his chair, sweat dripping.

"She was going to quit, you know. She had plans drawn up to open a business. She was going to announce her resignation that evening. The promotion was already yours anyway, you bastard. She already knew about it, but you didn't. She wasn't a threat to you at all."

Still slumping, he raised his face, not believing. I stood and, for once, towered over him.

"You didn't have to do it, you idiot. If you had just waited, you would not have lived the rest of your pitiful life with it."

His mouth contorted like he was struggling to say something, something I had to lean forward to hear.

"Burn in hell you bitch," he said. His voice was strong and clear.

He came up with a gun. I had not seen it coming. All along, he had been faking weakness so he could slump forward and take the gun from the briefcase on the floor.

"I should have sent you to hell the first time," he sneered, pointing the gun at me.

"I wouldn't do that," Clara said behind me, wheeling herself in.

Knight turned his glare to her. I could almost hear the disdain in his thoughts - a woman, and in a wheelchair at that, thinking she could tell him what to do. He turned his pistol to Clara.

Clara did not hesitate. In one fluid motion she picked up her gun - a big, black one that looked like a single piece of metal. She had it in her lap. She shot him cleanly through his right shoulder.

The shot disabled his arm, but his gun still fired. The slug passed between Clara and me, splintering into the wood paneling of the wall behind us.

Knight slumped backwards in his chair, his jacket already showing red at the shoulder and his right arm limp. Awkwardly, he fumbled in his shirt pocket with his left hand. Clara raised the gun again, but I waved her off. I knew he was going for the emergency pillbox he kept there - for the tablets he put under his tongue when he felt his heart twinge.

Really sweating now, he struggled with the little pillbox, unable with only one hand to depress the tiny button that opened the lid. His gun slipped out of his useless right hand. He held the pillbox against his belly, struggling with the latch. Finally, it sprang open, raining its contents over his desk. With panicked, bulging eyes he struggled breathlessly to grasp one of the pills with his left hand and then to bring it to his mouth. It dropped.

"Help him," Clara said. With him disabled, her professional duty now was to help him - to save his life.

But I could not be so generous quite so quickly.

I hesitated, watching him. Clara, unable to move any closer with me in the way, told me again to help him and I went to him reluctantly. I picked up a pill and Knight, with his mouth hanging open, nodded. But first, I took a pencil from the desktop holder and used it to slide the gun out of his reach. I slipped the pill under his slimy tongue, shut his mouth and held it closed, but he was gone.

Clara rolled herself beside him and thrust her fingers against his neck, feeling for the artery. "He's dead," she said.

"Go to hell," I told him.

I took the recorder out of my pocket, turned it off and set it on the desk.

"You are really starting to piss me off, Jack," Clara said. "I thought you were going to wait for me."

"But he was getting ready to leave," I said. "We were going to miss him."

"Then we come back another night!" she said. She reached for Knight's telephone and started punching the buttons.

"Did it never, ever once cross your mind that this man was a killer? Did you think that he would hesitate for one second to kill you too? Your stupidity nearly got us both killed."

She held the receiver away from her ear. "It's dead."

"Night setting," I corrected. "You'll have to use the one at the switchboard."

Clara told me to stay with Knight and wheeled herself down the hall to the receptionist's desk, still scolding me as she went. I heard her pick up the telephone and dial the number, "Detective Clara

Carson, KCPD. We have a shooting. I need backup immediately at .
. ."

I went to the door and shouted the address down the hall at her.
She gave the address and added, "I think the shooter is dead. I took
him down, but send an ambulance, too."

In the moments before the sirens began, I stayed at the door to
Knight's office, just looking at him. He sat back in his chair. His
mouth hung open, slack and wet, but his cold blue eyes still stared at
me.

Clara, waiting at the front door, flashed her badge at the officers
when they arrived with guns drawn. If they were surprised to find an
officer in a wheelchair in charge, they hid it well. Clara briefed them
expertly, using summarized police jargon to describe how she fired
only when the shooter aimed his gun at her. She fired solely to
disable him. They would find the slug from his gun in the wall
where she and I had been standing. He apparently died of a heart
attack after being shot. She told them that I attempted to administer
his heart medication and there was likely a partly dissolved tablet
under his tongue, the rest of his pills were scattered about.

I was amazed how calm and collected she was. She played the
tape for them. Since I had forgotten to turn it on at first, it started
while I was already talking to Knight - asking him about killing
Madeline. After the shots were fired and they could hear Clara and
me fumbling around to get his medication, they shut it off. It was
everything they needed.

Somewhere in the chaos, Knight's wife arrived. She was
wearing a raincoat over a two-piece velour track suit. Someone had
called her at the country club. When her afternoon golf game was
rained out, her foursome simply moved to the nineteenth hole - a
cocktail lounge at the end of the course. She came right over without
changing. Unlike most of the women her age who wore running
suits, she was in peak physical condition. Otherwise, she was over-
tanned, over-tucked, over-processed, and still looked old. She
walked in, sat down weakly in the chair across the desk from Knight
and stared at him, stunned. Then she looked around at the uniformed
policeman.

"What happened?" she asked.

"Is he your husband?" the officer asked.

"Yes."

"Ma'am, we have reason to believe your husband drew his gun on Detective Clara Carson here, and in self-defense she fired her weapon to disable him. She shot him in the shoulder, and then he appears to have suffered a fatal heart attack."

She was silent for a while, looking at Knight. I thought she was going to cry, but she said, "Good."

"Ma'am?" the officer asked, not sure he had heard her correctly.

"I said, 'good,'" she looked calmly at the officer. "He was a first-class bastard. He's had a bad heart for years. I'm glad it finally happened."

Then, to Knight, she said, "Good riddance, you old fuck."

We all waited in stunned silence while she stared at her dead husband. Then she looked around the room and settled on me, "I know you, don't I?"

"Jack Jackson, ma'am," I said. "I used to work for your husband."

"Oh, yes," she said, nodding slowly in agreement. "You had two first names - or almost, anyway. We met at the firm's Christmas party of 1977, or was it 1976? He fired you too, didn't he?"

"It was 1976 - and yes he did, ma'am."

"And he probably told you that the best you could ever do was become a teller, if a bank would even hire you, didn't he? He used to love saying that. Every time, after he fired someone, he would have to go through the entire speech again with me at home."

She turned back to Knight. "You were never content just telling someone they were fired, were you, you filthy snake? You had to completely tear them down and then then kick them, too - make them feel totally worthless, lower than the scum that you were."

She turned back to me, reaching for my hand. "The ones he fired were the ones he thought were threats to him. He couldn't stand anyone he thought might be stronger or smarter than he was. If he fired you, it was because you were good. But I'm sure you have figured that out by now."

"Yes, ma'am."

The officer spoke, "Detective Carson and Mr. Jackson here believe they have evidence that your husband may have caused the accidental death of a woman. Can you say anything about that? We can wait until you contact your attorney if you like."

"No, I don't need a lawyer, and it wasn't accidental. He killed that woman back in 1953. She was a doctor's widow and worked with him. Mrs. Montrose - Madeline, I think was her name. She was his supervisor at work and Keith hated her from the get-go. He was sure she was going to get his promotion, so he ran her car off the road and into the old quarry. I guess it worked because he got the promotion."

"You knew about this?" I could not help saying. Clara looked at me sharply and shook her head for me to shut up.

"I only put it together later on," she said, shaking her head. "Keith always said I wasn't the sharpest tool in the shed and, with a new baby to take care of by myself, I guess I was pretty dull-witted back then.

"As soon as Keith got the promotion, he insisted on buying this brand-new convertible that he said was more befitting of his new position. I thought our Dodge was still fine - even though it was five years old - but he wanted that 1954 convertible like a kid wants a new toy. It was light blue - just like the one in the song, but he hated anyone saying that since the singer, Eartha Kitt, was a . . . was a colored woman.

"Keith would never let me drive, but I still saw the front bumper of the Dodge before he traded it in. It was pretty banged up. It was locked in the garage from the morning after the Christmas party until the dealer came around and picked it up. I eventually put two and two together: how much he hated Mrs. Montrose, his worries about her getting the promotion he wanted, and her death the night of the Christmas party. Keith made me stay home that night, even though I was already dressed to go and had the sitter there when he got home from work.

"He said I was an embarrassment to him in my homemade dress and left without me. He said that right in front of the sitter and I was so humiliated. It was a nice dress - all my friends said so. I only realized later on why he did that. He meant to kill her that night and I couldn't be with him. He must have followed her, looking for his chance. I just couldn't believe he would intentionally run her off the road like that, crash her into that old quarry and just leave her to die - and all for that lousy promotion and another forty dollars a month.

"When I confronted him with it, I still didn't want to believe it. It was months later, he told me to shut up and we had a big fight. He said the cops already decided it was a suicide. He said nobody would ever believe me; they would think I was a lunatic or hysterical and would send me to an asylum. He gave me a big black eye and said if I ever said another word about it - to anyone at all - he would do the same thing to me that he did to her, and the baby too. It would look like an accident. I was too scared to say anything about it ever again.

"There wasn't anything I could do," she said, her voice wavering. She immediately cleared her throat, regaining her composure.

She stood and walked around the desk to Knight. Almost like we weren't there she leaned in and talked to him in a hissing whisper.

"You drove our son away, didn't you, you bastard. When he wasn't just like you, you called him a mama's boy and said he had sugar in his pants. That nearly killed him. I was so glad he could get away, but I told you the day he left that I would spit on your grave someday, didn't I?"

She hawked and spat in Knight's face. His unseeing eyes did not flinch.

"But this will have to do. Don't think for one minute that I am going to stick around for your lousy funeral. For all I care, they can stick you in a can and set you on the curb like the trash that you are."

She turned back to the officer, "My sister has a place in Florida. She says I can use it anytime, but he never wanted to spend the time or the money to go there. I'll stay there until the house is sold - unless you have to arrest me." She looked down at her hands, "I guess I'm an accessory to murder, aren't I?"

"A woman cannot be forced to give testimony against her husband," he said. "Besides that, he threatened your life, so I don't think the district attorney would even consider pursuing it. We will need for you to come to the station to make a statement before you leave. After that, if anything else is needed we can contact you in Florida, or through your attorney if you want."

As soon as Knight's widow was gone, the paramedics wrapped his body in a rubber blanket and transferred him onto the gurney. They would still take him to the emergency room for a doctor to issue a death certificate. There would probably be an autopsy, however limited, to confirm his heart attack after the shooting. The detective asked Clara if she could hang around a day or two, in case they needed any more information. He didn't even ask for my telephone number or identification.

Clara's bullet went through the back of Knight's chair and into the wall. The crime scene team extracted it from the paneling, as well as the bullet he fired at us. They put Knight's gun in another plastic bag; also his pill boxes and all the pills they could find. Clara did not have to, but she still handed over her gun for their tests.

She also answered every question, commanding me with her eyes to keep quiet. They assumed Clara was in charge and since she was the fellow officer on whom Knight had fired, they were satisfied with her answers. They did not cross examine me. It was enough that Clara said the door was unlocked when she arrived and the telephone system was already shut down when she called for backup. I did not have to tell them I used my old duplicate key to let myself in the locked front door, or that I had transferred the telephones to the night answering service, or that I had baited Knight into confessing Madeline's murder. Clara handed over the tape from my pocket recorder. They could hear his words for themselves.

It was still early in California. I would call Eva as soon as we got home. I wanted to be the one to tell her. She needed time to process the news and collect herself before the police or the reporters called her.

And they would - Knight had been a leading citizen and his death could not go unnoticed. The story of the old murder he had committed finally being solved went out later that night on the Associated Press wires and was immediately a news sensation. By Monday, Clara's face, and footage of her rolling her wheelchair from the doors of the Springfield Police Station to her van, would run on all the national networks. Clara declined all interview offers, but the story ran for days until the next big story replaced it.

I also made the call that evening because I wanted to be the one to deliver the final truth to Eva: that we proved Madeline had not killed herself, and that her killer had received justice - of sorts.

When Eva and I talked, I said I wished that Addie was coherent enough to know we had proved that her mother did not commit suicide and all suspicion for her death had been removed from Addie. Maybe Eva could make her understand that. My only regret was that Madeline's daughters could not have received this news decades ago. Their lives could have been so much better.

Even so, Madeline was vindicated - and she was released. She could rest now with Jordan. Martin, who had been the continuation of Jordan in this life, could rest too. The part of me that had been Madeline was gone. The rest of this lifetime was my own. I could stay in my house, and sleep in Madeline's bedroom, in peace.

But before the media storm that was to come, after the evidence collectors were gone and we were left alone, Clara motioned for me to come to her. I knelt beside her chair. She hugged me tightly, released me to give my shoulder a powerful wallop, and then hugged me even closer than before.

"Don't you ever do anything like that again," she said with tears in her eyes. "I can't lose you, too."

There it was. With her words Martin was there with us again. He always would be.

"Thanks for saving me, Clara," my voice was thick. "If only for that one thing, never doubt why you are still here."

She leaned back and stared at me a long moment as a new understanding came into her eyes.

"We really are here for each other, aren't we Jack?"

"Always have been," I nodded. "Always will be."

THE END

Acknowledgements

No book is a solitary effort and I wish to express my continuing gratitude to my editors, proofreaders, and cheerleaders: Walter and Irene Bailey, Katherina Kalman, and Dawn Smith.

I also extend my appreciation to Createspace, Amazon, and Barnes and Noble for providing the platform that allows writers like me to get their work to readers in a changing publishing industry.

And last, but never least, thanks to my partner, Mark, for your ongoing and unquestioning support of this compulsion I seem to have for making up stories.

ABOUT MIDTOWN AND THE AUTHOR

Springfield Missouri's Midtown neighborhood is an area rich in cultural, economic, racial, and architectural diversity. The area was originally called "between towns" due to its location between the original town of Springfield and the new town of North Springfield that was built in the 1870s when the railroad tracks were brought a mile to the north. Today the neighborhood includes the campus of Drury University, Central High School, the Midtown Carnegie Library, magnificent churches, the city and county government offices, and a richly diverse inventory of homes ranging from small railroad workers cottages to estate-like properties.

Alan E. Bailey lived in midtown for eighteen years and draws inspiration for the fictional *Midtown Murder Mystery* series from his time there. The setting of *My Lady's Chamber*, first in the series, was inspired by the Midtown house he restored. He is currently writing *Down the Stairs*, second in the series.

The author is a certified public accountant and holds a master's degree from Drury University in Springfield, Missouri. He was a technical writer in accounting during much of his career. He retired in 2010 to pursue his love of travel and fiction writing on a full time basis.

Beginning in 2012, *The Alexander Saga* was published in three volumes: *Myrtha, Louie G*, and *Dolores. Letters to Myrtha*, a supplement to *the Alexander Saga,* was released in 2014.

While writing *The Alexander Saga*, the author published *In Good Time,* a novel also set in Midtown during the 1930s.

The author shares his time between his home in Springfield and San Francisco.

Follow the author and his books at
www.facebook.com/Myrthathebook.

Made in the USA
Coppell, TX
31 December 2019